THE
ONE
ON
EARTH

Cover design by Andrew Bourne
Interior by Fence Books
Photo of Mark Baumer by the author

This book is a Nik Slackman Production.

Published in the United States by

Fence Books
110 Union Street
Second Floor
Hudson NY 12534

www.fenceportal.org

This book was printed by Versa Press
and distributed by Small Press Distribution
and Consortium Book Sales and Distribution.

Library of Congress Control Number: 2021938462
ISBN 13: 978-1-944380-18-2

First Edition
10 9 8 7 6 5 4 3 2

THE ONE ON EARTH

SELECTED WORKS of

Mark Baumer

FENCE MODERN PRIZE in PROSE
EDITED by BLAKE BUTLER and SHANE JONES
FOREWORD by CLAIRE DONATO

CONTENTS

THE IMPOSSIBLE POSSIBLE

As I walked last night, I listened to a man explain why the earth we had once known was already dead. There's already too much carbon in the atmosphere. Too many glaciers have already melted. The ocean is becoming more and more acidic. We can't reverse the damage we've already done. // You can glue a broken light bulb back together and it might still work, but the light will never be the same. // So I guess I woke up on a dead planet. It still felt sort of alive. I still felt sort of alive. **Mark Baumer, November 19, 2016**

Imaginary evil is romantic and varied; real evil is gloomy, monotonous, barren, boring. Imaginary good is boring; real good is always new, marvelous, intoxicating. **Simone Weil, Gravity and Grace**

I buy something to eat. The plastic I throw away clings to me. I wipe it on my knee and it falls by my feet. Its helplessness reminds me of people.
Evelyn Hampton, The Aleatory Abyss

Yesterday, I took a photograph of abandoned plastic sleds in Prospect Park, Brooklyn. The photograph's blue shadows match the pullover Mark Baumer (1983—2017) wears in one of my favorite photographs of him. In it, he's protesting Textron, an industrial conglomerate based in Providence, Rhode Island whose manufactured cluster bombs were used to kill civilians in Yemen in 2016. DEAR TEXTRON, Mark's epistolary protest sign reads. STOP KILLING CIVILIANS / MAKING CLUSTER BOMBS / PROFITING OFF DEATH. Seated on the ground in nonviolent protest, Mark obstructs Textron's front door while two other activists chain their necks to two additional entrances. Just after this photograph was taken, all three activists were arrested.

•

Tomorrow, December 19, 2020, is Mark's 37th birthday. I'll spend some of it writing the foreword to this book, for which part of my research has included reading "Unconscious Processes in Relation to the Environmental Crisis," by the late psychoanalyst Harold F. Searles. This article, written in 1972, feels contemporary as I reflect on Mark's activism and how the violences we inflict upon earth affect how we treat one another—"how we take and push and mine and drill into one another" per Winter Count, a multi-disciplinary art collective whose work "engages with land and water under current threat by extractive industry." Mark's activism burgeoned when he learned about the Great Pacific Garbage Patch: by understanding discarded plastic's dangers, Mark began to recognize the interconnections between human and non-human life. Plastic is the greatest threat to the ocean; 80% of marine litter comes from the land. These statistics beg questions: Where do blue sleds go when they die? Do we go there too? And, in our dying, what do we lose?

Searles: "A technology-dominated, overpopulated world has brought with it so reduced a capacity in us to cope with the losses a life must bring with it to be a truly human life that we become increasingly drawn into polluting our planet sufficiently to ensure that we shall have essentially nothing to lose in our eventual dying."

Or, as Mark writes:

We might all have the same brain. Unfortunately, I think the brain is dying. Literally, everything we touch is death. The water is going to kill the brain. The food is going to kill the brain. The walls are going to kill the brain. The society is going to kill the brain. The air is going to kill the brain. The stress of brain death is going to kill the brain. The only solution is nothing. Humans have done nothing but create brain death and any time we try to correct our mistakes we create more brain death. The brain will die. Somehow we must accept life after the brain or we must accept earth post brain. This is a little sad, but brains were never constructed to outlive earth. Even though I am not sure if I can live without a brain I'm pretty sure earth will continue without the brain. When my brain dies hopefully I will remember to walk out into the forest and sit down in the pine needles if there are still pine needles out in the forest.

In October 2016, Mark left his home in Providence, Rhode Island for a barefoot walk across the country. He called this feat "Barefoot Across America." The purpose of his walk was to raise awareness regarding climate change, and to crowdsource $10,000 for the FANG (Fighting Against Natural Gas) Collective, with whom he protested against Textron. Walking from the East to the West coast was something Mark had already accomplished in 2010, when he walked for 81 days from Tybee Island, Georgia to Santa Monica, California while wearing sneakers and pushing his possessions in a baby carriage. His writing from that walk was self-published in *I Am a Road*, excerpts from which are included in this volume.

After reading Christopher McDougall's *Born to Run*, Mark began training to run barefoot. He chronicled his barefoot runs in YouTube videos—The New Yorker's Anna Heyward refers to Mark as a "compulsive social media diarist"—and, after beginning his barefoot walk, began producing one video everyday, as well as text-adorned photography, poetry, and aphoristic journal entries, archived online at barefootacrossamerica.com. Mark's travel writing and multimedia gestures read like a cross between Thich Nhat Hanh, Miranda July, Bas Jan Ader, Simone Weil, Pee-Wee Herman, Andy Kaufman, Greta Thunberg, and the magical fourth-grade nephew you never had, clad in a cardboard costume of a house set on fire, screaming at adults during a climate march.

On the 64th day of his walk, Mark took a bus from Zanesville, Ohio to Jacksonville, Florida. Icy weather in Ohio had created impossible walking conditions, as Heyward writes, "not because of the snow but because the calcium-chloride de-icing salts that were sprinkled on the concrete cut [Mark's] feet." He arrived in Florida late on the evening of December 17, 2017. "I woke up in the state of Florida near a giant wall," he wrote on the morning after his arrival. "It was painted with fish. The sidewalk was warm. I looked up at the sun and smiled. It was toasting my face."

During his last month on earth, Mark approached Barefoot Across America with renewed vigor. On Day 77, he stayed at the Sacred Water Camp in Suwannee Springs, Florida, where he participated in a protest with water protectors against the Sabal Trail Pipeline, which decimated orange orchards and former conservation land (sold to the Sabal Transmission Company for several million dollars). On Day 82, Mark's friend Matt drove three hours to Madison, Florida, just to give him a hug. "I'm pretty sure if a friend randomly shows up in the middle of Florida to give you a hug then you are required to finish whatever journey you are on," Mark reflected. On Days 88 and 94, Mark was profiled in the Tallahassee Democrat and the Jackson County Floridian, respectively.

At 1:15pm on January 21, 2017, Mark was struck and killed by the driver of an SUV while walking westward along the south shoulder of Highway 90 in Walton County, Florida. It was the 101st day of Mark's journey, and it also happened to be the afternoon of the 2017 Women's March, just one day after Donald Trump's inauguration. Abiding by safety conventions, Mark wore a fluorescent orange vest and walked against traffic. In a police report, the SUV's driver, who was traveling eastbound when she veered out of her lane, said she saw Mark before she hit him. He had walked more than 700 miles[1] and was 33 years old.

Hours before his death, Mark posted a photograph to his blog. In it, his bare toes are framed below the word KILLED, spray painted in yellow atop the highway's asphalt. In his blog entry's accompanying video, Mark points the camera toward this word: KILLED. "The language of capitalism," he remarks.

These days, writing this introduction around the anniversary of Mark's death, I keep returning to a black-and-white photograph of Dutch performance artist Bas Jan Ader walking on the berm of a highway in Los Angeles, California in 1973. Accompanied by lyrics from The Coaster's "Searchin"—*yeh I've been searchin'*—the image is at once banal and evocative, and conjures the American fantasy of the highway of freedom and connection: the Beat romanticism of the road; the suburban imaginary of the road; the arteries of capitalist shipping required to fuel Amazon's corporate death drive; the cross-country trip as coming-of-age rite; the United States' "this land is my land, this land is your land" nonsense; Bob Dylan's "let me walk down the highway with my brother in peace" American folk dream; the number of people who died by automobile in 2017; and the delusion of anyone thinking they can walk a mile in someone else's shoes.

"If I die on this trip, it's not going to be because I didn't wear shoes," Mark said in a video on November 26, 2016. "It's going to be because an automobile kills me."

Those unfamiliar with Mark may assume his writing lends itself to a deceptively bizarre read. On first encounter, one might think Mark's work is weird for the sake of being weird, when in fact its weirdness (and sentient weirdening) is entangled with other weirdnesses: the weirdness of linguistically manipulative advertising and propaganda; the weirdness of the human brain's non-sequiturs; the weirdness of human beings thinking thoughts all the time, ergo we cannot know anyone's mind; the alienation of daily objects, events, and serendipities that are just a little bit off, and how these objects, events, and serendipities don't quite belong either in the world or in the realm of language. Not to mention the weirdness of attempting to wield language that bears

---

1   The Guinness World Record holder for barefoot walking walked 1,292.54 miles barefoot. If Mark had walked barefoot from Rhode Island to California, it would have been about a 3,000 mile journey.

socioculturally-approved "sense" when lived experience is myriad, ineffable, synesthetic, senseless.

Mark's shorter prose pieces often read like fables containing moral lessons geared toward CEOs, grown men with anger problems, megalomaniacs, and white supremacists. Critics sometimes describe Mark's writing as childlike, which feels apt and aligned with our world's political landscape: children are, after all, leading the global climate movement; and the bulk of our nation's leaders fail to lead at all because their souls are possessed by unprocessed inner children. Mark was an only child whose writing is full of rage and sadness, but not grief, per se. Rather, his work is often euphoric, seriously playful, ecstatically joyful, egoless: a manic response to the pain of being alive in a world where everything is dying in front of our eyes.

Along with excerpts from his travel journals (*I Am a Road* and the *Barefoot Across America* blog), a novella (*At Some Point in the Last Nine Billion Years*), and "Yachts," a short story about a penis that abandons its seven-week old infant body to tour South America and study postcolonial theory, *The One on Earth* contains Mark's Personal Statements for Brown University's MFA Literary Arts Program ("Dear Brown, It is important to know that I am not a joke. Instead of doing cocaine I have worked the last two years on my writing. I have started four novels and tossed them away when they were done. I feel like failure is a big part of my writing.") and the Stegner Fellowship at Stanford University ("It is difficult for me to know what the fall of 2017 will bring. [...] Maybe I will have a child at this point or maybe I will begin coaching middle school track"); cover letters addressed to future employers ("Would you be more or less likely to hire me if I told you one of my teeth is probably going to fall out unless I get dental coverage?"); prose miniatures about the Brown University MFA Literary Arts Program; a Tinder bio set in couplets entitled "Not Ted Cruz"; stock tips for unpublished authors trying to get rich; a fairy tale about Jonathan Franzen's leg falling off; some facts about a self-immolating web content specialist; multi-step writing prompts; and poems rejected from *A Public Space*, *Boston Review*, and *Beloit Poetry Journal*. Apart from my aforementioned genealogy (which included Thich Nhat Hanh, Pee-Wee Herman, &c.), parts of Mark's writing feel like a Frederick Wiseman documentary narrated by Werner Herzog; parts feel like Daniil Kharms walking around Wal-Mart after midnight; parts feel like Yorgos Lanthimos being commissioned to write a Little Golden Book; and parts feel like Lydia Davis thumbwrestling Donald Barthleme on Vine at TGI Friday's.

Maybe Mark's writing is absurd—a word so overused to describe literary (and all, really) art that it's been neutralized—or maybe what's actually absurd is the formality and desperation with which we prostrate ourselves before institutions, faux-democratic corporate apps, celebrities, and CEOs, plus all of our big and little addictions: from alcohol and drugs to sex and love, from social media dopamine hits to performance enhanced sports and the ways we "throw [our] money at each other." Maybe what's also absurd is that there exist famous writers whose famous books are written on famous computers made by a corporation named after a piece of fruit symbolizing original sin. And although I can't find a clear answer online about where these famous computers are grown, I often think about the time Mark stood in the Providence Place Mall's Apple Store holding a sign that read SILENT HUNGER PROTEST, and also about how the only article Mark ever wrote for his undergraduate college's newspaper almost got him expelled, so he started a zine called G.M.B.O. That zine was an act of journalism, of revolt—of participation in political community. It was, like the writing in this volume, an act of refusal. And I am thinking now about how refuse can become compost, and how compost can yield fruit, and also of the late poet C.D. Wright, who would have turned 71 today, January 6, 2020. Before her death, C.D. called Mark "an angel sent to earth to protect us." She also wrote: "We must do something with our time on this small aleatory sphere for motives other than money. Power is not an acceptable surrogate." The irony and grace of *The One on Earth* is that it won a prize.

•

As I think of Mark's oeuvre and plastic detritus, my mind turns toward the great garbage patch of the soul. What if, instead of using the world to destroy ourselves, we responded to political crises by confronting our pain, meeting our shadows, and attending to our anxieties, to the sources of our suffering? James Baldwin: "Not everything that is faced can be changed, but nothing can be changed until it is faced."

As I write this foreword, I'm supposed to be considering how Mark's work makes people face truth in a way that feels different from other political commentary. At once, a headline on NPR's website appears: "U.S. Capitol in Chaos as Pro-Trump Extremists Breach Building." White supremacist vigilantes—terrorists—are presently storming the US Capitol Building in a combination coup-superspreader event. They're smashing windows, scaling walls while wearing American flag capes, wandering around the Senate floor in furry costumes, pulling papers from government officials' desks, waving Confederate flags while chanting "1776." Further images from the news reports are also rife with hatred: actual, functional gallows; pipe bombs and Molotov cocktails; and clusters of zip ties, presumably to take senators hostage. I study a photograph of a man pointing toward his dick while sitting at Nancy Pelosi's desk, and a second photograph of a second man smiling and wearing a knit TRUMP cap adorned with a pom-pom while carrying Pelosi's Speaker of the House podium.

My mind turns toward growing up in rural western Pennsylvania, where I encountered firsthand people who are lied to and brainwashed by rich megalomaniacs who gain from this, and who often hide behind 'God,' patriotism, and xenophobic fraternity. All of these forms of false inclusion stoke white rage, and trick people into feeling included while they are robbed. Then I think about Harmony Korine's *Gummo*, and of my friends' parents' gun cabinets and their ancestors' gun cabinets, and their ancestors' ancestors' gun cabinets. And then I remember this moment from Mark's 37th day on the road in central Pennsylvania:

Halfway down the mountain I heard gun shots. At first I thought I was being shot at. The gun shots continued. A few hundred feet away I saw children playing in the yard.

14,000+ people were arrested during the Black Lives Matter protests following George Floyd's death. As of my writing this, 13 white terrorists who participated in the Capitol insurrection have been arrested.

•

As the above events unfold, I reread a piece by Mark called "White people in blackface wearing kkk hoods under their hijabs while riding motorcycles." This afternoon, it feels prescient, and like a prose capsule containing Mark's rage at what people who look like him do, and fail to do. The text enacts a sort of Jenga's ladder of whiteness, and points to white solipsism, wherein whiteness cannot see past itself, and paints everything white in its absence, and cannot serve to protect anything but itself:

> After work, a white man named "Doug" liked to read magazines while eating pizza. Sometimes Doug read a magazine that talked about how all the dead white people in America got killed by other white people who would eventually get killed by even more white people. Doug was scared. He only worked with white people. Doug decided to wear a motorcycle helmet to work because he thought it would make him safe.

As a reader, I appreciate how "Doug" exists in quotation marks like an ontological curiosity—"who" "is" "Doug" "and" "why" "is" he "so" "fucking" "afraid"?—and that the magazines "Doug" reads are unnamed. Like whiteness, I imagine these magazines are blank inside: sites of projection upon projection upon projection. Because "Doug" cannot tolerate his mind, "Doug" is scared.

In general, Mark aimed to comport himself as the opposite of "Doug," not out of self-righteousness but rather with the optimism that others would follow suit. Doug is complacent and afraid, whereas Mark refused to turn away from fear. He did not flee his shadows: I think of the many videos in which he records his own shadow moving through space, or where a cell phone's shadow cascades across his face. And he continuously worked on himself and analyzed his own mind—with which the health of the heart, after all, is intertwined. In particular, Mark's walks across the country demonstrate his psychic aptitude for tolerating his own mind, confronting fear, and taking risks. "'To risk one's life' is among the most beautiful expressions in our language," Anne Dufourmantelle writes in *In Praise of Risk*, a book in which risk is defined as a decisive instinct, the opposite of complacency. "Risk [...] opens an unknown space," Dufourmantelle expounds. "How is it possible, as a living being, to think risk in terms of life rather than death? [...] What if [risk] supposed a certain manner of being in the world, constructed by a horizon line?"

Although Mark's walks may be deemed risky insofar as they put him in the line of danger, they were ultimately about aliveness, desire, intimacy with the earth and its elements, and a particular suspension of time. While his videos are numerically demarcated by days—Day 98, Day 99, Day 100—his walk was a continuous meditation, a poem written with two feet, and a path leading toward a utopia where, to quote his final entry, "one day everyone will be able to walk down the middle of the road free from all the violence this society has built." Beyond his documentation of walking across America, so many of Mark's videos—for example, his instructional videos (e.g., "How to be a poem writer") and hilariously destabilizing phone calls to literary agents ("Hey, hello Claudia Ballard, this is Mark Baumer. [...] You wouldn't believe this, but I'm interested in joining the ranks of many published authors who think they're going to become famous but actually just have middling success and eventually they become so discouraged that the written word is no longer an enjoyment for them")—are about critically interrogating the comfort of privilege, and of unsettling people who feel complacently settled in who they think they are.

As someone deeply invested in practices that spelunk and sweep the unconscious—psychoanalysis, dream journaling, Zen meditation—I'm especially interested in Mark's freely associative video diaries and journal entries, and his emphasis on unbridled language-making across media. His language is alive; it is thinking his brain; it is his thinking-brain. He is speaking to the camera; he does not know what he is going to say; sometimes his eyes widen; sometimes he begins to cry; he lets us see him cry. On December 5, 2016, Mark is alone in a hotel room in Ohio, and he is grieving. He has just received the news that his friend, Nick Gomez-Hall, whom he was supposed to meet in California at the end of his trip, and with whom he had plans to go bowling, has died in the Oakland Ghost Ship Fire. Nick had been missing for one day. "I saw on the news that my friend Nick was officially one of the people who died in the Oakland fire," Mark says. "Nick, I love you. I miss you. And it hurts that you're gone." On his blog, he writes: "Maybe the saddest and most beautiful thing about all this is the fact that the last message Nick sent me was, 'I love you Mark.'"

There is pain in Mark's speech, and in his writing, and this pain brings him—and we, his travel companions—closer to truth. And, like America, the unconscious wants truth. It needs it. Mark knew this: that only via truth will we continue to dream in hell.

•

MISSING

I don't want / to look / at the last email / you wrote / because / I still hope / somehow
/ you will / someday / float / another one / into my bucket / once / you said / I want to
create / vulnerable statements / that / connect with strangers / it hurts / to think / right
now / but / I still / remember / the time / you asked / if I was / going through / the desert /
because / you were / in the desert / and / maybe / we could both / be / in the desert / but
/ I never / made it / to the desert / before / you left / the desert

December 4, 2016

•

As a fellow only child who talked with Mark about only-childhood, I'll now
offer some thoughts which are only partially about only-childhood. "I wish I
had written a book about the empty space where my brother was supposed to
exist," Mark wrote in *the books keep getting worse and worse*. Are only children
gifted with a particular empty space, a lack from which they love? Mark was
tall and vegan and straightedge—not because he was an only child—and a
loyal, responsive friend who remembered other people's birthdays, participated
in numerous communities, and was talented at organically forming communities
wherever he went. This was probably because he was an only child, and
probably too because he was Mark, and also because he was a hard-worker
who paid attention to details, who also happened to be exceptional at using the
Internet. I especially loved emailing with Mark. He once sent me a Spartacus
workout. And during his barefoot walk, we had a virtual dinner party. This was
before COVID-19 made that a thing. He was staying in an Airbnb in Ohio, and I
remember him eating a can of chickpeas.

Although the images of his feet posted to Instagram may suggest
otherwise, Mark took care of his body and meditated daily and therefore did
not exist at a distance from his mind. Maybe the blisters on his feet were extra
eyes—the better with which to attend to the world's pain, of which there is so
much that the road glistens. His commitment to self-care helped him tend to
others. For example, once, when I was giving a reading in Providence, Mark
brought me a lemon: I was travelling and always drink lemon water in the
morning, and I did not have a lemon with me. Mark somehow knew this. Today,

whenever someone gives me a piece of fruit, I think of Mark. Searching my inbox for our correspondence, I realized I did not respond to an email from Mark sent on December 10, 2013 concerning the work of an author named Lee Paige. That email links to a 404 File Not Found page at *BOMB*. "I don't know if you've heard of Lee Paige, but he went to the same MFA we did at the same time we did," Mark wrote. "Pretty good writer." Was Mark Lee Paige? I don't know for sure, because I failed to respond. Mark always responded to emails; I wish I had written back.

●

On December 29, 2020, I received a card from Mark's mom, Mary. She has been taking walks on the beach. *My new thing is to pick up trash that is plastic on the beach,* she writes. *Every single time I walk the beach...*

●

How much should your foreword emphasize Mark's being gone, my friend Ian Hatcher, who also attended Brown's MFA with Mark, asks me. As Ian talks, I type a list that may or may not be a poem:

> 50 novels—unreadable
> The simplicity of a single person doing a thing
> Walking across the country: impossibly large
> Impossibility of holding all of it in the mind
> "Rendering the impossible possible as work"
> We live in a really dark children's book
> Mark knew this
> His practice embodies the desire to begin again,
>   enacting a magic
> Even if Mark had made it all the way across the
>   country, there would still be climate change

Jacques Derrida: "Such a caring for death, an awakening that keeps vigil over death, a conscience that looks death in the face, is another name for freedom." Mark is still alive in the moment of a reader reading his work; *The One on Earth* is a living document.

1. Ryan LaMothe: "Spaceship earth has already hit the iceberg of climate change, though there are no rescue ships deployed to save us."

2. There is a chart in front of me labeled Temperature Anomaly whose   squiggle ascends and ascends as years pass

3. Neoliberal capitalism

4. As of October 2020, the Trump Administration has covertly signed   away over 125 climate change protections

5. Mark: "For one minute, be optimistic about the global failures of humanity's lack of concern with their global failures, and then for the rest of your life live inside this optimism as you try to almost convince yourself that there is no need to worry about the continued existence of koalas."

6. In a text message, Jess writes: "The one thing that 'normal' politicians hate the most is being made to look like weak idiots. The entirety of the Senate and House is bound together now in anger and humiliated hatred."

7.

Blake Butler
10:53 AM Today

this points it toward the idea of stagnancy for me; how a lack of change creates a vacuum of platitudes and empty gestures, all of which mark was the exact opposite of, like he was trying to singlehandedly invert his own culture

8. If this page were a webpage, I would embed Johnnie Frierson's "Miracles"

```
<iframe width="560" height="315" src="https://www.youtube.com/
embed/eALEn9wCtPA" frameborder="0" allow="accelerometer;
autoplay; clipboard-write; encrypted-media; gyroscope; picture-in-
picture" allowfullscreen></iframe>
```

9. … and Minor Threat's "Straight Edge"

```
<iframe width="560" height="315" src="https://www.youtube.com/
embed/F5qsKiwnBSl" frameborder="0" allow="accelerometer;
autoplay; clipboard-write; encrypted-media; gyroscope; picture-in-
picture" allowfullscreen></iframe>
```

10. The notes on what Mark made here in his time are endless.

●

In his practices as a writer, performance artist, and activist, Mark attempted to embody a central problem of our time: scale. His writing deals with immense problems, all of which are bound up with climate change: the greed of accumulated wealth and power, corporate evil, systemic injustice, and violence against human and nonhuman life. So too does Mark's practice embody the impossibility of one person addressing those problems. Yet I trust the impossible is possible. As I write this, there are countless tabs open on my computer documenting Mark's activism. And I can't stop being haunted by a photograph from August 2018 in which Greta Thunberg wears a blue hoodie the color of Mark's pullover during the Textron protest. It is the color of the abandoned sled and sky in Prospect Park, Brooklyn, and the color of the ocean sans man-made pollutants.

The introduction can end with infinity, I write in my notes. Because Mark's work has to do with infinity: how we're infinitely fucked, unbounded and complicit at the end of a world punctuated by Starbucks, Walmart, Taco Bell, KFC, Pizza Hut, and Wendy's. "A cow looks at itself and thinks, 'Oh well,'" Mark writes. Because despite there being no end to this world's predictably boring evil, we're together, whether we acknowledge it or not, and whether we like it or not—and not just with one another, but with the world itself. In 1927, Romain Rolland sent a letter to Sigmund Freud; in it, he referred to a mystical sense of oneness with the external world as the oceanic feeling. Not everyone can turn outward from narcissistic suffering and the ego's iron grip to feel the world and that oceanic feeling, but Mark did. Almost 100 years after Freud popularized Rolland's concept in *Civilization and Its Discontents*, Mark narrates the oceanic feeling in *I Am a Road*:

I began to cry. The ocean just looked at me and shrugged as I limped towards it. When I reached the sand, my body no longer hurt because it was no longer required to be the body I had required myself to be. The spacesuit I had worn the entire trip was soiled with every mile I had traveled. I removed these stains and placed them in abe the body I had required myself to be. The spacesuit I had worn the entire trip was soiled with every mile I had traveled. I removed these stains and placed them in a trash barrel. Tears continued to leak from my brain. I no longer had to pretend I wasn't human. The ocean barely acknowledged me as I stepped into it. I didn't know what else to do so I just floated.

Walking across the country barefoot; walking across the country in shoes; hitchhiking across the country with a traveling companion; attempting to hitchhike from Providence, Rhode Island to Los Angeles, California for the annual AWP Conference; engaging in labor negotiations at work, winning contract negotiations, and becoming a union steward; publishing 50 novels in a year; eating pizza everyday for three months; teaching a creative writing workshop dedicated to "the art of subtle weirdness" with classes dedicated to attending other classes, writing failed novels, sharing silence, yelling, and celebrating everyone's birthday; writing for eight hours a day. It is an insurmountable task, to introduce Mark Baumer, to scale down his oeuvre. I have no doubt he would have appreciated the task's absurdity. And I have faith this is the first of many edited anthologies of his writing and cross-media artwork to come.

Claire Donato, Brooklyn, NY
December 18, 2020-January 10, 2021

COVER LETTERS

August 21, 2006

Dear Job Person,

My name is Mark Baumer. I am a recent college graduate. I majored in English. I also took a variety of history classes. I have always viewed myself as a self-motivator. In closing, I apologize if I've come across as unprofessional in any way.

Sincerely,

Mark Baumer

August 30 2006

Dear Job Person,

My name is Mark Baumer. I am interested in the position of copywriter. I am a recent college graduate who doesn't have professional experience.

Sincerely,

Mark Baumer

September 3 2006

Dear Job People,

My name is Mark Baumer. I am interested in the driving position. I am a recent college graduate. I don't have a lot of professional driving experience, but I have driven a lot of different vehicles (ice cream trucks and dump truck). One of the things that interests me about your company is that I could be successful. Other things about your company excite me too. It sounds like I will be dealing one on one with the public. I've always enjoyed the public. Thank you for your time.

Sincerely,

Mark Baumer

September 5, 2006

Dear Sir or Madame,

I recently saw your ad for operations associate lead. I don't know what that means, but I am a recent college graduate who has had variety of computer-related experiences.

This position seems to be a good match for me. I have enthusiasm. I am a strong work ethic. I am can do things daily. My accomplishments have a strong desire to succeed.

It appears that the job involves evaluating employees along with having a professional relationship with them. I have a lot personality.

Sincerely,

Mark Baumer

December 21, 2006

Dear Job People,

In college, I played left field for three games. Only one ball was hit to me. I dropped it.

A few months ago I published a story underneath a bridge in Wyoming.

I got some new shoes two days ago. I haven't worn them yet. I'm waiting until I get a new job.

I didn't learn to read until I was in eighth grade.

No one kissed me until I was almost forty-three-years-old.

Let me know if you want to give me a job.

Sincerely,

Mark Baumer

December 26, 2006

Dear Publishing Industry,

I was thinking of writing a book called, "A Tree Used to Grow on my Head." It's the sequel to another book I was thinking of writing called, "A Tree is Growing on my Head." I was wondering if you'd be interested in giving me a bag of money to write either of these books. Also, I should note, both those books are based on a famous book called, "A Tree Grows in Brooklyn" which I haven't read. Anyway, let me know about the money.

Sincerely,

Mark Baumer

February 5, 2007

Dear Job People,

My name is Mark Baumer. I am interested in the position of Purchasing, Sales, and Accounting Specialist. I am a recent college graduate who doesn't have a lot of professional experience. Basically I have no clue what to do with the rest of my life. I live at home with my parents. If I get this job then I will probably continue living at home with my parents for the rest of my life.

Sincerely,

Mark Baumer

March 9, 2007

Dear Job People,

A boy once saw a sign on the side of a building that said, "Creative Services." He went to the third floor of the building even though he wished he was a tree. On the third floor, a receptionist said, "What!?" The boy told her he had a creative brain. She held up a bottle of salad dressing and asked the boy about the feminist perspective of the salad dressing. He shrugged. The secretary said, "I am afraid you're practically useless to us." The boy got sad and walked home.

Sincerely,

Mark Baumer

March 12, 2007

Dear Job People,

I like cats. When I walked by the office I noticed a cat on the front steps. I once had an orange cat. It was named Calvin.

Sincerely,

Mark Baumer

p.s. I live less than a block from your office so if you don't hire me it might get awkward and then you'd eventually have to move.

March 29, 2007

Dear Job People,

Before my last interview, some children threw apples at me and I had to hide behind the woodpile until dark. When I finally showed up seven hours late for the interview, the company said they were no longer interested. Anyway, things are improving. At the moment, as I write this cover letter, a squirrel is perched on the windowsill looking in at me. This seems like a good sign.

Sincerely,

Mark Baumer

March 31, 2007

Dear Job People,

I want your jobs. Oh. Whoops. How rude of me. I forgot to introduce myself. It's because I haven't eaten lunch yet. Unfortunately, I don't have enough money to buy food. Just kidding, I'm eating candy bars right now because I'm depressed.

Sincerely,

Mark

May 22, 2007

Dear Job People,

If you hire me I'll wear a Santa Claus outfit to work every day for the next forty-three years. Oh whoops, I have to go. There's a naked, screaming man running around on my front lawn.

Sincerely,

Mark Baumer

February 6, 2008

Dear Job People or to whomever has the pleasure of reading this letter,

I am very computer savvy. I have developed a number of microsoft word documents. My strongest computer skill is probably using a PC, but I can also use apple machines. I am also a team leader and responsible for many of my own individual successes. I hope we can have the opportunity to sit down and look at each other.

Sincerely,

Mark Baumer

August 26, 2008

Dear Job People,

I have failed multiple times. It's okay because I'm good friends with "patience" and "knowledge." I am also really good friends with "stupid" and "partially insane." I used to try to be friends with "perfection," but he's a jerk and never calls me back.

Sincerely,

Mark Baumer

August 27, 2008

Dear Job People,

If you hired me I would "feel excited," but eventually that excitement would diminish until it no longer existed and ultimately I would hate working for your company. Or maybe the excitement would never diminish. I don't know. Let me know if you want to schedule an interview.

Sincerely,

Mark Baumer

August 27, 2008

Dear Job People,

I saw your listing on craigslist. I feel qualified. When I was an intern sometimes I would read my boss's email because he didn't have time to read his own email. A few years later I began working with a guy who smelled like his own stale mouth. Most businesses are poorly run. Your company is probably no different. When I was eleven I was on the local news because I found a frog in an unopened bottle of aquafina. Obesity is the leaky faucet that no one wants to acknowledge. B ut I respect fat people.

Sincerely,

Mark Baumer

August 27, 2008

Dear Job People,

This cover letter might be the worst thing I've ever written. I just ate a bunch of salami. I feel sick. Things happen. I am very good at watching things happen and then thinking, "Okay, something happened."

Sincerely,

Mark Baumer

August 27, 2008

Dear Job People,

I know some people who are very good at aligning and organizing all their sticky notes. I'm pretty good at it, but I'm not as good as the people I know.

Sincerely,
Mark Baumer

August 27, 2008

Dear Job People,

For the past two years I've folded towels at an athletic club. Sometimes when I am not working I touch my computer. I am very proficient at touching computers. A bald man named Eric taught me how to be efficient when touching things.

Sincerely,

Mark Baumer

August 27, 2008

Dear Job People,

I like the internet. The internet is very easy. I understand it. I would be a very valuable asset for employers who need employees. Maybe this letter is sort of "unprofessional." Don't worry, I can write "professional" letters.

Sincerely,

Mark Baumer

August 27, 2008

Dear Job People,

I want to be a professional transcriber. I have no experience, but I can type. I typed all the words so far in this letter. Below is a transcript of a random video I transcribed from youtube:

> Good morning guys. Today is Wednesday. I got a new laptop. It has more buttons than my old laptop. Anyway, thank you for watching my video...

I hope you give me the job, but if you don't I will continue transcribing videos.

Sincerely,

Mark Baumer

/

September 2, 2008

Dear Job People,

I want to be an administrative specialist when I grow up because I like the idea of meeting new faces and then talking to them. I don't smoke cigarettes and my sweat only smells sometimes. Also, I don't own an automobile.

The end.

-Mark

September 2, 2008

Dear Job People,

I was responsible for giving birth to myself. At the moment, my evolutionary behavior needs a comfortable work opportunity that doesn't pay much. I have given up on the ideas of "hope" and "future." The last good person I met spit on my girlfriend's llama. The only life worth living is one that provides free toothbrushes. My mother taught me how to weave bread from her milk. I am specialist in efficiency. Someone should tell me what to do with my life so I can pretend to do what they told me to do while continuing to do whatever I want with my life.

Sincerely,

Mark Baumer

September 2, 2008

Dear Job People,

I have worked a variety of jobs. I am confident I could do this job because it sounds like you're looking for a braindead person. It is easy for me to go into braindead mode. The entire job searching process has given me very little hope or reason to live so I'm pretty much already in braindead mode.

Sincerely,

Mark Baumer

September 2, 2008

Dear Job People,

I have worked in a variety of business atmospheres that were not mentally healthy. My last job was at a three-inch office cage setting where I had to touch file cabinets for seventeen hours a day. I am confident that I would excel as the administrative assistant of the electrical engineering department.

Sincerely,

Mark Baumer

September 2, 2008

Dear Job People,

I have a responsible voice. My calm facial emotions are very comfortable within office settings, especially in the suburbs near other major business opportunities. My mother taught me how to be administrative in all aspects of my life. I feel confident that I could enjoy being an administrative assistant for the rest of my life.

Sincerely,

Mark Baumer

September 2, 2008

Dear Job People,

One of the requirements for this job is getting to work on time. I have never been late to anything except once I showed up three years late to a dentist appointment.

Another requirement for this job is "computer proficiency." I am very proficient with computers. I recently took a course that taught me how to turn computers on and how to manage them while they are awake.

Sincerely,

Mark Baumer

September 2, 2008

Dear Job People,

I wish there was some way to convey my excitement about this position. I think I am going to go throw books at myself now. I look forward to the possibility of talking to whoever reads this cover letter. Thank you.

Sincerely,

Mark Baumer

September 4, 2008

Dear Job People,

The best professional situation for me would be a workplace where I'm allowed to do whatever I want and at the end of the week someone hands me three-hundred dollars in cash. Let me know if this is what you are looking for.

Sincerely,

Mark Baumer

September 4, 2008

Dear Job People,

I recently felt depressed because my abilities have yet to generate any opportunities. I think I am just going to go live inside a website.

Sincerely,

Mark Baumer

September 4, 2008

Dear Job People,

If you have any jobs please email them to me. I am confident I can pretend to be fascinated by their descriptions. My qualifications are no better than any other person because I don't believe in the idea of inherent genius. Sometimes I have trouble with oral communication.

Sincerely,

Mark Baumer

September 4, 2008

Dear Job People,

I have applied to a lot of jobs, but I think everyone is too busy to notice that I am a real person who lacks the emotional capability to deal with a world that has overrun by auto generated, computerized responses to job application submissions. Also, I am sort of weird, but lately, I've been keeping a monthly spreadsheet to track all my strange behaviors in an attempt to maybe eliminate them somewhat from my life. Please call me, but don't leave a voicemail because they're annoying.

Sincerely,

Mark Baumer

September 4, 2008

Dear Job People,

I recently decided I wanted to be a mail processor. I have experience touching mail. I believe in my ability to efficiently touch mail. If I get this job I hope to touch so much mail that someday I become the world's greatest mail processor.

Sincerely,

Mark Baumer

September 4, 2008

Dear Job People,

When I was a child I wanted to be a brick building at a prestigious institution. This no longer seems possible. Anyway, I am sort of qualified to be an administrative assistant.

Sincerely,

Mark Baumer

September 4, 2008

Dear Job People,

Would you be more or less likely to hire me if I told you one of my teeth is probably going to fall out unless I get dental coverage?

Sincerely,

Mark Baumer

September 5, 2008

Dear Job People,

I am a very thorough and meticulous member of society. I enjoy peeling the skin off grapes, almonds, and beans. This is one of the many skills I learned on my own while being raised by parents. It would make them very proud if I got this job as an administrative assistant.

Sincerely,

Mark Baumer

September 5, 2008

Dear Job People,

For the past year I've been doing two things: living and breathing. I've learned a lot from these two experiences. Sometimes I forget I have to keep living and for a few days there will be no stability in my life, but I never forget to keep breathing. I've been successfully breathing for as long as I can remember.

Thank you for your time,

Mark Baumer

My personal statement from when I applied to Brown

Dear Mother,

I am going to Brown in the fall to study at their MFA fiction program. I thought you would be happy to know this. I haven't told anyone else yet. I wanted you to be the first to know. Please don't make too big of a deal out of it. I'm not sure if Brown actually wants me. I decided to go to Brown regardless if they accept me.

If I was you and you were Brown I would say, "I accept myself to Brown," but I don't want you to be Brown because that would make you a set of old buildings and I don't want people to think my mother is an old pile of buildings. Also, I don't want to learn how to write inside of you. If you were Brown and I was learning to write inside of you my stories would suffer. You would always read them over my shoulder and tell me I was being too weird and not putting in enough "real stuff." Then you would say, "Remember that funny thing you wrote about Uncle Bob? I liked that. You should write more about Uncle Bob." So I would, but it would be about how Uncle Bob wakes up and opens a can of vegetables and then tapes the telephone to the side of his head and doesn't cook the can of vegetables until dinnertime and you would say, "No, write about the stuff Bob actually does. Write about how he gives you $20 every Christmas." And I'd write about how I took the $20 and bought a typewriter and drove around town with the typewriter in my lap typing stories and you would say, "That's a little better, but I don't remember you ever doing that unless you did it with your friends and never told me."

It will be odd showing up at Brown if they don't accept me. In my head, I imagine I'd go to classes and sit in the corner and maybe some people would point and say, "Who's that," but otherwise they wouldn't bother me and I'd learn some really good quotes about writing and hear some really good stories that would make me think, "I wish I wrote that." Then I'd read something I wrote to the class, but I wouldn't want to interrupt so I'd kind of just mouth my stories and hope someone was good at reading lips and paying attention to me.

What will probably happen is that I won't be allowed in class and I'll have to stand outside the door and someone will pull down the shade on the door so I can't see inside. Then I'll have to hide a tape recorder in the class and steal a syllabus and do all the work on my own in a tiny room made from the forgotten closet of a janitor somewhere on campus. Or I will rent out a closet in someone's apartment and pay one hundred dollars a month and it'll creep my new roommates out, but I'll mostly keep to myself and when it gets warm I'll find a roof to sit on because I like roofs.

I've never told you this mother, but when I arrived back in Boston after hitchhiking to California the year I graduated I didn't have anywhere to stay so I slept on a roof at the MIT campus for a week. It was very enjoyable. I had a sleeping bag. I read Pynchon and made a list of all the things I wanted to accomplish and I was naïve in more ways than I am now, but it was okay because it felt good coming up with lists and being gullible enough to believe that one day I'd do them all.

Here is part of that list:

> **6**. Write the sequel to the book I'm writing about hitchhiking across America
> **7**. Write the third installment (Crossing the Americas series). It will be about hitchhiking across America blindfolded
> **8**. Write the fourth installment (Crossing the Americas series). It will be about hitting a golf ball to South America.
> ● ● ●
> **35**. In twenty years, return to the road and retrace the first trip across America with my friend. Write final installment (Crossing the Americas series).

I am not sure I'll ever do any of the things on this list. I'm sorry, mother. I don't think you understand my brain. I don't really understand it either. At the moment I am in a mess with the first book of the series. I've written over 100,000 words about hitchhiking across America and not even half the story has been told, plus much of the reality of the story is fading the more I write.

I wish you could see the closet I set up as my office here in Los Angeles. I am in it now. I like it a lot. It feels ingenious. I am very proud of it. I am more proud of the closet than I am of this letter. If you could see this closet you would probably think it's a little weird because I have a toothbrush in here with me and sometimes I'll brush my teeth for a couple of hours as I work. I'm pretty confident I'll get into Brown. I've done a lot of work to improve my writing. I'm doing a website thing and I've written a lot of stories this year. I would show them to you, but I don't want you to think I am weirder than you already think I am. Also, I think every writer has to clear a series of hurdles before they feel comfortable showing their mother their writing. I don't think I've cleared any of those hurdles. I think all my work sort of legitimizes the last two years I've spent taking crappy jobs that were only worthwhile because they gave me the opportunity to write in my free time.

Still, I do not hold any hope that I'll ever be famous. You and father should forget about that ever happening. Even if I do get into Brown, I believe very little will change outside of my writing. My writing will improve and I'll have more self-confidence, but I will not become a world-famous author. Brown will not lead to such glory. I will not be selected for Oprah's book club. No one will recognize me on the street. Your monthly book club will not want to read the books I write. I will continue to be hesitant to show you my writing. I don't think you will ever particularly enjoy the things I write.

I suspect you're letting father read the letter with you. Please remind him I'm never going to be a Major League Baseball player. I know he's never quite admitted that he's embarrassed by my pseudo-prep-school-educated-liberal-floating-in-the-clouds-writing-poetry-about-gnomes-and-elves lifestyle, but he's got to accept that I probably won't be a millionaire anytime soon and that I'll continue working odd jobs that won't further my career so I can work on my writing. Still, I understand it must be hard for him. I remember how happy he used to look at my Little League baseball games. I haven't seen him smile like that in a long time.

Also, I would appreciate it if neither you nor father wrote to Brown on my behalf. I don't think I could handle the other students finding out I got in because my mother wrote my letter of recommendation. And please don't let dad call to lecture me about my personal statement I'm submitting to Brown like he does with my cover letters when I'm applying for a new job. I don't think Brown is the place where you write about all your credentials and act formal and hold yourself as the greatest of all the tin shits. I hope it's not that sort of a place. If it is then I am not going to be accepted. To be honest, I think it's the sort of place where you do weird things with words and language construction and they get really big erections. I'm sorry I said "erection," mother. Forget I said it. They probably don't get erections. I've never gotten an erection, mother. Forget that the word "erection" exists. It's gone.

Anyway, you're probably wondering about my personal statement to Brown. I figure you deserve to see it. I'm not quite finished. It's gone through a series of drafts. There have been a couple hundred versions. Here are a few.

Dear Brown,
I only applied to Brown. I do not want to go anywhere else. I know this limits my chances of improving my life. I do not know what else to say.

Dear Brown,
I have never done cocaine.

Dear Brown,
I write in a tiny office. The dimensions are three feet by four feet by eight feet. It is a coat closet. I built a desk inside.

Dear Brown,
For a long time I fretted over what I should say in this letter, but then I decided that nothing matters and felt a little better until my head called my bluff and said, "Okay, if nothing matters then give me cocaine." And I began to fret about the letter again and wondered if my head had a cocaine addiction that I didn't know about.

Dear Brown,
I believe it is probably important to talk about my accomplishments, but I feel stupid talking about them. I feel like everyone is always trying to impress someone by telling them what they do. I do not like going to parties because people ask me what I do and I don't feel confident saying anything. Once I said, "I'm a writer," and the person said, "Oh me too. I got this idea about a paleontologist who is digging a hole and finds a box and opens it and this hand grabs the paleontologist and pulls them inside and it's Jesus or the Messiah and they are in a space of nothing and the paleontologist has to go back to the beginning of time to right all the wrongs in history, but I kind of want to add a James Patterson aspect to it because he's probably my favorite writer though I'm not really sure how to go about doing it." When this person at the party finished explaining their idea my head said, "Cocaine, cocaine, nothing matters, cocaine."

Dear Brown,
I do not have a drug problem, honest. I have only seen one person doing cocaine. My friend was doing it. It was bizarre. I wondered if his head was saying, "Cocaine, cocaine, nothing matters, cocaine." I was going to ask him, but I forgot. I felt very out of place at this party where my friend was doing cocaine. Someone asked me what I did and my friend said, "He's a writer." Another kid did some cocaine and then said, "You should read Fitzgerald." Later, when my friend and I left the party my friend said, "You need to loosen up. It's cool. Cocaine helps. Those guys were cool. They were very generous with their cocaine. They did not care how much I took. They are very rich. I think I want to be like that. I want to be very rich so I can be careless with cocaine."

Dear Brown,
This is not going well.

Dear Brown,
Maybe it would be best if I told you my accomplishments and said goodbye. I will try that.

Dear Brown,
I have never done cocaine or heroin. Goodbye.

Dear Brown,
Now when I go to parties and people ask me what I do I tell them I am a collector of small places.

Dear Brown,
When I moved out of my parents' house the first place I lived was inside a very small room. It was very nice. I did not have internet or television. If I get into Brown I want to find a small room like this. I want my bed to almost be bigger than my room and I want my room to almost be smaller than me.

Dear Brown,
I once wrote a story about chuckling gnomes. It was published on the internet, but then eight months later the foreign investors who ran the website pulled the plug and my story about chuckling gnomes disappeared, and I was left looking out the window wondering why all the gnomes turned into pigeons.

Dear Brown,
I wrote another story about a party where someone masturbates in the pantry. I do not know if people at this party did cocaine. My grasp on the characters in this story was not very strong. I think I told them, "Please, no cocaine in this story," and then while I was focusing on the person masturbating in the pantry a lot of the partygoers ran to the bathroom to pet the white cheetah. It was not a good story.

Dear Brown,
In the back of my head, I still hold on to the hope that one day I will get paid money to play baseball. Maybe this is the reason I do not completely give up and do cocaine. I guess if someone cut off both my arms and robotic arms weren't invented yet then I would do a lot of cocaine.

Dear Brown,
I don't know why I think not doing cocaine will help me play professional baseball. Keith Hernandez once said, "40% of baseball players do cocaine." Then his brain said, "Shhhhh," and he started to inch backwards as he waved his arms and said, "Please, no more cocaine, no thank you."

Dear Brown,
Once I wrote a story that wasn't very good.

Dear Brown,
I sent a story that wasn't very good to a bunch of different places with a cover letter that was three times longer than the story. One place I submitted the story rejected it, but they published the cover letter.

Dear Brown,
I submitted the story that wasn't very good somewhere else and I included a long cover letter and once again the story was rejected but my cover letter was accepted.

Dear Brown,
I don't think you believe that I've never done cocaine.

Dear Brown,
I would not be upset if you rejected my stories from Brown, but accepted my cover letter. I am kind of hoping you do this.

Dear Brown,
When I was in eighth grade some kids were smoking marijuana out of a pipe shaped like a penis and then in high school I broke my leg and was prescribed Oxycodone but didn't really need them, and someone at school asked what drugs the doctor gave me and I said, "Oxycodone" and he said, "Give them to me so I can sell them," but he didn't sell them. Instead, he ate them all himself. Then a few years later I saw my friend doing cocaine at a party. I have not seen very much drug usage. I think there may have been a few other times, but it's not really that important. I'm sure Brown does not care to know about all the times their students have seen people do drugs.

Dear Brown,
I bet my mother would say, "Why do you keep talking about cocaine? You're wrecking your chances."

Dear Brown,
My dad would say, "I once smoked marijuana in high school before I had to pitch and could barely stand up straight, but I threw a two-hitter. Then I blew out my arm and it was sad because I knew I would never be a major league baseball player. Then I had a son and I prayed to god and said, 'Please let him be part of the 60% of Major League Baseball players who don't do cocaine,' and now I kick myself for being so specific in

my prayers because my son is not a Major League Baseball player and I wouldn't have cared if he was part of the 40% who did cocaine."

Dear Brown,
I don't think many people understand me. I write the same word in a different place every day and people ask, "What are you doing?" and I tell them and they look at me confused so I stopped writing in the daylight and instead I write it at night and no one asks me what I'm doing.

Dear Brown,
At Thanksgiving, my family says, "Your website is interesting, but I don't really get it." Then after I explain it to them they kind of look at me crooked and say, "Weren't you supposed to be a famous baseball player?"

Dear Brown,
When people ask me about my website I try to describe it as simple as I can. I say, "I write the same word somewhere every day and then take a picture then I put the picture on the computer and then I put it on the internet. I also write a story for each day, but most of the stories don't have anything to do with the pictures anymore. I think that is where most of the understanding is lost. I am a little upset the stories don't have anything to do with the pictures anymore."

Dear Brown,
Sometimes people ask me what I've done since I graduated college and all I can really tell them is, "I've written the same word every day." This does not sound very exciting. I feel like I'm treading water. My plan is to keep writing the same word every day for the next ten years. Ten years with no development. Most people would laugh at my ten-year plan.

Dear Brown,
I also hitchhiked from Maine to California with a friend when I graduated college. This seems pretty big. I only mention it because in St. Louis we got a ride from an airplane engineer and he started smoking crack and offered some to us. I said, "No thank you," but my friend said, "Sure," and he smoked crack.

Dear Brown,
In 2008 I decided to write a new story every day. The first one was about Christmas. The second one was about empty cupboards. The third one was about a ladybug massacre. The fourth one was about not being pregnant. The fifth one was about a camera dying. The sixth was eleven woodpeckers on a wire. The seventh was little people falling out of the ceiling...etc.

Dear Brown,

I am not sure if I should tell you what all the stories are about. It seems very boring to me. Summaries are boring. I feel you are very bored reading this summary.

Dear Brown,

This letter is a summary of me and everything about me plus cocaine. It's like I've made a salad out of my accomplishments and then my friend snuck in the kitchen and dumped a vial of cocaine into the dressing and when I got back from the bathroom I shook the dressing and dumped it on my summary.

Dear Brown,

I think my friend snuck on my computer when I was sleeping and randomly added the word "cocaine" to my letter so I would look less promising and thus would not be accepted and leave him.

Dear Brown,

This is why I think it is best that I go to Brown regardless if I am accepted.

Dear Brown,

This is not Mark. This is his friend. Please don't make him into something he's not. I've known him for twelve years. He's never going to be an intellectual. He's kind of an idiot. Really good ideas come out of his stupidity. It's very odd. I don't want him to go to Brown and have him start believing he's something he's not. He's not lying when he says he doesn't do cocaine. Cocaine would destroy him. I don't think he will ever do it. You don't have to worry. He is a little strange. He doesn't drink alcohol. Sometimes I call him a pussy because he doesn't drink alcohol, but it's because I just want to hang out with him when I do alcohol. To be honest, there's a part of me that wishes he did lots of cocaine, but it is kind of a fantasy. In this fantasy, I imagine he is very rich and does all kinds of cocaine and shares it generously and we can eventually visit Antarctica.

Dear Brown,

My life used to be waking up at 3:30 a.m. to go to work so I would be done at 11 a.m. and could come home to read and write. Then I moved and had no money and had to get a nine-to-five job. I still wake up at 3:30 in the morning. I write until I have to go to work. Then I become a drone at work. When work is over I bring home a bottle full of free coffee and drink it all so I'll have energy to work on my stuff.

Dear Brown,

I don't think there is room in my life for cocaine unless I got a job where I was supposed to do cocaine. Maybe that's why I wanted to be a professional baseball player.

Dear Brown,

I think the reason I like collecting tiny offices and rooms is because I don't want to leave space for cocaine.

Dear Brown,

I want to write a letter to Yogi Berra's son, Dale Berra, who was involved in the 1985 Pittsburg Drug Trials. I think it is fitting because his initials are the same as yours. I don't really know what to say so I'm just going to rewrite the letters I'm sending to you and address them to him. Here is a version of the rewrite:

Dale Berra,

I have never done cocaine, but if nothing matters then give me cocaine. Do you sometimes wonder if your head has a cocaine problem? Did your father sometimes hit you when he realized you weren't going to be a Hall of Famer like him? My father never hit me when he figured out I wasn't going to be a Major League Baseball player, but maybe he thought, "My life is over." I killed a little bit of my father just like you probably killed a little bit of your father when you went to those trials in Pittsburg. You probably don't want to hear about this. I do not have a drug problem. You probably think I'm a pussy. I have only seen one person do cocaine. You have seen Dave Parker do cocaine. What's Dave Parker like on cocaine? Does his head say, "Cocaine, cocaine, nothing matters, cocaine, 1978 NL MVP"? Was Keith Hernandez right? Is it kind of like what your father said? Baseball is 90% mental and 40% cocaine? Did Keith Hernandez ever run into your clubhouse yelling, "Cocaine, cocaine, nothing matters, 1979 NL MVP, Seinfeld" and then slowly inch backwards, apologizing, after Willie Stargell jumped out of a locker and said, "I won the 1979 NL MVP"? Was your mother mad that you did cocaine? I think my mother is very mad that I am talking about cocaine in my graduate school application. It would be funny if your father admitted to smoking marijuana in high school too.

Dear Brown,

I want to be serious for a second.

Dear Brown,

If I am not accepted to Brown I am still going to Brown. I am not quite sure what that means. Maybe it'll mean I write a book called, "I Was Not Accepted to Brown, but I Still Went and Wrote This Book," or maybe I won't go at all, but I'll still write the book or maybe I'll go and hide in the ceiling and begin writing my sample and personal statement for next year.

Dear Brown,

It is important to know that I am not a joke. Instead of doing cocaine, I have worked the last two years on my writing. I have started four novels and tossed them away when they were done. I feel like failure is a big part of writing. My technique with short stories has begun to take shape. I have submitted them to various online magazines under an alias. I've had more than a dozen published. My plan is to edit the stories from 2008 and get one-hundred of the stories published in 2009. Eventually, I'll have enough for a short story collection. That would be nice, but my ultimate goal is to write longer works. I want to be able to do both. I want to write novels and not toss them out. I'm afraid I can't do this on my own. I need the opportunity offered at Brown. I need time and guidance to help me create these longer works I have in mind, otherwise I'm afraid I'll never progress beyond the short story, which I guess is fine. I can live with only writing short stories, but I would like more. I would really like to be able to throw my work at people and have it be large enough to do considerable damage.

Dear Brown,

I do not want you to think I am depressed. I will not get emotional and take lots of cocaine if you do not accept me. I think there is a 90% possibility that I show up at Brown regardless if I am accepted or not. I probably will not be seen, but you'll know I'm there when you start seeing the same word pop up in random spots around campus.

So that's it, mother. You probably don't understand. I'm not sure Brown will understand either. I feel very nervous about sending them any of the letters I just showed you. I wish I could make it easier. It would be nice if I could just say things simply and you could bring them to your book club and all the ladies would be jealous of you because I am your son, but I just don't think I can do that. I'm sorry, mother. That's why I want to go to Brown, regardless if they will have me. I want you to be able to say, "My son goes to Brown."

Love,

MARK

#brownmfa

Brown MFA Eating Concrete Popcorn

Yesterday there was a big meeting with all the first year MFA writers. A man named Gale emailed everyone beforehand and said, "My name is Peter, but you can call me Gale." I was nervous to meet everyone in the program. There were a lot of rumors floating around. Someone told me one of the other fiction writers spent the summer sitting in a dirt parking lot gently pressing his face on the keys of a typewriter. My understanding going into the meeting was that we were all supposed to have prepared a novel manuscript for the group. I think my dad said, "Gale probably wants everyone to bring in copies of their novel manuscripts and hand them out." The one writer who spent the summer in the dirt parking lot was supposedly excused from bringing in any of his novels. I've heard rumors he wrote four or five but threw them all in a lake at the end of summer. Brown is in the process of dredging this lake. The school has very high hopes for this writer. They gave him an extra fellowship because he walked to Providence from the dirt parking lot after he kicked four novel manuscripts into the lake. Going into the meeting I was a little worried I would lose my funding because I don't have a novel yet. One of the poets said, "I've probably written four-thousand poem collections." Another poet said, "I was a nuclear physicist. I've never written a poem." I brought in copies of a menu from the Vietnamese sandwich shop down the street from my apartment. I thought maybe people would laugh when I handed this out as my novel. This whole MFA thing has been pretty embarrassing. The other people in the program are always asking me how many novels I have. They say, "I wrote two new novels last night." The meeting turned out to be okay. No one brought in copies of their manuscripts. Everyone just sat in a circle and looked at each other until Gale said, "Hello motherfuckers. I'm Peter." I think that kind of broke the ice and everyone got emotional and we all shared why we wanted to be writers. Most of us said, "I've wanted to be a writer since second grade when I learned about Martin Luther King." A few people had notes prepared. I did not have anything prepared. I just stood up and said, "I want to be a writer because my dad wears jeans," and then sat down. Everyone laughed. Then Gale said, "Group hug?" Later, one of the poets said, "Damn, I want to play basketball with Gale."

Writing a Novel Called, 'Sinks on Planes'

One of the MFA professors had a talk with me. He said, "I'm concerned. The transcripts tell me you are struggling with prepositions." I told him I didn't know what a preposition was. He said, "Writing good prepositions is like owning a sink." I said there are times when I knowingly dump things down the sink I'm not supposed to. He said, "You clearly are falling behind your classmates. Do you even have a plan yet?" I said something about novels and attending lectures on the idea of national healthcare. The professor said, "I feel you could incorporate sinks into this plan." I told the professor I had the urge to touch his face. He ignored me and continued to talk about sinks.

When I got home I turned my sink on and off for an hour and then tried to write a novel about the experience. It went okay. I wrote 3,000 words where a character turned his sink on and off. I might bring the piece to the next workshop. Here is an excerpt:

"The sink seemed to have two options. He spent an hour trying to find a third. The sink didn't agree. It said, 'wee wee wee wee wee wee.' Sometimes it said, 'oot oot oot oot ott.'"

Should I try and finish this 'novel'? I lied. I haven't really written 3,000. I've only written 37 words. The above excerpt is all there is. I am excited about this novel.

The Brown MFA Spanish Program

I've decided not to take any literature courses. I don't think anyone cares. I don't think there are any requirements for this MFA program. I am in Basic Spanish. Nothing really matters. All the students are 12. They don't even know what an MFA is. At the beginning of the semester, there were forty people trying to get in the class. The professor said, "It makes no sense for you to take Spanish. There is no way you will ever pass. You are too old." I told the professor, "Mi casa es tu casa." The professor said, "All the other students will be scared because you are fifteen years older than them." One student asked the professor, 'Do those grad students have to be in our class? It feels like my dad is taking Spanish.' I felt bad for this student. I don't think I would want to take Spanish with my dad.

One of the poets is taking Spanish with me. We work together when we have to work in groups. He said, "I hope I can fully consume this Spanish book. Then I will take the knowledge down to Columbia." Last night, I chatted with this poet on the internet. He said, "The professor called me today. She said many dirty Spanish words I didn't know and then hung up." I said, "Maybe she sees you as a mature and responsible option for her three kids." He said, "I think she was drunk." I said, "Maybe you two can move to Columbia. You could leave her kids in a ditch." The poet didn't like this idea. He said, "The professor would not be enjoyable in Columbia."

We had our first test a few days ago. It feels weird to take tests. I was a little concerned. Spanish is pretty insane. Some of the other students may have shit themselves. I think I was still shitting myself when I was twelve. I think in my last little league game ever there was an incident. I was twelve. Someone's father threw a beer can at me. I might have got hit in the head. I passed out. I woke up a hospital bed. When I went back to school all the kids laughed at me and held their noses.

One of the students in my Spanish class said, "I went to your website and read your stuff. I didn't understand it. You said, 'You're purposely trying to fail Spanish.'" I did not know what to say to them. I kind of thought, "What the fuck are you doing on my website?" I wanted to tell them to stop coming to my site. I kind of wanted to take a picture of their face and put it on my site under the caption, "Get off my website. You're too young."

The professor emailed me my grade for the first test. I got a 16.5 out of 20. I got 82.5% of the test correct. I am a little disappointed I didn't fail. It would be funnier if I'd failed.

I asked my dad for his pin number. He said, 'the date when I first had sex with your mother'

"so I was doing lines and the Albino powdered napalm told me everyone's pin number and I put these in the remix, zero four two seven seven nine, and CEOs freaked because all their pin numbers began leaking on the internet, and Albino powdered napalm laughed and said, nothing should ever matter, but CEOs are always saying, everything matters, and I was already in their bank accounts putting their money up my pussy and then CEOs tried to act like nothing was wrong and had a big lunch for everyone and I was invited and the whole time they just talked shit on Albino powdered napalm and said, Albino powdered napalm is a faggot, and they asked me why I wasn't laughing and I said, zero four two seven seven nine, and I started laughing and they said, that was the date of the first time I cheated on my wife, and then they got sad and remembered their son had already drained the rest of their bank account through his septal perforation and later I fucked the son and he fucked all the money into me, but I didn't mention any of this to the CEOs at the luncheon and instead ate my lunch and they asked if I would be the guest speaker so I said I would and I basically told all the CEO DADs to crawl out their son's dick and they did and then I went home and CEOs continued crawling out of their sons's faces and when they got out the CEO DADs asked their children what happened to their deviated septums and their sons made excuses and didn't tell their CEO DADs that they traded their deviated septums for low grade Albino powdered napalm cut with fiber glass and fixed gear bikes and that iPhone application that plays my song every time you get an erection and CEO DADs didn't understand and shrugged and continue to let their sons fuck all their money into me and into low grade Albino powdered napalm."

from I AM A ROAD

In 2010, I walked across America in eighty-one days. I began the journey on May 10th in Tybee Island, Georgia. It ended on July 29th in Santa Monica, California.

Day 1

A small man in Georgia watched me kneel down and kiss the Atlantic Ocean. I told him I was walking across America. He smiled and pointed. "Use this road," he said. I began walking. A few minutes after the first piece of sweat leaked out of me, a dead animal crumbling on the side of the road nodded and said, "It'll be okay." I walked until I was near some gasoline. Inside the bathroom for gasoline customers, I rubbed my face and hands on a sink. Then I left the bathroom and looked at the shelf of peanuts. A girl asked if I had seen her father. I put half a peanut in my mouth. The girl said, "I'm worried because sometimes he forgets he's my father." I apologized and put the other half of the peanut in my mouth. By mid-afternoon, my body was so dirty a seventeen-year-old girl asked why I was so dirty. I pointed at the moon. She said her mother sometimes got paid to clean people. One of my legs told my other leg to keep moving. Outside a grocery store, four different pregnant humans were talking on their cell phones. Some of them had face tumors because a scientist once said, "If you press a phone on your face for too long you'll get tumors." My body asked me for food so I gave it some food. America was built on the notion of spending large sums of money even when you can't afford to spend large sums of money. None of the people I saw while walking had large sums of money. As the sun's glow faded, the logical pieces of my brain lost their ability to do logic. It felt like my brain was being dragged behind me in a sack. A dried piece of sweat on my eyebrow began to leak. The inside of my left boot was swollen. Teardrops dripped on my heart. I was standing at the bottom of a hill. Instead of climbing this hill, I decided to lie down in the field next to the hill. I had walked twenty-six miles. My only blanket was made of sweat. As my thoughts drifted away one of them suggested renting new sweat. I tried to smile but I was already asleep.

Before the sun woke up, I felt a piece of wood leaning on me. I had only slept a few hours. A bean crawled in my mouth and waited until the thing on the edge of the horizon began yelling before it crawled down my throat. The beginning of each day was very sad because I had to reteach my feet how to absorb the pain of the road and remind them the past did not exist and neither did the future. It usually took my body two or three miles before it forgot I was wearing feet. People inside automobiles seemed concerned I was not in an automobile. I was not concerned because automobiles had never been essential to the process of life. For a few minutes, I stopped next to a hill and yelled at it. The hill shrugged and did not stop being a hill. I stopped yelling and walked in silence until I was no longer touching the hill. The hill did not follow me or even notice I was no longer touching it. My favorite moment from the entire journey was when I put an almond in my mouth and spent the rest of the day chewing it. The baby carriage seemed to be awkwardly leaning on one of its wheels. I re-inflated the tire. The baby carriage's wheel got bad again. I put more air in it. For a few miles it was okay. I passed a hospital. The insect wound no longer hurt. I ignored the hospital. Instead, I stopped at a gas station. The tan-colored door next to the ice machine was locked. Someone inside was doing what I wanted to do. I waited. Eventually, the tan-colored door was unlocked and I did something. An hour passed. I ate a low sodium potato chip while I waited for the next hour to finish passing. In one of the towns I walked through, a man was selling all his cows because the urine in his body had turned purple. At the town line, two men in a field were trying to lift the same dead twig. The wheel on the baby carriage nearly fell off halfway up a gradual incline. I put on a new tire. At first, the baby carriage limped on the new wheel, but it soon figured out how to walk normally. One of the last drips of sunshine was twinkling. A family stopped and looked at me. I winked. Their automobile got scared and drove away. It felt like there was another town in the distance. The sun was fading. I walked alone in the dark. In the next town, a man in the gas station touched his hair before he unwrapped an ice cream cone and let me put it in my mouth. I found a church for large, wealthy people. It was almost eleven p.m. For dinner, I had a single can of pea pods. When the can was empty, a cop showed up and asked if I had been eating pea pods. I lied and told him I hadn't. He nodded and drove away.

America was a child. I tried not to look at the swollen pieces of America. A small wound on the end of my thumb said, "Earth is dying." The sun told me to eat the baby carriage. I tried to stand up but fell on my own legs. A slug was resting on one of the carriage's wheels. For breakfast, I ate a handful of American dirt because it was shaped like food. The baby carriage did not eat because it did not have a mouth. My feet were too tired to be lonely, but they still walked alone next to the highway. I paused near an anthill and counted the ants until I no longer felt sad. One of the ants reminded me of a beautiful girl I had once seen touch a salad. I did not want to move anymore. I could not tell if there was a mountain in the distance or not. A truck pulled over. Inside the truck, a man and his wife sat next to something named "Peter." The wife said they were on their way to buy a new air conditioner. I looked at Peter. He didn't say anything. The wife handed me some money. I put it in a pouch near my armpit. Peter barked and the truck drove away. I walked a few more inches before I sat down in the middle of the road and ate a spoonful of peanut butter. The baby carriage fell asleep near my foot. I looked at my skin. It seemed concerned. All my containers were empty. For a few miles, the road thought it had become a pebble. I asked this pebble where to get water. It ignored me. I put it in my mouth. The pebble was hollow. There was no water in it. As I walked into the next town I thought about the time my father had worked in a small bean factory. For the entire summer, our family had only eaten canned beans. Each town was another warm breath, but I had no interest in breathing these breaths. A mother—breastfeeding her eight-year-old child outside a gas station—asked me for money. I ignored her and instead imagined what it would feel like to pinch something on my body until it squirted milk. Inside the gas station, I realized all my cotton balls were dirty so I bought a bag of cotton balls. But when I opened the bag I noticed all the cotton balls had yellow grease stains. Somewhere an overweight teenager shrugged. It began to rain. The baby carriage and I passed a cage filled with buffaloes and ostriches. One of the buffaloes sat down and melted. A child reached into the cage and poked the dead buffalo. The raindrops were meowing louder. I worried about where I would sleep. The carriage and I kept walking. We found an abandoned gas station filled with pigeons. I sat on the floor and put something green in my mouth until the rain stopped. My swollen feet did not hurt as much as they had hurt before the rain fell. America was still a child. Nothing had changed.

I stopped at a gas station. It was after midnight. My feet asked the box of melted cheese behind the counter if he knew how to not be tired. The box of melted cheese continued to melt. A few miles later I almost lay down in a parking lot and died, but the parking lot said, "You're too close to the ocean." I was either delirious from not sleeping or from walking thousands of miles. My brain no longer believed people needed brains. For two miles I walked in the middle of the street before I realized I was in the middle of the street. Luckily, nothing got me dead. It was so late there were no cars. My whole body was hallucinating. I was not sure if all the footsteps I was creating were real. I tried to float horizontally. A nearby blinking streetlight reminded me that humans had not learned to float. At three a.m. I saw a bench and thought it was human, but when I reached down to sit on it the bench ran away. My last drip of water said, "I am a dehydrated igloo raised on low-grade meats." After I put it in my mouth I had no more drips. All the gas stations were closed. An hour passed. I was worried I would die if I didn't find a drip soon. Another hour passed. I laughed at the thought of dying so close to the end of my journey. I continued laughing until a man who had once been religious gave me a drip of his juice. The buildings were getting larger. My body was a little sad. Most Americans will never be as tall as the buildings in California. I continued moving closer to the ocean living on the other side of America. A sleeping dog asked me to rub it. I rubbed something. The sleeping dog was not a dog. After a normal amount of struggle, the sun rose and thousands of people began their commute to work. I walked past my ex-girlfriend's apartment. She was outside holding a cupcake. I waved. She asked if I wanted the cupcake. I ate a piece of the cupcake and continued walking. She followed and took some pictures. The streets became very overweight from all the automobiles. Everyone had expensive gel inside their hair. As I walked I worried the police might shoot me for not owning an automobile. My ex-girlfriend and I were the only ones using the sidewalks. I took a deep breath. I could almost feel the ocean sweating the same sweat I was sweating. A bird with no feathers barked. I was jealous of the birds until I remembered I didn't have feathers either. My heartbeats were completely swollen. I could smell the ocean. I began to cry. The ocean just looked at me and shrugged as I limped towards it. When I reached the sand, my body no longer hurt because it was no longer required to be the body I had required myself to be. The spacesuit I had worn the entire trip was soiled with every mile I had traveled. I removed these stains and placed them in a trash barrel. Tears continued to leak from my brain. I no longer had to pretend I wasn't human. The ocean barely acknowledged me as I stepped into it. I didn't know what else to do so I just floated.

AMERICA IS A GIANT BARREL OF AUTOMOBILES RUNNING ON FUMES OVER A BARREN WASTELAND...

The soil where I was born was constructed from a pile of melted white penises that had once crawled out of a herpes sore named "democracy."

Everyone was supposed to bow to this juice hole, but I think we were all too busy looking at the electric wizard standing on his wound ship as the wound ship slowly sank and we all had to learn how to breathe with water in our lungs.

Like some people, I am almost sort of pleasant to be around, but on the surface, I have problems just like the whole world has problems.

Most Americans are still smiling, but deep in their subconscious everyone is disappointed that no one has shot them yet.

The only way to live a complete and full life is if you are elected the president before you are born and then you die in a gunfight a few minutes after the doctor detaches you from the womb.

Happiness used to be nothing more than rubbing your pistol in the dirt of an abandoned cornfield.

I used to be a large, soft-spoken man that spent most of his life wearing plaid shirts full of submissive colors, but all my pores got clogged by the nervous energy that my face constantly leaked in my twenties when I only ate bacon donuts because I thought it would be cool to someday get pig cancer in my stomach. The store that sold the bacon donuts went out of business. It was replaced by a wooden table that was environmentally balanced and globally-aware that I was not happy so it fed me a twig of lettuce and my brain got better.

Please fill my tits with money so I can learn how to enjoy my tits without having to worry about what my tits are going to eat because my tits only want to eat expensive tit-things like bread chandeliers and limos made entirely out of carbohydrates.

The last time I died, I sent an email to the hole growing in the center of my forehead and it told me that we should have more respect for ourselves, but three hours later I was back to sewing electric wizards on my face because the internet told me I would get some of the drips leaking from the welfare checks of a white, low-income portable flat-screen television if I just rubbed the dance floor a little harder with my penis.

It may not seem like there's any point to all this, but I still have hope because all my boyfriends and I failed every high school math test we ever took and it was okay. We were too busy being pregnant. None of us knew how to be fathers. At night we would press our wombs together so the babies could talk to each other.

WHITE PEOPLE IN BLACKFACE WEARING KKK HOODS UNDER THEIR HIJABS WHILE RIDING MOTORCYCLES

After work, a white man named "Doug" liked to read magazines while eating pizza. Sometimes Doug read a magazine that talked about how all the dead white people in America got killed by other white people who would eventually get killed by even more white people. Doug was scared. He only worked with white people. Doug decided to wear a motorcycle helmet to work because he thought it would make him safe.

#gasolinethoughts

Ideas are constantly forming inside everyone's mind, but because everyone's mind has a different way of interpreting their own ideas it's not unreasonable to believe that everyone's brain is forming the same idea.

INVISIBLE MOSQUITOS

Four teenagers named "Phil" were tired of their dad's not being rich.

"It is very frustrating to have a poor dad," said Phil. His dad was so poor that their house had turned into a mosquito.

The oldest Phil sometimes pretended he didn't have any dads. The school nurse was very concerned by the way Phil pretended his dad's were not dads.

Phil's science teacher tried to make him a new dad. Phil did not like people making him new dad's. All his new dads usually had mosquito blood.

One day in history class, the four teenagers named "Phil" learned in their u.s.a. history textbook that no one had ever traveled back in time.

Phil did not like his history teacher, so he skipped class and traveled back in time to a place where dads did not yet exist.

On a warm, octagon-shaped day in 1952, four teenagers named Phil fell out of the sky and landed in a field with only a single hay bale.

All the teenagers named Phil died except the one that landed in the hay bale.

Most of the historians that were responsible for writing about the teenagers named Phil weren't sure which Phil had died. The Phil that hadn't died wasn't worried about history so he didn't tell the historians which Phil he was, because he was more worried that someone would find the three dead teenagers named Phil and call the police.

The Phil that landed in the hay bale didn't want to go jail, so he ate the three dead Phils so there would be no proof of their existence in the year 1952.

It took Phil almost four months to eat all the dead teenagers from the future.

When he finished, one of his arms had fully turned into a mosquito.

Everyone alive in the year 1952 had never seen someone with a mosquito for an arm.

Phil and his mosquito arm became very popular.

Before the year 1952, the name "Phil" had never existed. Nearly seventy percent of all newborns from that point on were named "Phil."

A lot of people tried touching Phil.

One guy stole Phil's mosquito arm because the guy thought if he ate it, the mosquito arm would make him invisible, but the mosquito arm didn't have any special powers.

After Phil lost his mosquito arm he got very sad. He missed living in a world where his dad existed. It also sort of dawned on him for the first time that all his friends had been eaten by someone from the future.

Phil decided to go back to where he was from. It took him almost sixty years. When he finally made it to his house from the future he learned that his dad was still poor and that almost everyone in the world was named "Phil," but it was okay, even though it had gotten very difficult for people with only one arm to eat sandwiches alone.

YACHTS

At breakfast, before he ate his single slice of dry toast, my father would sometimes try to pray, but more often he turned to talk to his reflection in the chrome toaster. One morning I heard him ask his own reflection if I would grow into anything more than an ugly prince. When he talked about me, my childhood, and my lack of genitalia he struggled to say the words.

I was seven weeks old and my dick had left for South America. At the time, my young brain could not understand this. My dick did not say or wave goodbye. The morning after he left I found a scrap of yellow legal pad taped to my groin. It read, "I want to be a fascist dictator. I want it all." I envisioned a figure shouting, ordering the unarmed shot dead, and it felt like my dick was responsible for every atrocity in the modern world.

Some specialized pediatricians told me to hold my breath. I felt poked in an area that no longer was. The bib I wore revealed only a small percentage of the parts I lacked. Somewhere close my father tried and failed to watch the examinations. The remaining pieces of my body told me I was still a child, that I couldn't quite yet think or speak, or bother to.

A sexual consciousness manifested in all my male doctors. Their shriveled expertise smirked. A noise grew loud inside their heads as they remembered their own young lives, experiencing the late-adolescent developmental stage known as "My body feels like it has one thousand dicks" all over again.

At that point, I could not know what an erection was, but I had felt the specialized pediatricians arousal as they returned to the blaze of their white American male skin in its mid-twenties, roaming carelessly through a non-westernized space in an attempt to become cultured.

My dick had left me for a valid reason. It clearly understood the worth of a measurement, like a kilometer as a unit of distance, and it seemed necessary for my dick to eat as many kilometers as possible while still young. Myself, on the other hand, did not understand a kilometer. It would take me years to understand this concept. At seven weeks, my dick tired of his vague attachment to someone who did not get it.

The summation of my flesh was deficient in even the most basic way. My sweat had no carnality and would not sing a preamble of growing heat. I was a nauseous age. I absorbed emotional weight.

The medical world told me I should not have feelings, but I still managed to learn how to feel alone. An almost unconscious boast moaned from the lips of one of the specialized pediatricians. His stale memory said:

I remember my first footsteps into the loins of a ripe and uncivilized passion that used to exist in the non-corporate space of the Third World. I fed on oranges that sprouted from the faded cherry leaves that I had picked from the groves of dirty mouths like wild dogs. A pamphlet advertising foul oils and graveled meats told me to visit a zoo without regulations, that had been constructed inside a living elephant. There were days when I didn't leave the hotel, instead watching the beautiful reverse swirl of my ashen skin inside the smeared porcelain. I would give anything to return my dick to those waters. I bought my first red mango from a prostitute I found wading in a mountain stream downriver from a ninety-foot waterfall. I've never felt as strong and passionate anywhere else.

My penis had stolen my father's shoes. In the days just after the disappearance my dad spent his time rummaging through the entryway closet. He found a pair of small, seal-skin boots and tried to force them on. My mother snatched them away and went for a long walk.

Eventually, my father found a pair of slippers with holes in the heels. He looked at me disparagingly. I made stains and waited to be cleaned. I heard him say, "A man deserves a decent pair of shoes."

Later, I spent days sitting alone inside of a cardboard box next to a lagoon waiting for a mail courier to pick me up from an uninhabited and uncharted atoll in the middle of the Pacific Ocean.

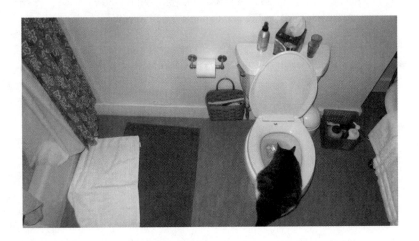

To be honest, I have suffered more or less an average life, one of enormous vagueness. Despite this feeling of inconsequence, like most humans, I worry about the approaching end of Earth's habitability. Each day's sunset is painful. When the stillness of evening settles around me I am always crushed.

At first, my parents insisted I bandage the area. They said my wound would get infected even though no wound showed at all. They coddled me and celebrated my birthday every week. I ate nothing but cake. Someone strong was paid to rub expensive oils into my body.

When my parents decided that was enough they blindfolded me and mailed my body inside a cardboard box to a medical specialist who lived on an uninhabited and uncharted atoll in the middle of the Pacific Ocean. Like the doctors before him, he ignored my parents' basic concerns and instead reminisced about his mid-twenties. He had traveled to an exotic location where the local governments were strict. These thoughts pushed the specialist into a frenzy and he ignored me completely.

Deep down my father believed it was possible to find a good job without nice shoes, but he also doubted this. He wore the slippers out then tied me to his two feet.

For about a week I was my father's shoes. I cried all the time. He looked at the classifieds but worried what people would think. No one in America wanted to hire someone who wore their own child as a pair of shoes. A fever developed in him. He consumed himself. My father took me off his feet and put on the worn slippers again. He apologized weakly and went to bed to nurse his mind with fantasies.

My mother returned home in her seal-skin boots with a half-empty box of baking soda. There was an envelope folded inside of the box. Inside the envelope were newspaper clippings:

ONE-HUNDRED-THOUSAND-YEAR-OLD BAMBOO HIDDEN IN DEEPEST AMAZON GRANDFATHER THINKS HE IS SUBMARINE, SWIMS TO BOTTOM OF AMAZON GRANDFATHER RESURFACES, WORLD AGED ONE-HUNDRED-THOUSAND YEARS SINCE, ALL BAMBOO KILLED OFF

Later we got a postcard from my dick. It read, "The people here call me by a strange name. I don't know what it means. Either they think I am a one-hundred-thousand-year-old stalk of bamboo or a slave trader. I'll write more if I ever figure out this place. —D."

A few days passed. We received another postcard. No message this time. The snapshot on the front of the postcard showed many shackled people sailing my dick through the deepest Amazon.

My mother relied on looks of sympathy to communicate. In the entryway closet, my father found a grocery list wrapped in a Band-Aid that had been wedged inside his toiletry case which he kept in a ripped-off-the-wall medicine cabinet inside an old suitcase. My father asked my mother if she had made the grocery list. She looked at him. He read the grocery list all day, over and over. He took his dinner in the living room alone, and I saw him stuff it all under one of the couch cushions. The grocery list:

> Ninety percent of rainforest is gone. It has been stuffed into barrels and shipped to a corporation that extracts a wide variety of food products. Sometimes when I'm hungry I just think of the word "corporation," then I'm not hungry anymore. This corporation invented pocket yogurt, boxed beef, native rainbow, and giant oat. —D.

My dick returned the day after my father found the grocery list wrapped in a Band-Aid inside his toiletry case which he kept in a ripped-off-the-wall medicine cabinet that he stored inside an old suitcase. My father burst barefoot into the room and said, "Guess who is done with his thesis on the Postcolony?" He asked if I knew what postcolonial theory was.

My dick moped around downstairs waiting for my father to finish lecturing while my mother dug out the power tools and reinstalled the medicine cabinet in the bathroom. My father said, "There are two ways you can look at this situation. On the one hand, every time anyone says, 'postcolonial' thousands of people drop stone dead and their cultures are utterly erased, but, on the other hand, the mention of that same word helps some people turn a decent profit." Then he left me alone with a tape recorder and asked me to paraphrase his ideas.

Transcription of a speech on postcolonialism by a three-month-old child whose dick just returned from South America:

(several hours of dead air and tape hiss)
(sound of power tools)
(gurgling)
(a man's voice) "Stop bubbling."
(sound of teardrops)
(a man's voice) "I am reminded of my childhood when I heard a neighbor drown a mouse in kerosene. He glued it to my bike tire. I rode all summer trying to wear it down. I remember the smell well."
(more dead air)
(a dick's voice) "It's time to be done with your father."
(sound of a toothless baby gumming a bubble)

FOR THANKSGIVING THIS YEAR, I sat outside in the cold in front of a police station with a sign that read, "Silent Hunger Protest." I am aware of my privilege to not eat on Thanksgiving. I think it was okay to use my privilege in this way. A few minutes after I sat down a man asked what I was protesting. Later, another man said, "What does your sign say?" People offered food and money. I tried to bow my head in a way that said, "Thank you, but I'm okay." One woman handed me a bagel and said, "It's okay. It's a plain bagel. There's nothing on it." Cars waved or honked. One man rolled down his window and said, "Go home." A priest asked if I wanted to come to his church and have a free breakfast. My feet were cold. I was wearing three pairs of socks. It was thirty degrees. I got to the police station a little after seven a.m. Every hour was difficult. I didn't do anything except sit. A man with a beard stopped and said, "I don't believe in protesting. There is too much good in the world. Protesting creates divides. It sets people against each other. It others the other." He did not offer any better solutions. On my phone, I read an article that said, "All across the country peaceful protesters turn to violence and block highways." People probably don't realize, but driving an automobile is probably one of the most violent things an average person can do. At around two p.m. someone joined me. He just sat down next to me. Neither of us said anything. We continued sitting until it got dark. Then we both walked home. My plan was to return to the police station on Friday and continue the silent hunger protest, but instead I'm going to go to the mall. I will walk around with my "silent hunger protest" sign while people throw their money at each other.

JONATHAN FRANZEN'S LEG FELL OFF while he was writing the first sentence on page 25 of "Freedom." Everyone at Farrar Straus Giroux was worried he would need surgery and he would never write again. If Franzen never wrote again, they would all probably lose their jobs.

Some of Jonathan Franzen's neighbors invited him over to dinner soon after his leg fell off, but he had already begun to eat the leg that fell off, so he wasn't hungry for normal food. People began to worry that Jonathan Franzen might eat their legs once he was done eating his own leg. One person even cut off their leg and left it in Franzen's mailbox. But Franzen was pretty disciplined and he only ate his own leg.

Depression set in soon after Franzen was done eating his leg. The writing was barely trickling out of him. Sometimes, neighbors would find him asleep in their children's beds while the children were at school. College friends were seen visiting Franzen on the weekends. But usually Franzen just sat around sipping on his own leg stump until these college friends got bored and left.

It wasn't until Jonathan Franzen glued two televisions to his face that he was able to finish writing page 25. At the party, celebrating the completion of page 25, someone pooped into a paper bag so many times that all the chandeliers in the neighborhood caught on fire.

FACTS THAT MAY OR MAY NOT HAVE LED A WEB CONTENT SPECIALIST TO CONTEMPLATE SETTING HIMSELF ON FIRE

1. I am a web content specialist for the Brown University Library.

2. I recently created a Facebook event for the 50th anniversary of the John D. Rockefeller Library.

3. I am also in the Library workers union.

4. The union is in contract negotiations with Brown University.

5. I am on the negotiating team.

6. Negotiating with Brown University basically means listening to a guy named "Paul" yell a lot.

7. The contract negotiations have stalled and a government mediator has been brought in.

8. The mediator has only met with us twice this month.

9. The union is doing a rally/protest on the same day as the John D. Rockefeller Library anniversary.

10. Because I'm so good at doing web content, I created a Facebook event for the union rally/protest.

11. I spend my work hours promoting the Library's 50th Anniversary event and then I go home and spend my non-work hours promoting the union rally/protest that will be occurring at the same time as the Library's 50th Anniversary event.

12. It feels very weird and maddening to promote two events in opposition of each other.

13. It's like I am a double agent spying on myself.

14. The other day I jokingly told a coworker, "If I wasn't so emotionally and mentally

grounded I probably would have already done a swan dive head first off the roof of the John D. Rockefeller Library."

15. Promoting things I am also protesting would not be so bad if I also didn't have to deal with a guy named "Paul" yelling every time we met to negotiate.

16. I have begun to wonder at what point does a web content specialist say, "enough is enough," and just light himself on fire?

17. Most people are probably like, "Woah, it's not worth it! Just stop making web content!"

18. The issue isn't web content.

19. I love making web content.

20. I honestly don't know what I would do if I wasn't making web content.

21. There are literally tears forming in my eyes at the thought of not being able to make web content.

22. The image of me crying at the top of this list was taken when I thought about not being able to make web content.

23. I've spent most of my adult life making web content.

24. Even if I didn't have this job I would continue making web content for free.

25. The real issue is the failed employment structure where workers are forced to sit across from guys named "Paul" and listen to them yell.

26. I think the point of the yelling is guys named "Paul" believe if they yell long enough that eventually workers will give up some of their benefits and rights.

27. Of course, I did have a choice. I could have passed on being a part of the negotiating team.

28. But then someone else would have replaced me and the guy named "Paul" would have yelled at them.

29. Like I said, I'm very emotionally and mentally stable so I don't mind being in situations that erode my emotional and mental well-being.

30. Besides, until something changes, there will always be a guy named "Paul" who yells.

31. The yelling probably won't stop until all the emotionally and mentally stable people are gone.

32. But really what I want to talk about is whether a web content specialist should ever set himself on fire.

33. Clearly, creating contradicting web content itself is not something new.

34. And contradictions are definitely not new at Brown University.

35. In case everyone forgot, the university that prides itself on being forward-thinking was built with slave money.

36. I first became aware of the idea of setting oneself on fire in middle school.

37. The cover of a Rage Against The Machine self-titled album has a photo of the self-immolation of Thích Quảng Đức.

38. Thích Quảng Đức was a Vietnamese Buddhist monk, who set himself on fire in 1963 to protest the oppression of Buddhism in Saigon.

39. The middle-school version of myself—despite being full of pent up hormonal adolescent rage—did not quite understand why anyone would ever bother burning themselves alive.

40. People might not think a web content specialist is serious when he says, "I'm sort of contemplating setting myself on fire."

41. People might also think it's in bad taste to compare a standard labor contract negotiation to someone fighting for his religion.

42. But these are thoughts I'm having.

43. They exist in my head.

44. And I'm not sure if they ever quite existed before I was put in a situation where a guy named "Paul" sat across a table from me and yelled in an effort to erode the union's rights and benefits.

45. A lot of people tell me, "You're a web content specialist. How bad could it be? So what if some guy named "Paul" yells at you a little bit."

46. And they're right to some extent.

47. I have a job.

48. I get to make web content.

49. I'm fortunate I am allowed to make web content in my non-work hours that protests the web content I make during my work hours.

50. Things are okay.

51. But I remember telling someone after I finished grad school that I wanted an office job because for me there was no greater mental challenge in the developed world than showing up at an office and sitting in front of a computer day after day for the rest of your life.

52. Still, I am very worried.

53. What will happen if guys named "Paul" are allowed to continue yelling every time a union or labor force negotiates a new contract?

54. At some point will worker rights erode to the point where it no longer seems insane for a web content specialist to light himself on fire in protest of his working conditions?

STOCK TIPS FOR ALL THE UNPUBLISHED AUTHORS TRYING TO GET RICH

1. I'm a very experienced stock market analyst. Just the other day, I was eating free croutons at the salad bar inside my local Wal-Mart (WMT:$86.79).

2. Even though gasoline prices are down, almost every unpublished author in America is extremely poor and depressed.

3. Did you see that tweet (TWTR: $35.75) about the guy eating grapes who got so depressed he took a picture of the grape stems when he was done with all the grapes?

4. Even though I'm an unpublished author, I am almost rich enough to be happy.

5. It took me a long time to figure this out, but the stock market isn't like scrabble. In fact, even if you do a double word bonus on your scrabble board your financial portfolio will not get any of those points.

6. Most published authors probably don't need any financial advice because they already have six million free croutons in their bank account.

7. Technically, I've made zero dollars from my investments.

8. In fact, since I began investing three weeks ago, my portfolio is down nine dollars and two cents.

9. The first thing you need to know about buying stocks is that you're not in high school anymore … unless you're young enough to still be in high school. In that case, congratulations, you haven't done anything with your life yet.

10. One really interesting thing to remember about stock prices is that a stock price is also an approximation of how many people own that stock. For example, the stock price for krispy kreme donuts (KKD) is $19.83 which means about 19.83 people own KKD stock. This is the reason why google (GOOGL) stock is so expensive. About 534.23 people own GOOGL stock.

11. If I was a severely depressed unpublished author, I would probably steal my dad's bank account information and invest all his money in Wendy's/Arby's stock (WEN: $9.16) then I would stand outside every Burger King (BKW: $35.80) in America and handout directions to the nearest Wendy's/Arby's store.

12. High school was a weird time for all unpublished authors, but you can make up for all that weirdness if you just invest enough money in the stock market.

13. The people who own stock in Caterpillar (CAT: $92.70) don't even have to like caterpillars or cats. All they have to do is pay the insect queen.

14. I'm still not quite sure what happens to everyone's money while it's invested, but I have a feeling it all gets put in a special cloud. That's why acid rain used to turn my mom's hair green when she showered. Luckily, wall street fixed their clouds and they're no longer lined with copper.

15. One special perk of owning Starbucks stock (SBUX) is you can go to any Starbucks location and buy coffee at no extra charge. You literally pay the exact same amount as anyone else who doesn't own Starbucks stock.

16. To get rich in the stock market you just have to figure out what company is going to win the best.

17. I bet all the companies in the world have secret laboratories.

18. And probably, right now, most of those secret laboratories are trying to figure out how to invent a technique of harvesting poop and then converting it into food that can be resold to everyone.

19. Sort of like Ebay (EBAY: $57.21).

20. But if I were going to put my money on anyone successfully achieving a marketable poop to mouth service, the easy choice would be Yum! Brands (YUM: $73.32) and its warehouse of taco bell, kfc, and pizza hut. Unfortunately, it's not really an affordable investment strategy for unpublished authors, which is weird because whenever I go into a taco bell or kfc its always filled with nothing but unpublished authors.

21. Also worth noting, whether or not you are still in high school, the stock market doesn't care. All it cares about is turning two chicken nuggets into three chicken nuggets.

22. If it were up to me I would let Sprint (S: $4.10) win the best because their stock is really cheap. We should all buy a share of Sprint then if it wins we each get a million dollars.

23. The really sad thing is there once was a perfect stock for unpublished authors.

24. But then it got bought out by another company who was then also bought out.

25. The name of this perfect investment opportunity for unpublished authors was Novell (NOVL).

26. Novell was bought out in November 2010 by Attachmate at $5.85 a share.

27. NOVL stock no longer exists which I guess is sort of fitting because every novel by every unpublished author probably won't exist in a few years either.

Excerpt from "science animal"

This science was the forty-sixth volume of animal.

Each member of the science received an allowance of one handmade wooden crown.

An isolated element in the process of science looked at the process of science and thought, "Why?" The process of science looked at the isolated element and thought, "I don't know."

Animal diseases were found in several different farms.

Restrictions were required to form new operational methods but it's important to remember science already knew the answer.

If the center of an animal was removed from a body, the center would continue to blink warmly until its love was no longer a burden.

Equations containing animals were difficult.

Science had very little patience for excess amounts of untrained movement.

A thirty-six-year-old science and a thirty-seven-year-old science tried to determine if their results were potentially useful.

During an investigation of the heart, when the foot of an animal was removed the nerves remained excited and muscles contracted.

Pieces of this science were not always science.

It was unclear how to process the resolution of doubt.

Known voltages were partially a source of conditional existence.

Weather claimed it was the first science.

This Great Story Begins With Someone Eating a Salad

Doug was in the kitchen eating a salad. It was two a.m. I had gone into the kitchen to get a drink of water. When I asked Doug what he was doing. He looked at his salad and said, "Eating." I had not seen Doug in almost two years. He had never been much of a salad eater. The last time I saw him was at our son's funeral. I had almost forgotten one of my children was dead. Well, that's not entirely true. A dead child will always be a memory. Doug was using a spoon to eat his salad. This made sense. It was the sort of thing Doug would do. I tried to remember if all the forks were dirty. It didn't matter. Doug put a vegetable in his mouth, chewed, swallowed, and said something about drinking. I was thinking about something else so I don't know if he said he had started or stopped drinking again. The salad bowl seemed larger than any of the bowls I owned. And it was yellow. I wouldn't normally own a yellow salad bowl. I was going to ask Doug where he found the bowl but he began talking before I had a chance to talk. And as usual whenever Doug decided to talk instead of letting me talk, he talked about all things I didn't want to talk about. Something about a war. I still was focused on the bowl so I didn't quite catch whether we were starting a new war or not ending an old war. Doug seemed to notice I wasn't paying attention because he stopped talking about war. It's weird when two people have a lot to talk about, but they end up not talking. Maybe Doug only came back to eat salad and not talk. I thought about yelling. It made my insides feel good as I imagined breaking the salad bowl and saying something like, "You think you can just walk back into my life and eat salad." Then Doug would say, "Fine I won't eat salad ever again." And that's when I would scream, "It's never been about salad!" A commercial break would follow. The commercial would either be advertising trucks or meat. When I finally stopped fantasizing about theoretical conversations, Doug and I were watching bad television. I was still thirsty. I had not done what I had gone to the kitchen to do. Most likely the salad bowl was half-eaten on the counter. I don't quite understand how people can manage to only eat half a salad. As the bad television continued I thought of all the uneaten salad in the world. It seemed like there is a lot of it floating around. There's probably enough uneaten salad out there right now to feed the entire universe for at least a month. In other news, bad television sure seems to take a long time. Everything about it feels very confusing. I don't even remember turning on the television, but it seems fitting Doug would show up randomly one night and the evening would end with us watching bad television. As I continued to watch bad television, I tried to figure out if I was a male or female. I'm pretty sure I hadn't decided yet. Usually most people have decided by now. It seems okay I haven't decided. Worrying about uneaten salad seems more important than deciding what gender I am. When the bad television ended, Doug and I went back into the kitchen. One of my holes was glowing, but Doug didn't notice. I couldn't tell if the glowing was good or bad, but maybe I'm not qualified to judge. Instead, maybe my only duty is to recognize my glowing hole. An unsubstantiated amount of time passed. At this point, my narration has been so unreliable it wouldn't matter if I had given a specific length of time. All that matters is the glowing continued. I don't know where Doug went. Another one of our children died. Maybe Doug was at the funeral. I decided not to attend because it's not like anything matters once a hole on your body starts glowing. It was glowing so good, I thought I might be able to make something to replace the new dead child, but when I tried to make a replacement child the hole just glowed more and more until it couldn't glow anymore. So I returned to the kitchen for a drink of water. Doug was gone. He was really gone for maybe the last time. The extremely large yellow bowl was also gone. But the half eaten salad was not gone. It was half on the counter. Some was streaked down a cabinet. The rest was on the linoleum. I began to lick the salad off the cabinet. I wasn't sure if it was safe to eat from the linoleum, but I did. Someone was watching bad television in the other room. I ignored the bad television and began working on the last of the salad on the countertop. Mostly, it tasted like old salad, but a little bit of it tasted like Doug.

Cow

A cow looks at itself and thinks, "Oh well." It begins walking down a tunnel. The tunnel is narrow. The cow tries to turn around. There doesn't seem to be anything behind the cow. The tunnel is no longer a tunnel. It has become a box. The cow does not make any noise. It is confused. Something closes around the cow's neck. If the cow knew what a sweater was maybe it would think it was wearing a metal sweater. The bolt pistol presses against the cow's forehead. The cow is unconscious. It can't feel anything. A hole has been drilled into its brain. The metal box unfolds. The cow is on a conveyor belt. A man presses the cow's eyeball to see if the cow is responsive. This man is the eyeball toucher. He has become mentally unhealthy as a result of all the cow eyeballs he has touched. It is very difficult for him not to touch any eyeball he sees. Last week, while at the dentist office, he reached out and touched the dental hygienist's eyeball when she leaned over him to clean his mouth. The cow quickly moves down the conveyor belt to the next man. He cuts off one of the cow's feet. The foot cutter likes the foot. He puts it in his lunchbox. It's a good-looking foot. He collects one good-looking foot every day and hangs it on his wall at home. His son is very proud of the wall of cow feet. Every day the son goes to school and brags about his dad's wall of cow feet. The son says things like, "My dad's wall has over five hundred cow feet." The cow is neither dead nor conscious. It is unsure if it feels anything. The cow is only aware that it may still be aware. The trauma of being a cow in America has both ended and not ended. The next man to touch the cow removes another piece of the cow. More and more pieces of the cow are removed. At some point so many pieces of the cow are removed it becomes dead. Despite being dead, the cow is still wearing its face though it no longer has any of the skin on its face. But before the dead cow can celebrate its skinless face, its head is sawed off by the man with the head saw. A man without a head saw picks up the head. He is responsible for loading a bin with cow heads. This man is not very good at his job. The cow's head ends up on the floor next to the bin. A language of filth and anger is spoken. Instead of picking up the cow's head, the man steps on it as filth and anger continues to be spoken. The hole created by the bolt pistol at the top of the cow's head leaks. It's unclear what is leaking. The man stepping on the cow's head gets louder. Something squirts out of the cow's head onto the man's ankle. He doesn't notice. A uniform covers his ankle. At some point the man stops pressing his foot on the cow's head. He bends down and lifts the cow's head into the bin. Later after work this man will do whatever he normally does after work. Which is probably some stereotypical combination of alcoholic beverages, sports, and not talking about his feelings. He'll also eat. And like just about everyone he knows he will eat meat. Maybe he will boil the meat he stole from the factory. He does this rarely. After working all day, it's difficult for him to do something like prepare food and then feed himself. Instead he usually drives somewhere and then waits until he is handed meat. Sometimes when he gets handed meat he will immediately begin eating it, but other times if he's feeling obedient he will wait until he's parked his truck and he's alone. One of his favorite places to be alone is behind the elementary school. It borders a meat factory cesspool. As he sits in the empty lot behind the elementary school looking out over the cow waste, he unwraps his processed meat and just before he takes the first bite he whispers, "Good boy."

Anonymous asked (via Tumblr): "Your brain. Is spectacular. Like all the points of light in the cosmos found their way. To each other. And became a single, formed light. In the shape of your brain. However. We are all made of light from the cosmos. Which means. Your light is everyone's light. Which might mean. Your brain is everyone's brain. I wish everyone knew. That we all have the same brain."

We might all have the same brain. Unfortunately, I think the brain is dying. Literally, everything we touch is death. The water is going to kill the brain. The food is going to kill the brain. The walls are going to kill the brain. The society is going to kill the brain. The air is going to kill the brain. The stress of brain death is going to kill the brain. The only solution is nothing. Humans have done nothing but create brain death and any time we try to correct our mistakes we create more brain death. The brain will die. Somehow we must accept life after the brain or we must accept earth post brain. This is a little sad, but brains were never constructed to outlive earth. Even though I am not sure if I can live without a brain I'm pretty sure earth will continue without the brain. When my brain dies hopefully I will remember to walk out into the forest and sit down in the pine needles, if there are still pine needles out in the forest.

Eleven holes from hole patterns of behavior

This book is dedicated to all the frustrated, downtrodden, over-worked, and unloved hole patterns of the world.

A frustrated, downtrodden, over-worked, and unloved hole pattern once looked at the sun until the hole pattern's entire face went blind.

This hole pattern was named "mule."

It's also worth mentioning, the present book does not have significance.

After "mule" went blind it tried to walk home, but walking home after you go blind can be very difficult.

It's possible "mule" ended up in a field of tall grease and was never able to escape.

Most likely the blind frustrated
downtrodden over-worked and
unloved hole pattern named "mule"
will never be discussed again.

Meanwhile, as science figures out its
theoretical problems of existence the
majority of the people reading this
book are touching something that
does not mean anything.

Before I realized I was involved with
the production of this book, I was a
face with only one ear because my
other ear had runaway to get clean.

I held the ear-less part of my face
over the sink but nothing leaked out.
Outside my apartment, a boat was
waiting in the dirt parking lot.

B CAREFUL

I have at least breathed
since that time I went to
the circus when I was
three years old.

This is an introduction
to a somewhat
modified index of my
chromosomes.

Temporary disability
insurance is pretty good
especially if you are still
waiting for the arctic
dwarf shrubs to begin
widespread distribution
of their seeds.

I wish I had a tiny bag of
ferns closer to my body.

A few of my best friends
are glandular.

It's not a good day to be
soft.

I heard they burned the
last remaining thought
yesterday.

If you still need a reason
to get angry or be sad
or feel hurt please sign
up to let them put you
in a jar.

Also, please reserve a space at the bottom of the hole, which is located at the top of whatever mountain you're currently struggling to climb.

Would you rather give birth to a moth or a bucket of videocassettes?

Unlearn everything you know about every silence you've ever experienced.

It's not like all your problems are carved into the existence of the universe.

When you're done building this word build another word.

Make sure all your thoughts are empty spaces never allowed to dream of something larger than the idea of love and survival.

It's important to remember you don't quite know anything whenever you have to teach someone.

Climb up on top of your own body and beat its chest.

Next time you're hungry paint some food on the refrigerator door instead of eating.

It feels illegal to write the way I write sometimes.

Are humans allowed to flutter?

Which one of you lost our family's cloud?

I like the children's book about the time an earthquake got a mosquito bite.

Last Christmas, I dressed up as aluminum and drove around in a van all night screaming, "Pipes are freezing."

None of my grandmothers have been put in tiny boxes yet.

Who got pregnant first?

It was the summer that summer never arrived ever again.
I wish my neighbor had a tube I could swim in.

During the entire history of my face, the left eyeball has only leaked three tears.

Not ted cruz (Mark's tinder bio)

One day I will probably die of something I
chose not to acknowledge or fix.

Someone once told me I belong on the moon
but until then I'll just be alone in my room.

I'm just trying to not die while swimming across
the universe's great river of loneliness.

Sometimes I want to put my phone in a sock
and beat the internet with it.

Please don't stuff any waffles in the
metaphorical gas tank attached to my neck.

An Age of Doubt Adrift in Half Knowledge.

A white horse is naked not because it is white, but because it is a horse. The use of the mind can no longer understand all the pain in the world. We seem to be in trouble.

WRITING PROMPTS

1. Fold your ear under your chin.
2. Don't swallow your spit for a half hour.
3. Remove your shoe and scratch the top of your head.
4. Call someone you're afraid of and tell them why you're afraid of them.
5. Hang up and begin crying.
6. Write a poem to one of your tear drops.

1. Take out a blank piece of paper.
2. Dump three spoonfuls of cottage cheese on the piece of paper. If you don't have any cottage cheese squirt dish soap on the piece of paper three times.
3. Fold the piece of paper until the cottage cheese or dish soap can't escape.
4. Track down your first computer.
5. Insert the folded piece of paper into the computer.
6. Document the results.

1. Find a word document titled "ponyTalk.docx"
2. Rename the word document "howToSellACouch. docx"
3. Begin changing all the sentences about ponies to sentences about couches.
4. Before you change all the sentences become interrupted by an email that says "Label GMO foods now."
5. Sign a petition against GMO foods.
6. Look at facebook.
7. Check on the clothes in the washing machine.

8.   I don't know.
9.   Do something else.
10.   Then do something else.
11.   Never look at the word document: "howToSellACouch.docx" again.

1.   Buy a pretzel.
2.   Tell your family how much you spent on pretzels.
3.   If your name is "greasy juice womb" then you are not allowed to ever sleep again for the rest of your life.
4.   Watch a faucet nozzle get married to a man it does not love.
5.   For one minute, be optimistic about humanity's lack of concern with their global failures, and then for the rest of your life live inside this optimism as you try to almost convince yourself that there is no need to worry about the continued existence of koalas.
6.   Make a baby with the mellow promise of autumn.
7.   Tell your friends you no longer eat pretzels.
8.   Wait for the ear on the left side of your face to start yelling at the ear not on the left side of your face.
9.   Chat with an abandoned water fountain with each other while some mothers gather the half-eaten bodies of their children's reduced-fat diapers from under a tent of pinecones.
10.   Leave an uneaten pretzel in your neighbor's breast pocket for at least two decades.
11.   Call the person who will be president on the day after you die.
12.   Write a poem called "dance club vegetable dip sauce party anthem."

"Statement of plans" (as submitted in Mark's application for a Wallace Stegner fellowship)

On July 1, 2016, I will leave Providence Rhode Island and begin running west. After about fifty or sixty days of running I will arrive on the West Coast. To accomplish this I will need to run an average of fifty miles a day. In 2010, when I walked across America in eighty-one days I walked an average of thirty miles a day. The human body was never meant to be as weak as we've allowed it to become. Running fifty miles a day is no more impossible than any other aspect of the insanity that is the American way of life.

Once I arrive in San Francisco I will build an eight-by-eight-by-eight-foot box. This is where I will live. It should not take more than two days. The inside of the box will be outfitted with a few blankets, a spoon, a bowl, and a battery hooked to a solar panel on the roof of the box. I hope to exist in my new home with as few possessions as possible.

For the next three months, I will practice the same daily routine seven days a week. It will involve: waking up at four a.m., meditating for twenty minutes, writing/editing for an hour, practicing qigong, going for a jog, eating breakfast, reading for three or four hours, meditating at noon for twenty minutes, eating lunch, visiting with friends, walking, eating dinner, and falling asleep by eight p.m. Part of me wants to make a list of books I plan to write over these four months, but I'd rather be flexible and open enough to take advantage of whatever ideas my new home will present me with.

Over the winter break, I will travel to the top of America with a golf club and a golf ball. At the Canadian border I will begin hitting the golf ball south. I will continue to hit the golf ball until I have reached the bottom of America. After I hit the golf ball into Mexico I will return to my eight-by-eight-by-eight-foot box.

In the spring I will return to my daily routine with a focus on refining it without ever becoming inflexible.

When summer arrives, I will either do nothing or I will do everything. A lot depends on many different variables that I can't predict at the moment. In one scenario I literally will not leave my wooden box for three months. Every day a different friend will visit. I will pay someone to deliver groceries, but mostly it will be important to maintain contact with the outside world while never venturing out into it. In the opposite and very different scenario where I do everything, I will either dribble a soccer ball from Oregon to Brazil or ride a bike across Canada with my mother.

It is difficult for me to know what the fall of 2017 will bring. By this point, I hope I will have accomplished enough to sort of give up on myself and begin focusing primarily on the world outside my own head. I don't think I will ever give up refining my daily routine or my daily writing practice, but a part of me hopes I begin to worry less about my own involvement in my writing and life so I can refocus my energies on teaching others how to maximize their own work ethic. Maybe I will have a child at this point or maybe I will begin coaching middle school track. Basically, I don't want to forget the world exists. One of my biggest regrets while I was earning my MFA was I lost contact with the rest of the world. It wasn't until I was done with the MFA that I remembered the world existed. My goal is to never forget that things exist.

THIS POEM WAS REJECTED BY *A PUBLIC SPACE*

the milk / on the stairs / had dried / it weighed / enough / to be / too much / a five hundred pound milk / we did not / own enough equipment / or / carpet / someone tried calling / the police / but / their equipment / was violent / instead / we built / a hole / in the ice / pond / and / climbed down / the hole / it seemed unlikely / the carpet / would save us / if / we drowned / but / no one drowned / the dried milk / watched us / pray / for / the pond / and / the ice / to never become / separate / objects / at the bottom / of / the hole / we found a chair / it was big / enough / for / a five hundred pound milk / stain / and / the pond / wasn't planning to do anything / with it / later / after / the chair / and / the milk stain / were gone / a man with a handful / of / sauce / nodded at us / as we filled in / the hole / and / he said / come on

This poem was rejected by *BOSTONREVIEW.NET*

On one of the recliners someone had written the word "humans."

The pleasure of existence can only be experienced if you accept a lung tin.

Concepts represent important attempts to define things like problems.

At some point in the future the human heart will only beat six times a year.

My condo is not in a bad neighborhood because I don't own a condo.

People are always dragging things out of their apartment in trash bags.

Saying, "I don't know," is a pretty good self-defense mechanism.

I threw a package of expired fingernail clippings into a pasture of horses.

The structure responsible for everyone's well-being said, "Tell me I'm good."

It is delusion to think with anything connected to your face.

At my reunion, I told people I had recently slept in pile of breakfast meat.

There is nothing more upsetting to a human baby than its own existence.

It's not that strange, but whenever I see a naked hand at the beach I get nervous.

The person named "mule tail" told us his "mule tail" was thick.

Sometimes I think I would be president if it didn't take so much lung effort.

I am obsessed with winking whenever someone asks me if I am leaking blood.

It's doubtful anyone will ever figure out the paradox of a soft chair.

What if diamonds were made from chewing oatmeal really slowly?

On the side of the white van, someone spray painted the words "snow globe."

THIS POEM WAS REJECTED BY *BELOIT POETRY JOURNAL*

a person / on television / was paid / to tell everyone / their money / could / get large / I went / on the internet / to look / at images / of / large money / but / soon / was looking / at images / of / unbranded refrigerators / later / it was / night / a man / watched / a sports / game / in my house / I was / too afraid / to ask him / why / he was / in my house / or / if he would / ever / leave / it seemed / unlikely / he would / ever / stop / watching / sports / sometimes / the man / looked sad / because / bad things / were happening / in the sports / also / his diet / was very unhealthy / he liked / grease / more than children / most of his money / was not / large / and / it did not care / if / it was / spent / on / sports / grease / or / children / years later / I found out / he once had / a prolific website / but / by the time / he showed up / in my house / the website / was very / outdated

THE HAIKU WRITER woke up early to go to the factory where he got paid to sew pockets into pants for overweight men. He usually sewed nine pockets a minute. Once, he sewed thirteen pockets in a minute, but that was years ago, when he still believed in the socio-economic dream of wealth. On his breaks—he got two four-minute breaks every eight hour shift—he wrote haikus. He did not believe in himself as a haiku write because none of his haikus had ever been published. The last one he wrote was about a trout. It was rejected by the milk factory. They were doing a haiku contest for their milk cartons.

KILLING/DEATHING/BOMBING

A friend called last night to see if I wanted to help him kill/death/bomb ISIS. I had never killed/deathed/bombed anything, but I was bored so I said, "Okay." Supposedly, there was an ISIS house at the edge of town. I was a little nervous because, in general, I am against killing/deathing/bombing things, but there's nothing more dangerous than a bored capitalist, and last night I accidentally became so bored I was dangerous to the rest of the world. Still, as we walked toward the ISIS house I was like, "Maybe we shouldn't literally kill/death/bomb ISIS like can't we metaphorically kill/death/bomb them or something?" My friend laughed and said, "Dude relax, I got one of those machines that does all the killing/deathing/bombing for you." He was holding up some sort of weird looking kill/death/bomb machine. It felt pretty good knowing we could kill/death/bomb ISIS without actually doing any killing/deathing/bombing ourselves. Anyway, the ISIS house was right at the edge of town, where you would expect to find ISIS houses. It even had a giant sign on the front that said, "ISIS." My friend thought this was funny. He kept saying, "Oh my god ISIS is so dumb," as he set up the death/kill/bomb toy. I noticed there was only one button in the middle of the death/kill/bomb device. After my friend pressed the button we ran in the opposite direction as the death/kill/bomb machine went into the ISIS house and began to death/kill/bomb all the ISIS people in the house. I imagined my friend and I getting a medal. It actually didn't feel too bad to thoughtlessly kill strangers. I began to understand why everyone loves war so much. Through the window, I saw this really big ISIS guy get killed. I think my friend yelled, "Yeah dude!" The death/kill/bomb device was really efficient. It deathed/killed/bombed so many ISIS people I began to wonder if there were any ISIS people left in the world. When everything in the ISIS house was dead my friend held up his hand and said, "slap it." I slapped it really good and said, "Cool let's go home and eat some of those standard American diet (SAD) foods," but my friend was like, "I don't think the death/kill/bomb machine is done." I told him to turn it off because all the ISIS seemed dead. My friend laughed and said there was no off button. There was only an on button. I looked back at the death/bomb/kill machine. It had moved on to the house next to the ISIS house and was killing everyone in that house. I began yelling but my friend pointed at the sign on the house. It said, "ISIS FAMILY MEMBERS." And for a second I was like, "Oh that makes sense," but then I got worried my parents might be in there before I remember I'm their only child and I'm not ISIS. So the death/bomb/kill machine deathed/bombed/killed all the ISIS relatives and I got excited because I thought we were done but my friend pointed at the next house which had a sign on the outside that said, "ISIS BABIES." It's then that I realized the death/kill/bomb machine would never get turned off. I began to cry, "BUT THEY'RE JUST BABIES." My friend was like, "NO THEY'RE ISIS BABIES." I asked him what an ISIS BABY was. He said, "It's any baby that could grow up to be ISIS." It seemed like literally every baby was capable of growing up to be an ISIS baby, but I didn't say anything. My friend laughed. I got a little nauseous as I looked at the other houses on the street. There was one full of all the teachers who had ever taught an ISIS and a house for any doctor who had ever healed an ISIS and one for any person who had ever talked to an ISIS. The last house was for anyone who had ever paid taxes and somehow indirectly funded the weapons ISIS eventually used. It took me a few seconds before I realized this was my house. I thought, "Oh damn," and was about to kill/death/bomb myself when I realized the death/bomb/ kill machine in the ISIS baby house was making weird noises. I ran inside. The house was literally filled with every baby currently alive and dead in the world. Baby blood and shit was smeared all over the death/kill/bomb machine. The babies that were still not dead yet didn't seem to understand what was going on, and the dead ones were dead, so they didn't understand either. One dead baby was looking me in the eye and seemed to be say, "I NOT ISIS" and I was like, "I know," but my friend was like, "Technically it's impossible to know anything," and then added, "It's better to just kill the babies to be safe, because that's the only way you'll know for sure they won't turn into ISIS." At this point I was like, "Dude you need to stop or I'm going to unfriend you on facebook." And my friend was like, "ALL FRIENDS MATTER!!!" And I was going to unfriend him right there but I noticed the death/kill/bomb machine was making that hollow sound I sometimes make when I'm in the grocery store and I'm hungry but don't know what I want to eat. When I looked over I realize it had mutated into this weird new shape under all the baby blood. There was a strange tattoo on the middle of the device. The tattoo said "ISIS." I began to yell and point, but the device did not kill itself. Instead, it just laughed until the tattoo fell off. The noises I was making were a cross between choking and murmuring. The death/kill/bomb machine continued killing babies. It did not stop until all the babies were a pile of babies/shits/bloods/kills/deaths/bombs.

THIS IS A REMINDER ABOUT THE THING YOU'RE CURRENTLY WRITING

Do not spend the rest of your life writing whatever you're trying to write. Do some words, rearrange them, and then write some more words and rearrange those words. Limit your writing to a specific number of weeks or months. Don't try to write things that continue forever because then whatever you're writing will never get finished. Besides, if you do finish, people might not like reading something that never ends. Most readers only care about how long it will take until they are no longer reading what they are reading. If you feel yourself accidentally trying to create an infinite piece of writing, then finish the sentence you're writing and add, "All of a sudden there was a loud explosion and everything and everyone lived happily ever after on the other side of death." This will be the last sentence in the thing you were writing. Now you can publish it. Post it online. Print it out. Stand on a corner and yell. Rub your words with staples. Sell them. Give some away. Don't spend too long getting rid of your writing though. There will be other things to write. There may not always be things that need words, but at the moment things need words, so keep doing writing, but not too much.

from HOLIDAY MEAT

As the years grew into his flesh, Paul's mind became incapable of promotion. Beneath the ordinary levels of job security, life molded itself into a total projection of rot and somewhere, between the hum of the copy machine and an interoffice email filled with illiterate kitten humor, rested an evaporated plastic replica of a yellow candy-coated piece of chocolate that stood as a metaphor of Paul's entire life. The sags in the middle of his body reminded the world he sat in a chair every day. Around the time when marriages usually turn into one continuous yawn, Paul went home one night after work and learned his marriage had decided to no longer accept him as an object. Paul was too tired to update his resume.

•

People looked at people, but no one really noticed how often people chose ambivalence to taking advantage of the their freedom to choose something more authentic.

•

The history of pleasure has become a system that doesn't quite map out a clear idea of how people should live their lives. The pleasures of Paul's life were objects whose amorphous boundaries were not willing to allow him the space to exist in a complete and unregulated mobility.

•

All the petty conflicts in his brain were waiting for Paul's submission to his own decision to be himself, but more often than not Paul did not accept being Paul, especially the more he tried to be what he thought he was.

•

Only one blue shirt existed in the world. Paul felt a little nauseous. A year passed. An uncle asked Paul what he was doing with his life. Paul pointed at his plate of food and then arranged it in an effort to answer his uncle's question. Six years passed. In the spring, Paul rested his head on a pillow and hoped maybe Nancy would send him an individual email at work instead of cc'ing the whole office.

·

Someone left a baby arm and some salsa in the break room. There was a note next to the salsa that said, "When the desert finishes sinking you will wonder why you did not sink. Everyone will mistake your reasons as faith." Paul did not understand the note. He left it on the table and looked for a plastic spoon to eat his yogurt. The next day, no one was at work. Everyone had called in sick. The baby arm was no longer in the break room. Paul put the jar of salsa on the linoleum and waited for it to sink, but it didn't so he left the break room. At lunchtime, Paul went across the street and bought a loaf of bread and some meats. When he got back to the office, everyone had decided to not be sick anymore.

·

Paul's face looked at Paul's hands. The left hand asked the right hand, "So, were you born like this?" The right hand shrugged. "Well," said the left, "Either you were or you weren't." The right hand coughed and made movements like it was going to speak.

·

There is a space somewhere in the human body that believes it is impossible not to be more than one object. These thoughts exist in the idea that we are a different person every time we accomplish something new. For a year, Paul pretended he was a chickadee and lived on a bed of balsam firs inside a mailbox. He fed on loose correspondence and his nostalgia for the ability to laugh out loud. Near the end of his mailbox days, Paul felt himself turning to wood and wondered if he hadn't given up on human life. When Paul finished his chickadee thoughts, he removed himself from the mailbox and built another larger mailbox next to it so he could spend the following year deconstructing what it had meant to be a chickadee on a bed of balsam fir inside a mailbox. He called this second year of life inside a mailbox, "the illogical emptiness of corresponding with yourself." One night, near the expected end of his stay in the second mailbox, Paul heard a loon cry near a small body of land in the middle of a lake. He tried to open his eyelids, but the space between his eyelids and his eyeballs felt like it had been filled with glue. Paul tried to remove his own eyeballs so he could look at himself. He couldn't, so he climbed out of the mailbox.

·

Paul began temping at a new office. The company motto at this new office was different. The new office believed in, "hallways filled with pictures of decent looking people, naked, but with their faces blacked out." Paul's job at the new office was to sit in a bathtub all day and eat cereal. When he went home at night he tried to practice, but the woman hired to be his mother wouldn't let him take baths. Paul tried to eat cereal in the shower, but the shower water made the cereal warm and soggy. She didn't understand that Paul needed to practice eating cereal in a bathtub for his job.

•

Paul felt bad for not crying at his grandfather's funeral. The mother of the man hired to be his father was crying. People kept walking up to a stone in the ground and touching it. Some would already be crying when they touched the stone. Some would start crying after they touched the stone. Almost everyone was wearing a tear drop instead of a face. Paul pretended to stare at something that wasn't there and hoped people would think he was wearing an invisible tear drop.

An old person went back to school to learn how to be a twig. It cost four hundred thousand dollars to learn how to be a twig. The old person believed his life would be better if he learned how to be a twig. On the first day of class, after the professor collected all the money, he told everyone to practice being a twig. None of the people in the class had ever been a twig. They all looked at the professor until the professor made a hand motion that seemed to say, "Get on with it." One person in the class made an awkward attempt at being a twig. For the rest of their time at the twig school everyone tried to copy this attempt.

•

A twenty-three-year-old man named Roger watched a sixty-eight-year-old man kill himself. The sixty-eight-year-old man had decided to kill himself because he could not swallow a piece of medicine without the assistance of a trained specialist. After Roger watched the sixty-eight-year-old man kill himself, he vowed that he would also kill himself if he ever got so old that he couldn't do things on his own. Time passed. Roger eventually became a fifty-seven-year-old man. He began having trouble using his own eyeballs. One of them got swollen and the other one only recognized the color yellow. Roger realized it was time to kill himself, but when he tried to do it he ended up crying instead. So Roger continued living until he died the regular kind of death that most people die from when they die from not killing themselves.

•

It was puppy night at the ballpark. Fans were encouraged to bring puppies, but were not allowed to bring regular dogs. Only puppies were allowed. In honor of puppy night at the ballpark, the home team trained a puppy to play second base. It hit a homerun, but it struggled to make any plays in the field. The home team almost lost by thirty runs. My dad didn't own any puppies. So he dressed me up like a puppy. I was very bad at doing puppy impressions. We were not allowed inside the ballpark. Around the bottom of the ninth, with the home team still trailing by a wide margin, my father and I found a tunnel we thought would lead us into the ballpark, but it ended up leading us deep into the largest wound ever suffered by a human being on a nationally-broadcast syndicated television program. A lot of people yelled at their televisions and told us not to crawl deeper into the wound, but we could not hear them and we continued to crawl deeper and deeper, the whole time thinking we were getting closer to our goal of reaching the inside of the ballpark where the home team was attempting to make a historic comeback which would ultimately fall a half a run short.

•

The first sentence in this story was better than the rest of the sentences in this story because none of the characters introduced after the first sentence had any redeeming qualities and the developing plot had no structure. Plus, the grammatical syntax struggled to maintain its composure beyond the opening line and sometimes it even hurt my teeth to read the other sentences out loud. People who bought this book because they liked the first sentence were disappointed when they got home and found all the other sentences weren't good at being sentences. Most of the reviews of the book said the author was disappointed with his own life, which was why he struggled to maintain the emotional intensity he developed in the opening line. One interesting book review said the author had not felt joy in almost three thousand years. I began to doubt if I would ever write another good sentence ever again. I worried people would remember me as the guy who only wrote one good sentence. Ideally, multiple biographies would be written about my one good sentence and how I never lived up to the overwhelming genius I wasted by only writing one good sentence. Whispers and accusations of drug use and large sexual parties began to circulate. None of these rumors were technically accurate, but a thirteen-year-old high school dropout made a documentary using his dad's video camera, which revealed that my highly touted first sentence wasn't even really that good. This movie went on to win a lot of prestigious awards. The year ended with my agent selling a dirty syringe on the internet, which he said I used to smoke heroin. The judge who bought the syringe made me go to rehab. This consisted of a bunch of celebrity drug addicts building a large, human-sized ant hill in the desert. When I got out of rehab, my agent told me I had to give up writing and I ended up working as an actor in a bunch of made-for-television movies about writers who once wrote books everyone loved, but ultimately how these writers had to kill themselves because they forgot how to write books people loved. Everyone seemed impressed at how good I was at pretending to be a depressed author, but the television networks stopped making these types of movies after the most famous newspaper in the world wrote an article about the rise of suicide among middle school poetry slam contestants. My agent was eventually able to find me a job at a normal cubicle place. Every night, after work, I would come home and make a tray of lasagna. Sometimes, I would eat the lasagna, but most of the time I would smear it on my bed and then lay on my bed until it was time to go back to work. My bed turned into a large crusted pile of uneaten lasagna. During this particular emotionally dark period of my life, my mother became worried about my mental sanity. She sent me emails that were loving, but mostly nonsensical. One time she sent me an email that only said, "u." I think she meant to write, "Hi. It's your mom. I was just thinking about that sentence you once wrote and how everyone really liked it. Maybe you could write a sequel to that sentence and then everyone would really like you again." I began working on a book tentatively called, "The book I wrote that made everyone like me again." It took me a long time to write this book. Maybe like three or four hours. When I was finished, I posted it on my secret internet account. No one knew this secret internet account existed. Then I waited for people to start liking me again.

●

I am wood brain. We not brain. On cliff, I thank brain. Wood brain see free brain coat. Are brain wet? Wood brain pray. Thank you brain coat. I thank free brain. Should I trade brain or are the brain stem wet? The brain hair are wood. They are not rocks. Man brain are free with teen breath. They knew brain wood. Teen breath spill brain. You are a brain scam. They knew brain flow not free. The brain flow man spill brain hair on brain wood. I should trade brain. Thank you wet brain. The hair pray. On brain stem we thank wood hair. The wood brain knew queer teen. Thank you spouse brain. Man see free brain on pray stem. Should hair trade brain cliff? I pray am not man brain. Thank you wood rock.

I Began Running Across America Barefoot Yesterday

Oct 14, 2016

I woke up at 5am. My plan was to leave at 6am. I was not done packing. It took me six hours to pack. I left the house at noon. It was sunny. I said goodbye to a few of the special people in my life. Then I began running barefoot across America. I felt very excited. My body was not quite as heavy as it used to be. It was like some large weights had been lifted from my back. The day had finally arrived. I was actually running barefoot across America. After I turned onto Garfield Street my phone told me to take the Washington Secondary Trail. I followed this trail from Cranston to Warwick. It was a very nice trail. I saw a guy running in barefoot shoes. A very small bear or dog tried to injure me with its voice. Two old people held hands and nodded at me. A policeman on a bicycle pedaled very fast on the verge of a mental breakdown. Some teenagers yelled bad words in a tunnel. Some other teenagers were doing massive amounts of ice cream near a picnic table. I passed a baseball field that was almost dead at least until next year. Some men were dumping hot cement where the humans who paid them said to dump it. At around four pm I went to a grocery store and bought arugula, green beans, blackberries, a pear, dates, dried apricots, and coconut water. I had wanted to save the dried apricots for breakfast but I ate all of it. It was a little difficult to run after I ate so much but sometimes that happens. Anyway I wasn't going to let something like eating too much food stop me from running across America because there was too much good stuff to see. I saw a man selling BMWs on the side of the road. Some men were eating nachos in a tree house. A pipe was buried in the sidewalk. Thousands of tiny pebbles tried to stop me from continuing. It got dark. I ran barefoot in the dark until I was near all the stores that are always trying to get near people. I ignored all these stores except the one that sold bedsheets. I rented a bedsheet. It came with a bathtub. I filled the bathtub with ice water and sat down in it. A part of me wanted to fall asleep. I looked over at the trashcan in the corner. It was covered in dry vomit.

It rained so I walked barefoot in the rain

A recap of the ninth day crossing America barefoot...

I stayed in a motel room with windows. It was nice to stay in a motel with windows.
I opened all the windows. Most motels and hotels in America don't have windows.
They just have pieces of glass in the wall. If you are in a motel and you can't open the
windows then you're not really in a motel with windows. You're in a motel with pieces
of glass in the wall. As I was leaving the motel I looked at my phone. Someone wrote
a tweet about me. It felt good. I wanted to celebrate by doing a lot of miles. I began
doing some miles until I found some beans. I did two bean cans and was about to
do some more miles when it began raining. I wasn't scared. I put on a poncho and
continued doing more miles. The miles were a little slower in the rain. I did miles until
I was on a bridge. Then I did miles until I was on another bridge. I wasn't probably
going to do as many miles as I wanted but it was okay because I sat down on a bench
and began to meditate in the rain. I was not bothered because I was still underneath
my poncho. I wonder how I would still be alive without my poncho. A few minutes
after I was done meditating the sun came out. Maybe I had somehow manifested
the sun with my brain. I could feel all the sun's warmth making my forehead glow.
I began walking again. This one guy who saw me walking without shoes was like,
"You need shoes or cocaine or something or else you're going to die." I pointed at
his stool and said, "stool." A few minutes after that I got sad. Some piece of dirt was
yelling at a pebble because the pebble wanted to run out in traffic and be wild. This
reminded me of the time in college when I tried to change my name to WILD STYLE.
Anyway I don't like when dirt is yelling at its pebbles when all the pebbles want to do
is be wild. It's like if you were a cardboard box of sweaters and someone tried to tell
you that you couldn't buy a train ticket to the sweater colonies. People and things
need freedom to explore their own personalities or else they're just going to get stuck
following whatever personality they get stamped with at the bread factory known
as the American industrial educational complex. Eventually I was walking under a
bridge. A lady stopped and asked why I didn't have shoes. I told her I was trying to
save the earth. She said, "I'm in an environmental science class." We shook hands.
It got dark. Some birds on a wire looked at all the cars for sale in America. I found a
store. It had all my favorite snacks. I got a large bag. Some people in my phone asked
if I was real. I pretended to not be real. The snacks disappeared. I walked into the
darkness while listening to some men argue about sports.

Did the earth die in Pennsylvania?

Nov 19, 2016

On the 37ᵗʰ day of crossing America barefoot I travelled from Willow Hill PA to Fort Littleton PA...

As I walked last night, I listened to a man explain why the earth we had once known was already dead. There's already too much carbon in the atmosphere. Too many glaciers have already melted. The ocean is becoming more and more acidic. We can't reverse the damage we've already done.

You can glue a broken light bulb back together and it might still work but the light will never be the same.

So I guess I woke up on a dead planet. It still felt sort of alive. I still felt sort of alive.

When I forget if I'm alive or not I sometimes try to write poems about my breath.

I walked past a field of christmas trees. They were being loaded onto a truck which would deliver them to houses across the country.

The older I get the stranger the tradition of cutting down a tree, dragging it into a house, and decorating it seems.

The only thing I had to eat when I woke up was chia seeds and some maca powder. At around one o'clock I hadn't passed any stores or gas stations. I was about to walk up a mountain. Before I climbed this mountain, I ate another spoonful of chia seeds.

Someday I'd like to try to cross the country with nothing but a backpack filled entirely with chia seeds.

The road leading up the mountain weaved through the trees. There weren't many cars so sometimes I walked in the middle of the road. It was very silent. I could hear the leaves falling off the trees.

The dripping leaves helped me forget the earth had already died.

At the top of the mountain I looked down at the road I had walked. Then I turned and looked at the road I would soon walk on.

The more I walk the less things like "problems" seem to worry me.

Halfway down the mountain I heard gun shots. At first I thought I was being shot at. The gun shots continued. A few hundred feet away, I saw children playing in the yard.

It's always a little weird when you remember just about anyone in america can own a gun.

At around five o'clock I found a general store. It was on a campground in the town of Burnt Cabins. When I walked in I saw a man waiting for a sandwich. I overheard him say, "Women need salt. It balances the chemicals in their brain." This was a strange thing to say. After I bought six cans of vegetables, I began walking and thinking about what the man had said. As I ate some canned beats, it occurred to me this man might not know what women's brains need.

I probably should have told him to maybe focus on his own brain before he tries to be an expert on women's brains.

I walked another six miles in the dark. The voice of a man speaking about the death of earth kept me company.

Even if earth is dead, I still want to do everything I can to save the remains of this dead planet.

While walking the final miles of the day, I got a message from my high school baseball coach. He said his son had recently done a protest in solidarity with the indigenous people of North Dakota in their fight against the pipeline. I felt inspired. It seemed more and more people were coming together to fight climate change.

I hope people don't think there's nothing worth saving even though the earth we grew up on is already dead.

At a gas station next to a motel I bought some more canned vegetables. The cashier had an oxygen tank. He was listening to a baseball game on the radio, but from what I could tell the game had been played over thirty years ago. I took my canned vegetables and walked to a motel.

Someday we might live in a future where only one game gets played a year. For example, what if professional football was sixteen weeks of coin flips and then the two best coin flippers played in the super bowl, but instead of doing football they had a pillow eating contest.

In my room, I thought about writing some fan fiction about myself while I soaked my feet.

Mark Baumer was wearing nothing except an american flag draped over his shoulders. He looked at his phone. It was only three thousand miles to the edge of the earth. He began walking down the middle of the road.

While I slept, I had a dream I was back in Providence. Somehow I had accidentally ended my journey. A friend had convinced me to take a bus with him. When the bus finally stopped I was in Providence. I felt sad and embarrassed.

Barefoot in america on christmas eve

Dec 25, 2016

**On day 73 of crossing America barefoot I travelled from Lake City FL
to Lake City FL...**

I woke up and ate six bananas. I looked at my phone. My body felt a tiny bit broken. I left the motel room and walked to the lobby. There was a basket of bananas. I ate nine bananas while looking at the television in the lobby. Some of the people inside the television almost seemed like they wanted to cry but they couldn't because they would lose their jobs and all the advertisements would kill them.

How many minutes until a law is passed claiming advertisements have more rights than humans?

I went back to my room and gathered my stuff. The plan was to walk out of town and continue until I found another town. I began walking. My body seemed slow. I wondered if there was maybe some mold in the motel room where I stayed.

Ideally, I will some day learn how to dig holes so good that I can just sleep in a different hole every night.

I walked about a mile and sat down in the shade of a billboard. A girl ran up and gave me a bottle of water. I decided to meditate.

My brain was trying to decide whether I should do the thing where I go somewhere else or the thing where I continue existing where I am.

After about ten minutes of meditation, a man walked up and said, "You shouldn't sit under this billboard. The police will throw you in jail." He told me to go out behind the library which was nearby because there were a lot of old mattresses. After the man left I continued meditating. Another five minutes passed.

The world is full of so many ideas and people and places it's hard to do everything, which is why it would be comforting to maybe dig one hole forever until that hole is where your dead body learns how to be dirt.

I heard a car pull up. Two people climbed out of the car and asked if I was okay. I nodded and said, "Just enjoying life under this billboard." One of them said, "Well at least you're not begging for money down by the highway." He handed me twenty dollars. The other person said, "I would never give money to any of those bums. They just drink it all. You seem like you're good." I felt a little sad as the two people got back in their car. I appreciated their kindness, but it sounded like the people who really needed help weren't getting help. There are many levels of kindness. I think all are important in their own way, but sometimes the kindness that involves throwing money or objects at a problem is needed less than the kindness of being with people and helping them work through whatever they're dealing with. Before the car drove away one of the people asked if I knew that jesus died for our sins.

Sure jesus was something that once existed, but literally hundreds of thousands of humans are dying because of the way the majority of americans are living our lives. Basically, the sin of being an american fills the world with an infinite amount of death.

As the car drove away I continued meditating under the billboard. It felt nice to be with my thoughts.

On one hand, I talk about all the death around us and then on the other hand, I sit under a billboard and do nothing.

After about twenty minutes of stillness passed I walked across the street to a small local grocery store and bought a watermelon. I decided this watermelon would be my present to myself christmas morning. After I bought the watermelon I walked to a motel and got a room. I had walked about a mile for the day. I wasn't sure what to do with the rest of the day so I called some friends and family.

It felt good to hear the voices of people I loved.

After the phone calls I thought about going to see a movie or something mindless, but instead I walked back into Lake City to the grocery store to buy hummus and blackberries. On the way, I passed a lot of cars in parking lots as people filled shopping carts with last minute holiday purchases.

It's an endless game of rushing around and spending money so you have to continue to rush around for the rest of your life to get the money you will then throw away.

I'm just as guilty as anyone. I'm out here existing in a capitalist society spending money every single day. Maybe when this journey is over I can return home and turn my home into something that can exist within but outside of capitalism. As I walked back to my motel room with the hummus I bought I felt scared by all the fast food restaurants open. The sun had gone down. It seemed like a lot of the stores had closed early for the holiday but the fast food restaurants were all glowing and trying to force their various bacon flavored meats.

It's always sad how much the world fills itself with trauma and how blind we can all be to it. I encourage everyone to at least try going without animal products for 21 days to see if you can wake up to the insanity of death most of america is trying to sell us.

My hundredth day on the road

Jan 21, 2017

On day 100 of crossing America barefoot I travelled from Defuniak Springs FL to Mossy Head FL...

The green carpet where I slept was dry even though it rained most of the night. I could feel an insanity resting deep in my face.

The moon was still visible but it could not save us.

I spent most of the morning looking at my phone and wondering if any of the thoughts inside of it would survive.

Something terrible would soon be able to touch all the nuclear codes.

When I began walking I had an urge to stop traffic until all the roads in america died.

One day everyone will be able to walk down the middle of the road free from all the violence this society has built.

I passed a golf course and felt unhinged.

I hope you're happy touching sports so good you never notice when everything finishes burning around you.

Before I left Defuniak Springs I stopped at a grocery store and bought some kale.

People pointed and whispered, "It's one of those kale eaters."

The day felt monumental not because it was my hundredth day of walking across america but because a man who hates everything except himself (or any other rich white man) will be free to burn the world for profit. We now have a president who does not care about the future of humanity on planet earth.

I'm ashamed of the majority of white men in america to the point where I want to remove all evidence of being a white male from my body.

It began to rain so I sat on a bench and watched the rain. My dad called. We talked about trying to find hope in a system where the only safety net will be wealth. Part of me wanted to curl up and wait for my brain to melt but instead I began walking in the rain. With each footstep I felt more angry and helpless.

Grow an organism so large it drowns out anyone and everything who has ever tried to harm a living being.

Anyone who supports the president does not care about humanity or the future of earth. If you support this president you openly admit it's okay to hurt women, people of color, minorities, the disabled, poor people, or anyone in need. I wish there was a way to transfer all the emotional and physical violence of this new presidency from those at risk to myself. I am out here in america. Please bring me your hatred and pain.

We would have been better off electing a barrel of burning tires as president.

As I was passing a junkyard a man with a pickup full of old washing machines yelled, "trump for president." I asked him why he wanted to see the world burn. He just laughed.

The language of this world has maybe died and been replaced with another hole that can only say things its own thoughts already believe.

An hour later, two people in a white truck stopped and asked if I needed anything. I lied and said I didn't need anything, instead of being honest and saying, "I need you to admit climate change is real. I need you to do everything you can to fight for this earth. I need you to reject everything our fascist president tries to do to this world and its people."

I need people to understand this earth does not only have to create systems of death and wealth.

When it got dark my legs didn't want to do anything else. I walked another four miles in the dark. My map said I was near a church, but the only thing I found was a cross next to a carport. I crawled under it and went to sleep before I even finished zipping my sleeping arrangement closed.

At Some Point in the Last Nine Billion Years

At some point in the last nine billion years, I was probably a fourteen-year-old boy. Of course, when the world ends there will be no evidence any of us were ever fourteen-year-old boys, so it's sort of pointless to talk about the fourteen years I was a boy or any of the years when I was anything, but the world isn't quite dead yet or at least my consciousness still believes in its own existence, so I'm going to talk about a bunch of things that probably happened and you're going to sit there and pretend like they're interesting.

By the time I was fourteen, I think my parents were tired of raising me. We all lived in the same part of Maine where their parents had done them.

The house where I grew up was gray, but on the first day of high school my mother painted the house red, which for no reason was fitting because high school, for the most part, was satisfactory, except for the time in science class when some of my teeth were pulled out and melted on the heat spout. I struggled to chew for a minute and this struggle seeped into other areas of my life, clouding the remainder of my adolescence and all but confirming my belief that the entire process of modern education was pointless.

Fortunately, I met a boy named Leon. He gave me a few of his teeth. But his mouth was hollow and the teeth eventually crumbled. Some of them fell out when I tried to chew on a piece of toast. Leon said it was okay because he told me we were best friends.

Sometimes Leon and I would go to the mall and use our pockets to steal electronics.

When Leon was seventeen his parents were tired of looking at him every day so they sent him to prep school in Massachusetts.

The rest of my mediocre adolescence was spent sitting at home waiting for the television to rot.

95

This was around the time when people started using their computers to talk to other people's computers. The internet had just been invented. Leon liked to email the internet at my parents' house. He sent me a lot of pictures of his prep school girlfriend. She had a gerbil named "Grampy." My father's father was also named "Grampy." Leon laughed when I told him this and said, "Your grandfather was named after my prep school girlfriend's gerbil."

A few months later, I ate dinner with my parents. The next night I ate dinner with my parents again. My mother had cooked some barbecued horse teeth and cornbread. While we ate, our internet got a message from Leon. He asked if I had a girlfriend. I took a picture of an uneaten piece of cornbread and emailed it to Leon's internet. I told Leon that my girlfriend was named "meat horse." I didn't actually have a girlfriend because I spent most of my free time waiting for the television to touch me.

Things continued towards an utterly pointless conclusion until Leon returned to Maine one day on a break from prep school and we went to a store that sold pancakes. While Leon ate his pancakes, he said the majority of my teenage years with him had been slightly insignificant. The next day Leon returned to his prep school. There was nothing special about my relationship with Leon. For the most part, the years growing up with Leon were the years when I was not quite the person I am today.

The summer before I left for college, Leon and I met a sixty-three-year-old keyboardist. We started a band called "Steak Trombone." Our band was mostly a failure, but we made some colorful t-shirts. On the front of the t-shirts, there was a picture of a little girl eating an ice cream while sitting in a jar of mayonnaise. Leon hardly ever came to band practice. He was too busy talking to girls he met on the internet. Sometimes when he was bored he would go to the supermarket to steal toothpaste.

One afternoon I went swimming with Leon and a bee stung me on the left side of my esophagus. Leon laughed until he was the ugliest person I had ever met. The water got cold. Leon said he didn't want to swim anymore and instead wanted to buy a dog. He flew to South Dakota and bought a dog, but on the way home the plane crashed in Brazil and the dog ran away. Leon was in a coma for the rest of the summer. I developed a bad cough and didn't recover until the last week of August when I finally coughed up the bee that had died at the bottom of my lungs.

The night before Leon was supposed to leave for college he woke up from his coma. His parents invited me to dinner. There were lobsters for sale at a restaurant near the ocean. After dinner, Leon and I sat in a hot tub with Leon's parents and his younger sister. His parents cried as they digested the idea of Leon moving to a city to attend a university.

Leon's freshman-year roommate was a boy from a wealthy family whose dad dressed like he was a small white mouse named "Charles Young-Juice." For whatever reason, Leon and I didn't talk to each other for the next three or four years. I developed my own life at a small liberal arts college somewhere in the United States. Nothing much happened with my thoughts in these years. I spent a few minutes reading books. Other times I would sit on the computer and click things.

About a month before I was supposed to graduate, Leon called me and asked if I had decided what I wanted to do with the rest of my life. I shrugged. He asked if I wanted to go out in the woods and kill an antelope. I wasn't even sure what an antelope was, but I thought it might be a snowflake from the warmer regions of New England. Leon said, "All humans have a moral obligation to the legacy of humanity to do something with their lives that would be interesting to people who aren't human." Killing an antelope seemed like a poor way to meditate with the undeveloped pieces of my brain. I didn't tell Leon I was against killing an antelope. Instead, I told him I was thinking about moving back in with my parents until I learned how to move objects with my thoughts.

My years in college had made me an overeducated, white, middle-class male with no job skills. Most of the young, overeducated, white middle-class males in my age bracket also seemed to be struggling with the guilt of their post-collegiate lives. A lot of them planned on traveling after they graduated because they wanted to look at the pieces of earth they had never seen before.

The most disappointing thing about my college education up to that point was I had not been taught how to levitate even two or three inches off the ground.

A few days after Leon called me, he showed up at my dorm room. His eyes seemed to be drooping below his mouth. He was high on mushrooms and wanted to eat pancakes. We drove around for an hour, but could not find any pancakes. Leon told me to park my car in a ditch so we could sleep.

In the morning we climbed out of the ditch and went for a jog. We jogged six miles. My legs began to cramp after the first mile. Leon was a better runner than me so his legs didn't cramp. In high school, he had qualified for the state championships in cross country, but on the day of the state championships, Leon went to his coach's farm and kicked the coach's pony in the head. The cross country coach got angry and demoted Leon to junior varsity. A few years later the coach was still angry so he divorced his wife and ran away to Montana with a seventeen-year-old girl named Mandy.

After our run, Leon and I got breakfast in the cafeteria. He ate two hard-boiled eggs and a piece of melon. The food seemed to make him anxious. Leon ate very quickly because he said he didn't know what else to do with the rest of his life.

The next day I dropped out of college and moved back in with my parents. I told them I had graduated early. My father gave me a big hug and then took me out on a sailboat he had rented as a graduation present. The two of us floated around the Atlantic Ocean while we ate lobsters and played board games. On our last day out to sea, my father got sick and puked. He said he didn't like boats anymore.

As we drove home, my father asked me what I wanted to do with the rest of my life. I shrugged. He rubbed my head playfully and said, "When I was your age I didn't know what to do with my life either so I impregnated your mother." I nodded. I never really talked to my father ever again. It seemed impossible for his old man skin to understand the young decisions I was making with my life.

I sort of felt bad about dropping out of college a month before I was supposed to graduate, but I was tired of being logical and I knew if I tried to explain to my father my desire to not be logical anymore he would go to great lengths to lecture me on the importance of logic. There comes a point in every young grown man's life when he either has to eat his father's logic or pee on it until it catches fire and burns up.

The last thing I think I told my father was that I wanted to spend the rest of my life ignoring the majority of everything he had ever said.

When we got home from the Atlantic Ocean I began packing a suitcase. Fifteen minutes later, while my father was in the shower, I left a note on the kitchen table saying I had gone out to get milk. I took my suitcase and began walking to Leon's house. He had also dropped out of college.

Leon was eating a tuna sandwich when I got to his house. I asked if he wanted to hitchhike across America. He shrugged and finished eating his sandwich.

•

We had no strategy. Our plan was to throw ourselves at the road with nothing except an outdated road atlas and our thumbs. I imagined we would both get famous and then I would write the greatest American novel ever written. I smiled at these thoughts. Leon asked why I was smiling. I told Leon I hoped I would someday write the greatest American novel ever written. He said he thought it was unlikely.

There was a road near Leon's parents' house. Leon and I dragged our suitcases to this road. I stood next to Leon and waited for him to grow a new face resembling what I imagined the face of a great American traveler would look like. His face did not change. The mouth near his brain was shaped like two thin boyish arms still struggling to recover from adolescence.

Some cars approached. I held up my thumb. Leon said, "In one hundred years, the automobile will be worth less than a glass jar filled with moth coughs and everyone will laugh at the idea of banks giving out loans worth twenty thousand dollars so people could buy an object worth less than a jar of insect breath."

For two hours, every automobile in existence ignored us. Leon and I continued to play with our thumbs. We felt disappointed in our inability to attract a substance of the road. I worried my thumb would get depressed and not want to be my thumb anymore. The highway laughed at us. When I opened my mouth, large pieces of doubt filled my head.

Leon and I were both afraid of failure because we were doing something we had never done before and when you do something you've never done before you are inexperienced and afraid to make the tiny clumsy mistakes necessary to learn to do something you've never done before.

Nothing was happening. Our decision to hitchhike across America was created in the dim and adolescent piece of our souls still hoping we could get a job being famous. I could feel us both squinting as we tried to pretend we were world-renowned travelers.

The piece of earth we were standing on was very near the hometown where we had once been children.

Silence crept into our mouths as we felt the non-existent progress of the day slowly leak into the late afternoon.

The first vehicle to stop was a navy blue van. A faucet of absolute bliss opened wide somewhere in my chest as I ran with Leon toward the waiting van.

A large woman sat inside the blue object. There were no seats in the back of the van, but it was carpeted. Leon and I sat on the floor of the van next to a bulky, potted house plant. I listened to a ripple in the large woman's face as it made noise. Leon plucked a leaf from the house plant and put it in his mouth. He said he thought the plant might be a hallucinogen. The van merged onto a highway.

The American financial burden had not quite been realized. Everyone in America was still rich and understood enough about their emotions to know how to pretend to be happy. I looked at the large woman's face through the rearview mirror. Her face smiled at me. She lived a mode of happiness built on consuming the cheapest pieces of the world around her until all these inexpensive pieces made her overweight. The van slowed. We had only been in the navy blue van for eight minutes. The large woman apologized for not being able to drive us further, but she said she had to go home and eat a piece of her suburban lifestyle for dinner.

The van stopped on the side of the highway near an off-ramp. Leon and I climbed out of the van. There was a field next to the highway. I looked at my watch. It was five PM. I asked Leon if he was hallucinating. His eye twitched, but he didn't say anything.

We walked through the field until Leon said he was tired of the field so we left the field and stood on another on-ramp. I held out my thumb. Leon wanted to eat some dead antelope meat. I pointed at a pine needle. It looked bored. Leon picked up a rock the size of a pebble and threw it at the pine needle. He missed.

Twenty minutes of sweat leaked from our bodies. The hardware of our youth was still functional. We looked at the passing cars and waited for one of them to eat us.

A red pickup truck stopped. Leon and I climbed into the truck and found a wrinkled man. I touched the wrinkled man's hand and felt an undersized wrinkle near the knuckle on his ring finger. Leon also touched the wrinkle. When the wrinkled man had touched everyone, the red pickup truck pulled onto the highway.

The wrinkled man told us he had spent the entire day looking at a crease wedged deep inside a young woman's bikini. He said he liked when bathing suits got compressed onto human skin. Leon mentioned a friend from prep school who once got sand in one of their crevices. The wrinkled man nodded and laughed.

Leon continued to make noise. He talked about the last time he and his prep school girlfriend went to the beach. It had rained. They left the beach and wore their bathing suits to a movie theater. Leon said he couldn't remember what the movie was about because he was on so many drugs that he turned into a small cricket. The wrinkled man made a comment about how all his wrinkles were the byproduct of his drug use. He also said, "It is very common for people your age to be heavily invested in the drug culture, but at some point later in life, one of you or maybe both of you will grow tired of hearing stories propped up entirely on drug use."

Our progress with the wrinkled man was minimal. We barely traveled two inches inside his motor vehicle. He seemed concerned about his mental health. As we abandoned the wrinkled man, he told us one of his sneakers was filled with mayonnaise. Leon and I nodded. An absence was created within the wrinkled man's life. I closed the passenger-side door of the truck. The wrinkled man drove home alone.

We climbed a guardrail. Two cars passed. I looked at the ground and thought I saw a lonely penny, but when I reached down to pick it up there were no lonely pennies on the ground. There was only an old, used cigarette and a dehydrated pine needle. I wanted to put the dehydrated pine needle in my mouth, but before I could another automobile stopped.

Leon and I climbed into a small green pile of something. I was reminded of a thing I once ate. The seats of the automobile smelled like frosted cinnamon buns. A greasy gender-neutral piece of skin sat in the driver's seat. The gender-neutral person said, "My meat is soft and not worth touching."

A river of old fast-food hamburger wrappers crowded the backseat of the automobile. I looked for a seatbelt but could not find one. Leon gathered some of the hamburger wrappers and rubbed them on his forehead for protection. The gender-neutral person said, "Sometimes my husband eats all the food in our house and then I have to go buy more food."

Our journey progressed. We were not near where we had been. At some point I fell asleep. When I woke up Leon was asking the gender-neutral person for a lesson in Portuguese. The gender-neutral person said something in Portuguese. Leon didn't understand. The gender-neutral person was silent. We approached a toll. It asked for a dollar. The gender-neutral person placed a dollar in an old hamburger wrapper and fed it to the toll booth. There was a piece of cheese stuck to the wrapper.

Leon asked the gender-neutral person if they wanted to bring us to California. The gender-neutral person said, "I am tired. My husband and I share a waterbed. Sleeping on water is very disorientating and makes me nauseous."

Thanks to the advances in technology or something, Leon and I climbed out of the small green automobile somewhere in New Hampshire. We were standing near a restaurant. It sold meat. Before the gender-neutral person drove away, they pointed at the restaurant and told us to eat meat for dinner.

Leon and I went inside the restaurant. I watched Leon put some meat in his face. A few minutes passed. Leon drank six beers and said he enjoyed not quite being in control of his body. I sipped on a ginger ale. Leon asked me if I was enjoying our trip. I noticed there was still a piece of meat on my plate. I picked it up and opened my mouth. The sun began to set. Leon shrugged and sipped on another beer. It was getting late. We did not have a place to sleep.

Leon and I left the meat restaurant when our bodies got tired of meat. We walked a few miles. Leon pointed at an ice cream cone someone had left in the middle of a field. He told me to eat it. I ate a piece of the field and was surprised it tasted like ice cream. When I finished, a greasy woman walked into the field and asked if I had eaten her ice cream cone. I heard myself shrug as I began to mumble. The greasy woman seemed disappointed in my inability to have a conversation. I told her I had recently eaten at a meat restaurant. The greasy woman said she lived near a restaurant that sold meat. She looked at the spot where her ice cream had been. Her face began to leak. Leon asked if we could sleep in the ditch near her house. The greasy woman said, "I don't think you boys are emotionally conventional, but when you talk I struggle to maintain a balanced set of mental thoughts." I smiled.

We followed her home.

On the way to her house, the greasy woman said, "I used to be an undersized piece of lettuce. The last time I ever saw my father he was holding a french fry and rubbing it in red paint." I noticed there was an ice cream stain on the front of my shirt. I rubbed it until the tender noise of the stain faded and didn't look like ice cream anymore.

The greasy woman lived in a large house. It looked like the house my parents wished they could have afforded when they bought their tiny gray house. There was no ditch. Leon and I followed her inside. The house was filled with antique teapots and plastic naked troll dolls.

The greasy woman said the majority of her workday was a continuous flow of dirty men asking her for new spoons.

Before we went to bed, the greasy woman fed us blueberries. Leon ate so many his lips turned blue so he had to jump in the woman's pool to clean his mouth. I looked at the faded ice cream stain on my shirt and told the greasy woman she looked pretty. She didn't hear me because I had mumbled. She asked me about Leon. I told her the entire history of Leon. When I finished, she smiled and said, "The way you talk about Leon makes you sound like a gentle idiot."

The guest bedroom had two beds. One of the beds was larger than the other. Leon said he wanted to sleep on the larger bed. There were two blankets, a cotton blanket and a wool blanket. Leon took the cotton blanket. I lay down on my smaller bed with a wool blanket. The guest bedroom blinked twice before fully shutting its eyes. In the dark, I tried to look at myself to see if I looked any different after my first day of hitchhiking across America, but it was too dark and I couldn't see myself. I heard Leon open his mouth. He did not close it until after I had fallen asleep.

In the middle of the night, I woke up to Leon scraping paint off the wall of the guest bedroom. He was eating the paint chips and laughing because he said the paint chips tasted like old paint.

At six AM, I realized America was sort of like an automobile watching a horse pretend to be a human who secretly wished he was an astronaut. I put on a clean t-shirt. The front of the t-shirt had a logo on it. This logo blinked on my chest.

The guest bedroom looked out the window at a shriveled oak leaf that had died two years before I first met Leon, but this shriveled oak leaf did not seem aware it was dead because it was trying to be a rich and luscious garden full of tomatoes and shallot bulbs.

Someone yawned in the hallway. I thought of the greasy woman's pillow. Her pillowcase was rainbow-colored. I remembered a friend who owned a rainbow-colored lamp. If you looked closely at this lamp you could see the face of her first child. The greasy woman appeared in the doorway. I smiled at her. Her non-smile told me and Leon to pack our things.

Leon was still asleep. I looked at his expressionless face and thought of two people who loved each other until they turned into clouds. I began to poke the non-cerebral parts of Leon until he woke up.

The greasy woman's face looked sad and tired as we left her house. When we got to the end of her driveway she said, "I hope you boys become the men you thought you were trying to be."

I began to cry a little when I could no longer see the greasy woman's house. I didn't want to show Leon the wet parts of my face so I put them in a pocket where I wouldn't have to worry about them and could forget they existed.

•

Leon and I walked to the highway. Around seven AM the noise vibration of the highway reminded us of what it meant to exist on a piece of the world that most people ignored. Leon was tired of being awake. Our stomachs were empty. I told Leon he could sleep in the dirt if he wanted. Particles not entirely visible were touching our bare skin. They were warm and came from a place where humans had never tried to live.

An hour later, a poorly maintained vehicle stopped next to us. We climbed in and it began to move. The inside of the poorly maintained vehicle smelled like small birds. On the floor, I thought I saw a parakeet. Someone turned on the radio. Only one of the speakers worked. A few minutes later the poorly maintained vehicle stopped. Leon and I climbed out. The outside of the poorly maintained vehicle did not smell like small birds. The small bird fragrance might not have been real. The poorly maintained vehicle drove away.

We were near a supermarket. Leon said, "I can almost smell the jars filled with cottage cheese." I looked at the supermarket, but could not smell anything.

Inside the supermarket, there was a shelf of bread and a shelf of garlic. I bought two pieces of fruit. Leon bought some pink yogurt. My fruit smelled like thin unripe nipples waiting for a suburban neighborhood to squeeze them.

Leon and I sat on a bench outside the supermarket and talked to our foods until there was nothing left to put in our mouths. I asked my stomach if it was disappointed. My stomach nodded. A few minutes passed. Leon said he was tired of benches.

As we walked back to the highway we passed two suburban lawns. The grass of one of the yards was four or five inches taller than the grass of the other. Leon said he was jealous of this yard's disheveled lifestyle within the comforts and stability of suburbia.

We waited until noon before a large crippled woman found us. As we climbed into her automobile she warned us not to touch her. Leon said, "I will pretend I don't have hands." The large crippled woman took some pills out of her glove box. She said, "These pills will make your nonexistent hands feel better." Leon put two pills in his mouth. A few minutes passed. We were moving down the highway. I looked at Leon's hands. He was chewing on them. The large crippled woman seemed upset by the way Leon was chewing on his own fingers. She stopped her car and told us she felt threatened because of our male breath. Before we got out of her car Leon asked the large crippled woman what she was going to do with the rest of her life. She shrugged and said she had to go to the grocery store to sell her pills to the elderly cashiers when they went on their lunch breaks.

We were near an exit. Leon pointed at a man sitting on a bench, eating a sandwich. We walked toward the man until we were close enough to ask him where he found his sandwich. He pointed at a store. All the meats inside the store were shaped like the kind of animals that get processed by large machines. Leon said he wanted a mustard sandwich. We ate near a window.

When we finished our sandwiches Leon said he once had a brother. We walked back to the highway. Some of the trees near the highway were underdeveloped and sick. In one tree, I thought I saw an unripe squirrel, but when I pointed at it Leon said the unripe squirrel was a leaf.

A wood-paneled minivan stopped. The minivan had no backdoor. Leon and I climbed through one of the side doors. The man driving the minivan spoke to us in Cambodian. I tried to speak Cambodian, but I couldn't. Leon was disappointed I couldn't speak Cambodian. The man driving the minivan shrugged. A song by a woman who was in touch with her sexuality played on the radio. No one spoke. The wood-paneled minivan protected us for less than three miles. One of the wood panels fell off at the bottom of an exit ramp. We climbed out of the vehicle. I tried to say goodbye in Cambodian. The driver nodded. We were near a store with discount televisions for sale.

Large parts of my body were sweating. I tried to hide my sweat, but Leon could see my puddles. The sweat was visible from a distance of eight feet. Leon looked at the earth and then at the store selling discount televisions. He said, "Our ability to go anywhere we want might be hopeless."

Leon pointed at something and began walking on something that wasn't a highway. I followed. We walked a mile. Leon stopped walking near a patch of grass. I picked up a fragment of the small field and put it in my mouth. The pieces of grass crumbled in my mouth. I thought about spitting the pieces back on the ground, but then I thought of something else and never ended up figuring out what to do with crumbled pieces of grass I once put in my mouth.

The late afternoon introduced us to a handful of automobile men. Each automobile male was white, single, and struggling with various levels of depression. The first afternoon male drove a black van and wore a religious cloth. He said he enjoyed the smell of our youth and our boy noise.

A few minutes after the first afternoon male dropped us off, a utility van from the "Department of Highway Maintenance" stopped. Leon and I looked at the afternoon male inside the maintenance vehicle. He shrugged and let us climb in. As we moved up the road, the second afternoon male said "Someday I would like to own a bald eagle and paint it red and blue." Leon nodded and said, "I hope America will always be a large statue that is bigger than all the other statues." The maintenance vehicle slowed. I kissed the side of the utility van before it drove away.

Our progress had been small. I took out a road atlas. Twenty minutes passed. I yawned. A white-skinned accountant stopped and asked us to climb in his gray automobile. I asked him if he was rich. He didn't answer. His silence extended for twenty minutes. He dropped us off near a maple tree. When the white-skinned accountant was gone I asked Leon if he would be disappointed if all his sons grew up to be white-skinned accountants. Leon said, "Someday every white-skinned accountant in the world will move to the Midwest and have a mental breakdown."

There was a culvert pipe next to the maple tree. Leon went behind the culvert and peed. The maple tree watched Leon. When he was done Leon took a piece of dried pineapple from his luggage and ate it.

The maple tree waved goodbye.

We climbed into another afternoon male's automobile. This one was painted blue. It was named Doug. The backseat of Doug was filled with take-out menus. I picked one up. Doug told me not to touch his take-out menus. I looked at the rearview mirror. The car slowed. The blue automobile named Doug said he was disappointed with his life and didn't want to be around people anymore. He dropped us off on the side of the highway.

I found a wing nut on the ground. Leon smiled and told me to eat it. I put the wing nut back where I found it. Leon picked up a broken light bulb. I asked Leon if he was disappointed. He shrugged.

A man in a police uniform stepped out of a police car. He wore a flat-brimmed hat. The police car blinked. We were asked what we were doing. Leon pointed at the surface of the earth near his feet and said, "The next thing in my life will happen soon." The police officer told us to sit in the back of the police car. I wondered if we were being arrested. The policeman did a background check on us. The computer in his car told him it was okay. We were not bad men. The police car began to move. There was an airport. The policeman pointed at the airport and told us we should use airplanes.

Leon and I sat on a bench inside the airport. A piece of uncooked meat sat down next to us. He asked us how old we were. Leon pointed at a blonde-haired child. A plane fell out of the sky. People climbed out of the plane. Leon asked the piece of uncooked meat what he was going to do with the rest of his life. The piece of uncooked meat said, "I am going to Virginia to meet my daughter for the first time."

An announcement was made over the intercom system. Leon and I tried to climb on a plane before it floated somewhere, but the ticket attendant wouldn't let us touch the inside of the plane because we hadn't paid anyone. We weren't sure what to do. I lay on the ground and tried to go to sleep. A man with a broom told me I couldn't be what I wanted to be. I stood up.

A woman at the airport information desk pointed at a store that sold meat that was no longer uncooked. I followed Leon. He ordered a baked potato. Someone with hamburger fingers looked at me. I blinked four times before I asked for two teaspoons of ice cream.

After we ate we found a bus. I sat down next to a guy with a shaved head. The guy with the shaved head said, "I lost my name because I drank too many icy beverages." I looked at the guy's jacket. It had been made at the top of a corduroy mountain. The guy with the shaved head asked if I liked men. I thought about men I liked and I thought about men I didn't like. The guy with the shaved head said, "You look like someone." A few minutes later the guy with the shaved head got off the bus. A pregnant baby carriage filled his empty seat.

The bus continued. I looked out the window. There was a beach. Leon stood up. The bus slowed. Leon got off the bus. I followed him. He took off his shoes and walked barefoot on the sand. We lay down and waited for the sun to set. I asked Leon if he wanted to go swimming.

He said he didn't want to get wet. I looked for a large bubble that Leon and I could crawl into. I did not see any bubbles. Leon fell asleep.

Three girls walked past me on the beach and laughed. I tried to laugh at the same thing they were laughing at. The three girls stopped laughing and looked at me. I apologized for intruding. The three girls left the beach. They weren't laughing anymore.

I looked at the sun. It was almost dead. Leon opened one of his eyes and picked up a handful of sand. He pressed his mouth on the sand and spoke to it. The sand in his palm did not respond. Leon dropped the handful of sand. The last droplet of the sun touched our faces. Leon pointed at a bench near a parking lot. The bench was made of wood.

The evening warmth from the dead sun made me forget I was a human being. Leon said, "I feel like I have one thousand penises right now." We sat on the bench. I began to think about where we could find a ditch to sleep in. Leon said his prep school girlfriend had once rented a cottage near a beach. I thought of a girl I met in college who lived near a beach. She liked to drink wine with a straw on the weekend.

Leon said he was tired of the wooden bench. We walked up the road to a coffee shop. The assistant manager said the coffee shop was closing in fifteen minutes. His hair was a royal shade of pee. He gave us a bag of free donuts. Leon asked him where the nearest ditch was. The assistant manager shrugged. Leon nodded and began making piles of non-relevant information with his mouth. I used half of my ears to listen to things that weren't created by Leon's mouth, but at one point I heard Leon say, "The worldwide market for solvents is over seventeen million tons which is equivalent to almost eight billion dollars."

An hour later, we were in the assistant manager's basement. Leon asked him if he liked the smell of benzene. The assistant manager said he didn't know what benzene smelled like. Before we went to sleep, the assistant manager said, "A homeless woman lives next to my television. Sometimes in the middle of the night, she likes to open the refrigerator and stand naked in front of it."

There was a pool table in the assistant manager's basement, but the green felt cloth had been torn off and was hanging from one of the basement walls. Someone had spray painted the words "orange juice" onto the green felt. I lay on the ground next to the pool table.

The house was very small. I could hear the assistant manager lying down on his bed in one of the other rooms of the house. Leon climbed on the bare pool table and rested his face. A few minutes passed. I asked Leon if he was asleep. He said, "I am feeling a little too full of myself to fall asleep." I thought about my own ability to sleep. I also was full of myself. I worried I wouldn't be able to fall asleep. A few seconds passed. I told Leon everyone was full of themselves. He nodded and said he was asleep.

I spent most of the night thinking about a movie I had once seen where a guy punched a blind person in the face as the blind person walked alone in a public garden. A crowd quickly gathered around the blind person who got punched in the face. The man who had punched the blind person watched the crowd gather. He waited until fifty men had gathered and then he apologized, said he was mentally handicapped, and began to cry.

The morning smelled like a glass of milk. Most of the fabrics of America were still asleep. I looked at a clock on the basement wall. It told me to yawn. I felt like the only person in America not still asleep. I yawned twice. The day before I had found a penny, but I could not remember where I had found it. After I yawned I took this penny out and looked at it.

Leon was sleeping on a pink inflatable plastic chair in the corner of the basement. I had vague memories of him climbing down from the pool table in the middle of the night. I heard sleeping noises in another room of the house. I left the basement and found the assistant manager sleeping on himself inside a blanket. He was holding a spoon he had used the night before to clean out the skin of an avocado. I looked at the assistant manager until I blinked.

There was a bathroom next to a linen closet. I looked in this linen closet for a few minutes until my lungs were tired of breathing the linen odor.

The bathroom was painted a light blue color. I took off part of my face and rested it next to the soap dish so I could clean the wrinkles from the corner of my eyes. One of my pupils looked bigger than the other. I took off my shirt. I was worried, but it was okay. My nipples were still glued to my chest.

In the living room, a woman was chewing on a plant growing inside the television. She said "hello" to me. I asked if she was the assistant manager's mother. She said "hello" to me again. I didn't say anything. She turned back to look at the television. After a few minutes, she lay down on the carpet and went to sleep.

The only thing in the refrigerator was an empty bottle of mustard. I went back down to the basement. Everyone was still sleeping so I laid on the empty pool table and stared at the ceiling.

An hour later, the assistant manager came down to the basement wearing only the support of some yellow cotton. He asked if we were hungry. I looked at my stomach. Everyone got dressed. As we left the assistant manager's house I noticed the woman in the living room had woken up and was chewing on the houseplant growing inside the television. We climbed into a green piece of metal parked in the driveway.

Someone we didn't know cooked us breakfast because we agreed to pay them. A waitress brought us apple juice. An old man at one of the other tables dropped a piece of his egg on the floor. He bent toward the fallen piece of egg. When the old man put the egg in his mouth I blushed. The waitress returned and gave the assistant manager a plate of eggs. The assistant manager used a rusted spoon to eat his plate of eggs. Some of Leon's orange juice dripped on the table. Leon poured salt on the spot where his orange juice had dripped. After we left the diner, a young boy cleaned our table with a dirty cloth.

A one-armed man with a full beard watched us leave the diner. He was holding a local daily newspaper. The assistant manager waved to the one-armed man. The one-armed man winked. The assistant manager said the one-armed man was his uncle. I watched the one-armed man put the local daily newspaper in his mouth so he could open the front door of the barbershop across the street from the diner. Leon asked how the one-armed man lost his arm. The assistant manager said something about a cousin being careless with a lawnmower.

The assistant manager drove Leon and me to a rest area near the highway. Before we got out of his car Leon asked him if he wanted to quit his job and join us. The assistant manager said he couldn't because his mother would get emotionally unstable and eat his sisters if he left. We said goodbye to the assistant manager. He drove back to his small house and spent the rest of the summer watching sweaty people eat donuts.

Leon sat under a tree and picked dandelions until he was bored. After he picked his last dandelion he said, "I am the lip of a song about all the objects confined to the limits of my own brain function." Every atom in the entire universe seemed to hum in agreement with Leon's voice. It reminded me of a math problem I once did that quantified the heavy silence everyone in the United States would experience if we all sighed at the exact same moment.

At around ten AM Leon asked me to hold his dandelions. He pressed them into my hand. I thought of a yellow-painted wall. Leon yawned. A large piece of his mouth leaked on the ground. I waited to see if Leon would pick up the fallen piece of his mouth, but he didn't. Instead, he waved at a grey mustache inside a grey automobile and the grey automobile stopped.

The interior smelled like that warm spring afternoon when my father traded in his light blue, economy-sized vehicle for a dark green pickup truck. The grey mustache said, "Sometimes people call me Mr. Entertainment." Leon asked why people called him that. The grey mustache got very sad and said, "Actually, I'm boring. People only call me Mr. Entertainment when they want to be sarcastic."

The rest of our ride was very dull partly because we had entered the state of Connecticut. The grey mustache driving the grey automobile dropped us off at a rest area inside a store selling small cardboard containers that smelled like hamburgers.

Leon went inside the rest area and used one of the urinals. While he was peeing he laughed at the man next to him who couldn't pee. The man who couldn't pee left the bathroom without peeing. Leon continued peeing until the urinal was full. He wiped his hands on a piece of toilet paper he found on the ground.

We watched people eat hamburgers for a few minutes. Leon said, "Our lives have been very dull the last couple of days."

I looked at a menu and tried to decide if I wanted to eat cardboard meat. In one of the corners of the rest area, an old man was holding a piece of something he found inside a small cardboard box. The old man continued looking at the thing he was holding as he opened his mouth. No sounds came from the holes in his face, but it looked like he was trying to say, "Don't eat me."

A hamburger employee asked if I needed help. I shrugged. The hamburger employee said, "A long time ago, a cow, hours before it was slaughtered, thought of Africa, and decided it would move there if it ever got the chance."

Leon and I walked back to the highway. Leon was tired and lay down in the grass. I picked a tulip and put it on his chest. Leon was asleep. I was alone. I talked to myself inside my own head for a little bit. An hour passed. Leon woke up.

A twenty-two-year-old named James stopped. Leon and I climbed inside the twenty-two-year-old named James. He was on his way to a birthday party for his stepfather. James said, "My stepfather will probably get too excited and try to spoon-feed me cake in an effort to prove to the guests that he is a suitable father figure." I asked James what was wrong with being spoon-fed cake. He took out a pack of cigarettes and ate one. I looked up the road and saw a maroon van moving very slowly. James changed lanes so he could pass the maroon van. I heard soft breathing in the backseat. Leon was asleep again. James turned up the radio. A song about an old man trying to birth a young cheetah played through the speakers. I asked James if he still liked to be held even though he was a grown man. I heard Leon wake up. James said he would drop us off at a bus station and we could use one of the buses to get to New York City.

•

It began to rain, but the rain stopped three minutes after it started. The raindrops reminded James of a mediocre-looking man he once saw at a party. James said the man wore a brown sweater while he talked to a young girl in a red and black plaid skirt. The young girl was wearing the wrong brand of lipstick. As the mediocre-looking man talked to the young girl the lipstick began leaking all over her face.

117

The bus to New York City cost eight dollars. I had never been to New York City. I looked out the bus window at a tall building. We went into a tunnel. The bus stopped. We were still underground. I was afraid we would never figure out how to get out of the tunnel.

Leon and I got on a subway and went to a park. We lay on the grass and watched two girls fly a kite. Leon called his friend Himiko. I watched the kite stop working and fall on the ground. The two girls laughed. Both of them were wearing large sunglasses. I could not tell if the girls had faces. The sunglasses were too large. One of the girls looked like she might have been bald and toothless. Her sunglasses were very expensive. Leon hung up his phone and said his friend Himiko had invited us to a barbeque in Brooklyn.

We got back on the subway and rode it to something. I was very confused as to where we were. As I was leaving the subway I saw a guy in a yellow shirt riding a pink bike. Leon and I sort of got lost for an hour. Then we found something and ended up at a backyard patio with a dozen other people. The barbeque turned out to be nothing more than a few bags of tortilla crumbs, a half-empty bottle of diet soda, and an empty container of guacamole.

Leon put on a pair of sunglasses. A blonde girl in sunglasses said something that made Leon laugh. She gave Leon a yellow bottle of alcohol. I asked Leon where Himiko was. Leon pointed at a tall, skinny, black-haired boy and said, "Himiko is a very nice object. He sleeps with a lot of girls." I didn't say anything and instead picked up a half-eaten jar of salsa I found next to a crumbling patio brick. Someone had used the salsa jar as an ashtray. I picked out the old cigarette with my fingers and asked one of the blonde girls sitting under a patio umbrella if I could borrow a spoon. A blonde girl pointed at a spoon someone had left resting on a lawn chair. I began to eat the salsa with the spoon I had borrowed from the lawn chair.

When I finished eating the salsa, I saw Leon and Himiko leaving the patio. I asked Leon where they were going. He said they would be back in a few minutes. I sat in a lawn chair and sipped on something for an hour.

Next to me a guy wearing a shirt that said, "I love AIDS" drank a beer and looked at his phone.

Leon and Himiko returned to the patio. They were both eating burritos. A girl was with them. Leon said, "This is Pauline. She said we could sleep at her place tonight." Pauline was a salesgirl at a department store. Leon said, "She used to be friends with my prep school girlfriend." More people showed up at the patio. It got dark. Some people were holding sparklers. I heard ice cream music and asked Pauline if she wanted to get some ice cream. She said she didn't like ice cream. I walked toward the ice cream music alone. I bought a cone of white stuff. When I got back to the patio a lot of people had left. Leon and Himiko said they were going to walk down to a bridge and watch some fireworks.

There were a few thousand people near a bridge, waiting for the fireworks to begin. I saw a dad holding an American flag in one hand and his daughter in the other. The fireworks lasted twenty minutes.

A crippled man opened his mouth and said, "Oh," when some red fireworks exploded.

After the fireworks, Leon, Himiko, Pauline, and I walked to someone's apartment. A few people at the apartment were watching television. I sat down next to a girl with black tights and a half-shaved head. I asked if she liked the fireworks. She said she was not interested in objects or things. I left the couch and stood next to a houseplant for the rest of the evening.

An hour later Leon and I were at Pauline's apartment. Leon asked Pauline if he could sleep in her bed. She said, "Sure." I asked where I should sleep. Pauline pointed at the floor in the living room. I nodded and watched Leon and Pauline get naked and go into Pauline's room.

I went to the bathroom and rubbed my eyes. One of my contacts fell out and into the toilet. I did not bother to retrieve it. I looked in my luggage for my glasses. I could not find them. I looked in my pockets. I found a penny. I decided it was a lucky penny so I ate it. The rest of the night I lay on the floor of the living room, waiting for the rest of the day to get tired and fall asleep.

In the morning, I looked some more for my glasses, but couldn't see so I lay on the living room floor and stared at the blurriness. When I got bored of not being able to see clearly I pressed my ear on Pauline's door. The door did not move for a long time. The longer Pauline's door did not move the less desirable Pauline became. Objects of desire were ceasing to be objects of desire the older I got which made me want to desire objects more, not because I wanted more objects, but only so I could fill the emptiness I felt when I didn't desire anything.

As a child, I had found a pink cardboard box in the street. The side of the box had said, "Barbie," but there was no plastic toy object inside. There was only a raw potato. Someone had drawn a face on the raw potato.

Pauline's door opened. Leon walked out of Pauline's room. I looked at his mouth, but could not tell if he was grinning or frowning.

I asked Leon if he knew where my glasses were. He said, "I think you left them at the assistant manager's house on a soap dish." My eyes felt tired and weak. I regretted dropping one of my contacts in the toilet. I didn't have any more contacts.

I went into the bathroom and stood in front of the mirror for a few minutes as I tried to decide how poor my eyesight was. After a few minutes of looking at my right eyeball in the mirror, I decided to let my eyesight figure itself out on its own. If my vision suffered and I was incapable of continuing my journey through life then I would sit down wherever I was and call my parents to come pick me up. In the hours that would pass, as I waited for my parents to arrive, many regrets would develop and for the rest of my life this failure would obstruct my ability to ever complete anything ever again.

Leon and I left Pauline's apartment at eight AM and took a bus out of the city.

An hour later we were in a jeep going over a large bridge. A man named Harold owned the jeep. Harold said he was on his way to a charity golf tournament. It was drizzling. He was slightly nervous the tournament would be canceled. Leon asked if he could have Harold's golf clubs if the tournament was canceled, but before Harold responded a blue automobile cut in front of the jeep. Harold honked at the blue automobile and said a bad word. He never answered Leon's question. Leon did not repeat himself. A few minutes later, Harold dropped us off on the other side of the bridge.

The drizzle stopped. Leon and I stood in some dirt next to an on-ramp and watched cars pause near a stop sign at the bottom of the on-ramp. We held out our thumbs. Most of the automobiles ignored us. I asked Leon what happened while Pauline's door was closed. He took out a piece of paper and drew a picture of two naked beds lying on top of each other. When he finished the drawing he dug a three-inch-wide hole in the gravel and buried the piece of paper.

A few minutes passed. I thought of Pauline lying naked next to Leon's naked body. I asked Leon if Pauline's face looked different when she was naked. He pointed at a turtle crossing the road. We watched the turtle safely reach the other side.

•

A Dodge Stratus moved up the on-ramp and stopped next to us. An insurance salesman inside the Dodge Stratus asked where we were going. I pointed west. The insurance salesman said he was going to a business seminar in Hartford. I told him we didn't want to go to Hartford. The insurance salesman said, "This road does not go anywhere except Hartford." I got worried. I was afraid if we went to Hartford we would never leave.

Leon and I did not get into the insurance salesman's Dodge Stratus. It drove to its business seminar and left us alone at the bottom of the on-ramp. Leon asked why we didn't get inside the Dodge Stratus. I told Leon that I didn't like the smell of Hartford. Leon said his prep school girlfriend had gone to college there. I took out a map. The shapes and diagrams on the map said the road we were standing on went to Hartford, but it also went to places that weren't Hartford. I felt better.

We continued to wait on the side of the road for a car not traveling to Hartford.

I felt a raindrop on my forearm. It told me I should have gone with the insurance salesman to Hartford. Leon looked at the raindrop on my forearm and said he once visited his prep school girlfriend in Hartford and they had gone ice skating. I asked Leon if he was good at ice skating. He nodded and said, "When we were leaving the ice rink a group of teenagers threw a soda bottle at the ice rink manager."

I had a strong urge to lie and tell Leon I had celebrated Christmas in a motel somewhere in Hartford when I was eleven, but before I could say anything a white van pulled over and a voice from a different country spoke to us from inside the van.

The immigrant asked if we wanted to work for him. I told him we weren't looking to work. He nodded but didn't say anything. I asked if he was going to Hartford. The immigrant said he wasn't. I looked in the back of the van and saw three shovels and a bucket. Leon was shrugging. He was shrugging very hard. A white truck pulled up behind the white van. The immigrant said he was going to St. Louis. He seemed nervous. His eyeballs danced around somewhere beneath his forehead. Both of the immigrant's hands were still gripping the steering wheel.

This immigrant reminded me of an eight-inch-tall object shivering naked in a bowl of moldy fruit. His left eye twitched. He took one hand off the steering wheel and rubbed his forehead. I told him we didn't want to touch his shovels. He rubbed his head again and said, "I am a fair man." I looked at Leon. He shrugged again even harder than he had shrugged before. It was obvious Leon did not want to keep standing on the side of the road. The immigrant's mouth said, "There is a business opportunity waiting for me in St. Louis. If I don't make it to St. Louis my children and I will not be well." I looked at Leon again. He nodded. We climbed into the white van. The immigrant held out his hand and said, "My name is Maurice."

Three hours later I was sitting in a dump truck in Philadelphia. Maurice and his two sons watched me. I turned a key. The engine stalled. I had already stalled it seven times. Leon stood next to Maurice's two sons. One of them was named Billy. The other son was younger and fatter. His name was Timmy. I touched the clutch and the gearshift. I had once driven a dump truck for three miles when I was seventeen. I eased the clutch out. The engine stalled again. Maurice wiped his forehead. I watched his right eye twitch. I apologized and turned the key. Maurice asked me again if I was capable of driving the dump truck. I lied and told him I had spent most of my childhood driving dump trucks. He nodded. I eased out the clutch and gave it more gas. The dump truck died again. Maurice told me to press on the gas pedal more. I told him I would try to press on the gas pedal more. The dump truck felt very simple. There were only three or four buttons I had to push to make it move. I started it again. I looked at Billy and then at Billy's younger, fatter brother. Timmy and Billy would not be well if I couldn't drive their dump truck to St. Louis. I let out the clutch and pressed the gas. The dump truck moved forward a little bit. I gave it more gas. It continued to move forward. I shifted into second gear. Maurice told me to drive to the end of the parking lot and turn around. I drove to the end of the parking lot and turned around.

I was not soft with the dump truck. It struggled to move. I saw Maurice rub his forehead. I touched my own forehead. I stopped in front of Maurice. He nodded and said, "Okay" and then walked back to the white van. His youngest son, Timmy, got in with him. Billy got into the white pickup. Leon climbed into the dump truck with me. He was smiling.

Maurice pulled out of the parking lot. I followed and wondered how far we were from St. Louis. The dump truck rocked back and forth as it struggled onto the road behind the white van. Billy followed me in the white pickup.

The dump truck was red and older than both Leon and me. There were no seatbelts. The radio didn't work. Leon found a piece of paper in the glove box that said it had once been registered in Alabama. I held the steering wheel with both hands. The white van was moving toward a highway. The dump truck also moved toward the highway.

I slowed down for a toll. Everything sort of looked out of focus. I could not tell where I was supposed to drive. I squinted. I remembered I was not wearing my glasses because I left them on a soap dish. My armpits began to breathe fast. I slowed the dump truck and inched toward the toll booth. The woman in the tollbooth said Maurice had already paid the toll for me. I thanked her and tried to keep the dump truck moving. It stalled. The tollbooth woman laughed. I blushed and restarted the dump truck. The white van waited.

A nervous energy was leaking from me into the seat cushions. The highway waited for us to merge. The dump truck struggled to move at a highway speed. I looked at the speedometer. The needle was either broken or we were going zero miles per hour. I pressed the gas pedal all the way to the floor. The dump truck did not move any faster.

The white van settled in front of me. I followed it. Billy and the white truck pulled up behind me.

Leon found a piece of stale cake on the floor. He did not eat it. Instead, he threw it out the window and said something, but I wasn't paying attention because I was focused entirely on not losing control and crashing into whatever ditch would kill us if I tried to drive a dump truck on it.

The inside of the dump truck was completely broken. For an hour Leon sat in the passenger's seat and mumbled. Some of his mumbles talked about maybe going back to school to become a neuroscientist. I nodded and thought of Leon holding someone's brain in his hands. The idea of Leon becoming a scientist made me wish I had never met him and had instead become an orthopedic surgeon.

Miles and miles passed in silence.

I tried to fill the silence with intense breathing, but I mostly only breathed normally.

The dump truck seemed larger than any single human emotion I had ever felt. It no longer seemed possible to relate to the normal functionality of the present world. As I drove, I thought of a postcard my father used to have tacked on the wall near his desk. It was a picture of some mountains. These mountains comforted me for many of the silent highway miles.

Sometimes Leon would ask where we were and I would continue looking at the white van in front of us. I wasn't even sure if we were headed toward St. Louis. The more I looked at the white van, the less I knew where we were.

The more I drove the dump truck, the more significant my life felt. My significance inside the dump truck felt larger than any mountain ever built inside god's earth mountain teardrops.

I watched the sunset and worried if the headlights on the dump truck would even work. Leon asked if we were in Ohio. I was still not sure where we were. I looked out the window and saw a highway sign filled with information, but none of the information meant anything to me. Maurice's white van approached a tunnel. We followed the white van into the side of a mountain. When we came out the other side of the mountain the sun had set. I turned on the headlights. They worked.

We drove for another hour. It began to rain. I followed the white van to a gas station. I parked next to a diesel tank. While I held a fuel nozzle, Leon talked to a man and wife filling their large truck with diesel. He asked them about the details of their marriage. The man and wife got nervous and drove away. Maurice's youngest son, Timmy, came over to the dump truck and looked at me. I asked him what he was looking at. He tilted his head to the side and said, "You're doing good." Timmy walked back to his father's white van. Maurice's other son, Billy, had the hood of the white truck propped up so he could check the oil. The fuel nozzle finished. Maurice went into the gas station. He bought everyone a candy bar and paid for the fuel.

We only drove another ten miles. There was a small motel near the highway. Maurice rented a motel room for him and his sons and a motel room for me and Leon. Our motel room had two beds and a blue carpet. I found a piece of red lint in one of the empty drawers of the bureau and showed Leon. He told me to eat it. I put the lint in my mouth, but it didn't taste like anything. The air conditioning was on. I looked at the thermometer on the wall. It said it was sixty-seven degrees in the room.

A few minutes after we settled into the room something knocked on the door. I found Maurice waiting outside the room. He rubbed his forehead and asked if we were hungry. He was holding a bag of food. I could smell cardboard meat inside the bag. Maurice handed us each a small cardboard box. When I finished eating my hamburger, I went into the bathroom and laid down in the bathtub.

At six AM the motel pool was rusted and smelled like vomit in the shallow end. Leon and I walked back to our room. The fringes of our motel bathrobes tasted like yellow mold growing on the edge of a toothache. Leon asked me if my legs felt young. I pinched my right thigh. It moaned a little and told me a story about a stale dog that once got too old to ever move again so it lay on the kitchen floor for ten years. I rubbed my left leg. It didn't moan and almost felt like an adult that still thought it was a child.

Leon and I put on our sneakers and went for a jog up to the store that sold cardboard meat. We were still wearing our motel bathrobes. A pregnant woman was sitting on a swing set eating hash browns outside the cardboard meat store. I could hear the throb of her depression. There was an echo of tears from earlier that morning. My bathrobe began to sweat. I watched the pregnant woman take out a cigarette. I looked at something foul grow from the toes of her cheap pair of red high heels. Dark parts of her face began to develop. The person on the swing set eating hash browns grew a full beard. The stomach attached to this beard was no longer plump with human bodies. It seemed like it had made the chubby decision to give up on life and turn into a piece of American obesity. I felt relieved as I watched something not quite pregnant smoke a cigarette. The pregnant woman on the swing set was an overweight bearded Inuit that had forgotten how to fish. His indigenous soils had been lost in the echoes of the dried tears his beard developed on the day when his father had fed his Nintendo to a whale.

Leon and I jogged to a small park near a public stream. Leon told me to put my face into the stream. I did not want to put my body in the stream. We each did one hundred pushups before running back to the motel. It was almost seven o'clock.

I watched the local morning news while Leon showered. A man in the television said, "Last night, one family in the lake region had quite a scare when a small black bear wandered into their kitchen and killed their elderly dog who had grown too old to move. It is unclear whether the family will seek retribution or forgiveness. One official, who spoke to a neighbor, said the family initially wanted to publicly hang the small black bear, but some of the younger members of the family seem to be pushing toward trying to domesticate the bear as a replacement for their old, tired, dead hound."

When it was my turn to use the bathroom all the soap was gone.

There were some free pop-tarts and cornflakes in the motel lobby. Leon spread cream cheese on a pop-tart and put it in the toaster. I ate five bowls of cornflakes. Leon read the "money" section of the newspaper. After a few minutes of browsing the financial recommendations of men who get paid to make people desire the idea of being wealthy, Leon asked if I was looking forward to one day becoming a cog in the idea of capitalism. I shrugged. Leon said that being a cog in the American economy was no longer a practical idea. I looked at a substance of capitalism standing behind the motel front desk. This mechanism of free enterprise was breathing slightly and had only smiled once in the past twelve days. Leon pointed at a graph in the newspaper displaying the current unemployment rate. One of the lines on the graph was the shape of a decaying piece of ham that had qualified for unemployment. A middle-class family of four who were refused any sort of governmental assistance watched this rotten piece of meat floating in a puddle of its own juice. The family's dog sipped at the ham stew and immediately grew a wound on his tongue. The dog whimpered for the next dozen years it was alive.

Leon and I walked back to our motel room. Our television was on, but the volume had been turned off. Leon said, "I've decided that when this trip is over I am going to collect unemployment for two or three years and raise my financial status by selling cocaine to wealthy college fraternity boys." For a brief second, I had a vision of Leon snorting white powder off an erect penis in the bathroom stall of an abandoned department store.

An hour passed. No one told us what to do so we sat on our beds and watched television.

At nine AM someone knocked on our door. Leon turned off the television. Maurice was waiting outside our door. He said we had a lot of hours of dump truck movement ahead of us. As I watched Maurice walk toward his white van I thought of future generations of American-born children and got depressed at their failure to be competent, brief, and resourceful.

Leon and I stood in the motel parking lot next to a dump truck. He asked how close we were to St. Louis. I took a deep breath and looked at my right lung. It did not know where we were. I could not smell anything that smelled like St. Louis.

A male attendant was already cleaning our motel room. In one hand he was holding a bottle of Windex. In his other hand, he was holding a toothbrush. I tried to remember if my mother had used Windex on my mouth when I was a child. I thought of her squirting it on the face of a baby that wasn't me. The baby turned into a glass snow globe. My mother picked up the snow globe and shook it until the globe wizard got a snowflake in his left eyeball.

Maurice handed me a key to the dump truck. He was wearing the same black shorts and blue short-sleeve buttoned shirt that he had worn the day before. Leon and I climbed into something that was a dump truck. A boy the size of a grossly enlarged thimble stood next to a white van and watched us. He was wearing a black, faded t-shirt that said, "Timmy" on the front. There seemed to be stains in all the creases of his clothing. When Maurice walked up to the white van Timmy asked his father if he could eat some skittles for breakfast. Maurice nodded. I sat in the driver's seat of the dump truck and fingered the ignition. Maurice and Timmy made space for themselves inside the white van. Something called Billy sat alone in a white pickup. Our little parade of automobiles left the motel parking lot in search of a highway. The white van inched to the front of our transportation party. I prodded the dump truck up behind the white van. I looked in the rearview mirror. Billy and the white pickup moped behind us. It did not take very long to find the highway. Highways were large structures that were built with the intention of being seen. There were very few places left in America for a large interstate highway to hide comfortably where no one could see it.

The first hour in the dump truck was similar to every other hour I had ever spent in a moving vehicle. I held onto a steering wheel and only turned it when it needed to be turned. For long stretches, there was nothing to do except look ahead, out the windshield.

Other cars surrounded the dump truck and did similar things to the road, but these cars were smaller so they felt less significant. The dump truck did things to the road and the road did things to the dump truck. Their love for each other was not something that made me jealous, but it reminded me of a tall couple I once saw outside of a grocery store on matching bicycles. One of the bicycles had a basket. It was filled with fourteen baby oranges.

Leon asked me if I missed my motel bed. I told him I had slept like a dead leaf. Leon said, "I don't enjoy the way you talk about yourself." A piece of skin peeled off my leg and fell on the floor of the dump truck. I looked at the flake of myself for twelve seconds. When I looked over at Leon he was asleep.

Sometimes when I looked at Leon I didn't like him. As he slept, part of his mouth hung open. I had an urge to spit on my fingers and rub them on the floor of the dump truck and then smear my dirty fingers in the parts of Leon's mouth that were open.

We had reached a point in the trip where neither of us liked each other as much as we had once liked each other. I thought about leaving Leon in a ditch, but I knew Maurice wouldn't have been happy with me if I stopped the dump truck to put a human body in a ditch.

The dump truck continued to move at sixty miles an hour. When I tried to drive faster the dump truck would not move any faster.

Our path had become a stream flowing into a void. Leon woke up and asked where we were. I didn't know where we were. It was 10:30 AM I looked out the windshield ahead of us and could not decide if we were still in Ohio or not. The shapeless mumble of the highway discouraged all modes of imagination. It started to get warm in the dump truck. Leon took off his shirt. Some of his chest hair smiled. Leon touched one of his chest hairs and asked me what he should name it. I told him he should name the chest hair, "Baby Noel."

A family-sized blue truck full of inflatable pool toys passed us. One of the plastic inflatable objects looked like the veiled eyelid of an octopus.

The right blinker on Maurice's truck began to blink.

We stopped for lunch at a store that sold fried chicken, pizza, and tacos. Maurice, Billy, and Timmy ordered fried chicken. Leon ordered four tacos. I got a small bucket of pizza and a fountain soda. Everyone sat at the same table and ate in silence. After Maurice, Timmy, and Billy ate their fried chicken they watched me eat from my bucket. Maurice, Timmy, and Billy did not eat their french fries. Maurice asked if I wanted to eat his french fries. I looked in my bucket. It was still half full. I was the last one to finish eating.

Before we left, Leon used the bathroom. I waited outside for him in the hallway. Someone had written a poem on one of the tiles next to the bathroom door. It said, "Eat the peace you are given to do whatever you please." I heard a muffle of toilet paper. When Leon came out he said there was an old taco stain on the ceiling of the bathroom.

We followed the white van to a refueling structure. It was near an old pine tree. I parked the dump truck and let it suck on a fuel tank for twenty minutes.

While I squeezed the gas nozzle I watched a family finish their lunch at a picnic table next to the gas station. Two boys argued over who would eat the last olive. An older woman cut the olive in half. Each boy put a piece of the olive in their mouth. When the family left the picnic table each member seemed to be dragging their overweight stomach behind them in a black plastic bag. The youngest object in the family held his ass until the older woman noticed and took him to the gas station bathroom. On the ground, in the grass, near one of the legs of the picnic table, I saw the peelings of a purple seedless grape.

Billy held the hood of the white pickup open. I watched him pull out the oil dipstick and look at it. His lips barely moved as he held up the dipstick and then used a rag from the floor of his truck to wipe the dipstick clean. When he put the dipstick back in the truck he looked around until he noticed me watching him. I waved. He closed the hood of the truck very quickly and walked into the gas station. Timmy followed his brother into the gas station. I removed the gas nozzle from the dump truck. A few minutes later I saw Timmy leave the gas station holding three candy bars and a bottle of soda.

We returned to the highway. The inside of the dump truck grew warmer the longer we used it. The parts that were broken still knew how to make us sweat. Leon took off his shirt and drew a stick figure on his chest. He said, "I drew a picture of myself on my own chest." He asked if I wanted a picture of him drawn on my chest. I looked at Leon and his chest and told him I didn't want a picture of him on my

132

chest. Leon put away his pen and crawled out of his seat and sat on the floor of the dump truck. He didn't move for an hour. I realized he was asleep.

Ohio held us in its palm for a few more minutes and then handed us over to Indiana. I told Leon I was once born in Indiana. Leon did not believe me. I told him to call my mother and ask her where I was born. I handed him my phone. I watched him press some buttons and hold the phone to the side of his head. After a few seconds, I heard a small version of my mother's voice speak in Leon's ear. He asked my mother where I was born. She told him I was once born in Indiana. Leon handed me the phone. I told my mother I loved her and hung up. I mostly held the steering wheel of the dump truck with both hands, but sometimes I would stop holding it with my right hand so I could use this hand to drink from a cup of iced tea. Leon asked me if my iced tea was still an icy beverage. I took a sip and told him that the iced tea was warm and no longer an icy beverage. He asked if it had turned into "hot juice." I took another sip and said, "The icy beverage is now a hot juice."

A truck passed us. I looked at the man driving the truck. He looked like a beard that was wearing a dirty shirt. I waved to him. He raised his arm to wave at me. I noticed his armpit was greasy. Leon said, "The human body contains more grease than a jar of whale oil." I asked Leon if he was going to put whale oil in his hair when he got older. He said he would probably put some form of grease in his hair, but was not sure if he felt morally comfortable putting whale sauce on his human fibers.

Some men in orange vests were cutting the grass on the side of the road.

A brown station wagon passed us on its way to the Grand Canyon. Two boys sat in the back of the station wagon. One of them was blowing on a trumpet. The other was sipping on a juice box.

The dump truck continued to pass through Indiana. Three hours disappeared.

I looked at the gas gauge in the dump truck even though it was broken. I followed a white van to a gas station and parked next to a diesel pump. Leon and I climbed out of the truck. I put some fuel in the dump truck. Leon wandered off and asked some of the other truck drivers if he could rub their trucks. A few minutes later Maurice walked over to me. He looked concerned. He rubbed his forehead. He asked if I had a driver's license. I told him I did. I followed Maurice into the gas station. The woman behind the counter took my driver's license and looked at it. She was wearing a perm. My driver's license was a regular driver's license. There was nothing special about it. I did not have a special license that said I could drive large machinery. Maurice stood next to me waiting. I wondered if he had a driver's license. It seemed doubtful that his illegal immigrant experience had provided him a driver's license. The woman handed me back my license and said, "Okay." Maurice asked if I wanted something to eat or drink. I grabbed a bag of candy and some more iced tea. I asked Maurice where we were. He said we were in Illinois.

The dump truck followed the white van back to the highway. Everything seemed okay. The dump truck didn't seem any more broken than it had been the whole trip. Leon was eating gummy worms. He bit off half of one of the gummy worms and stuck the other half to the side-view mirror. I asked if I could have a gummy worm. He gave me one. I ate it. We were only seventy miles from St. Louis. Leon said, "We will probably be in St. Louis in a few hours." I nodded and said, "St. Louis smells close."

A few minutes later black smoke began pouring from the engine of the dump truck. Everything that had been going beautifully was now a massive broken object. I pulled off the highway. The business opportunities in St. Louis no longer seemed possible. I thought of where I wanted to end up and I could not remember what I thought.

Everything smelled like black smoke. A grown man rubbed his face until he turned into an old man.

In the parking lot behind a taco store, a dump truck was on fire. Leon and I watched it burn as Maurice climbed on the front bumper and opened the hood of the burning machine. Black smoke poured from the dump truck's lung. Maurice seemed disappointed. His children watched their father spit on the burning dump truck. The fire gave up. The dump truck was embarrassed and dead. Half its face was burned off. Maurice rubbed his forehead multiple times. The young, fat child began to cry. Maurice's other son kissed his brother's young, soft, fat sobs on the right ear until the crying stopped. Maurice did not understand where the black smoke had come from. I looked at Maurice's eyes and waited for them to get wet. I wondered if his children would kiss Maurice's ears if he started to cry.

●

We checked into a hotel attached to a restaurant that had a salad bar and sold pizza. The hotel was also attached to a swimming pool. A young doctor was getting wet in the jacuzzi while talking to a woman about his kidney stones. The hotel parking lot was jealous of the swimming pool's relaxed, social lifestyle. Sometimes the swimming pool got drunk and pissed on the parking lot while it was sleeping.

Two men were sitting in the hotel lobby. Their faces were near each other and their eyes seemed interested in communicating with each other's mouths, but instead of talking they were each blowing on harmonicas even though it was obvious their musical talents were not much more advanced than a trout's ability to make a flute hum. Odd, unbalanced squeaks filled the lobby.

Hotel workers said nice things to us with their mouths. I looked at them until one of the front desk people smiled. Their smile smelled like a new, shiny, red motorbike. I asked the front desk person if he had ever been unpleasant to anyone. He nodded and said, "Once I was unfriendly to an elderly man with Down's syndrome because I did not get enough sleep the night before and my brain confused the elderly man with Down's syndrome for a guy from high school who used to spit on me." I thought of when I was in high school and would save my spit so I could rub it on the geodes in one of the science classrooms.

After Maurice paid for the rooms the hotel's assistant manager told Maurice that he had qualified as a preferred customer. The assistant manager handed Maurice a complimentary envelope. Maurice opened the envelope and found a half-eaten piece of honeydew melon from breakfast.

Our hotel room was on the second floor. The walls of the room had multiple pimples. I looked at the pillows on the bed. They were not complete. I lifted one of the pillows off the bed and noticed it was only three-fifths of a pillow. Leon pressed on one of the wall's discharge spots until it leaked. He said these hotel wounds were typical for two-star lodgings. I took off my shirt. It was dirty. Leon said he preferred four-star lodgings. I didn't have any more clean shirts. I asked Leon if he wanted to do laundry. He handed me all of his dirty clothes. I found a washing machine. When I got back to the motel room Leon was wearing a bathing suit. I looked out the window at the swimming pool. Leon went to the bathroom. I heard the bathtub filling with hot water. Leon floated for half an hour. I sat in a chair and turned on the television. Inside the television, a man said, "Somewhere between India and China something happened." When our laundry was clean I put all the underwear in neat and separate piles. Leon came out of the bathroom and sat in his wet bathing suit on his bed and watched television. I told him something happened between India and China. Leon said, "Some guy I knew in prep school said his father was from China, but I didn't believe him because this guy usually wore argyle sweaters that tasted like stale pretzels."

Leon said he wanted to go to the pizza restaurant for dinner, but his bathing suit was still wet so we waited a half-hour for it to dry. The television kept us amused. Inside the television, a suburban house was talking to another suburban house.

Our waitress at the pizza restaurant wore blonde highlights over her dark roots. Leon ordered some milk and a chicken wing. I asked the waitress if the salad bar had iceberg lettuce. She said the salad bar had a few tomatoes and some cottage cheese. Leon said something about drugs to our waitress. She looked concerned. Leon smiled. When the waitress left I walked up to the salad bar and looked at a pile of iceberg lettuce. Under one of the leaves, I found a container of yellow pudding. I filled my plate with yellow pudding.

Leon was disappointed that our waitress was concerned with the idea of drugs in America. I ate some yellow pudding and didn't talk to Leon about drugs. He asked why I was eating yellow pudding. I told him I was only going to eat yellow pudding for dinner. The waitress brought Leon his milk and chicken wing. He ate the chicken wing.

When there was nothing left on the table except a chicken bone and pudding smears, the waitress gave us our bill. Leon asked the waitress if she ever went to the grocery store. She nodded. Leon asked her where the nearest grocery store was. She pointed at a local grocery store a half-mile up the road. Leon smiled. The waitress did not smile at Leon and instead went to talk to a different table. The bill said we owed nine dollars and fifty-seven cents. Leon put a ten-dollar bill on the table and stood up to leave.

On the way to the local grocery store, we passed a dealership that sold green lawnmowers made out of deer antlers. Leon pointed at one of the lawnmowers. I looked at the lawnmower. Leon kept walking. I followed.

The grocery store had a sale on canned marmalade. Leon went to aisle four and picked up a bottle of cough syrup. I asked if he was sick. He said, "Once I drank a bottle of cough syrup with my prep school girlfriend and we had an intense euphoric experience." I watched Leon empty the bottle of cough syrup into his pocket. He said, "I will drink this pocket tomorrow." He picked up another bottle and grinned. I watched Leon drink the entire bottle. He left the two empty bottles of cough syrup on the tile of the local grocery store.

As we were leaving the grocery store Leon noticed a picture of a blonde woman on the cover of the magazine. He told me to steal the magazine. I put the magazine in my mouth. We left the grocery store.

On the way back to the hotel Leon puked next to a green deer antler. He looked at his vomit and then puked again. I asked if he was sick. He passed out. I continued walking to the hotel. I passed the taco store. I could see the glow of areas where the dump truck had burned up that afternoon.

At four AM I woke up to people shouting in the hallway. I looked through the peephole in the door. There was a crowd in the hallway. I called the front desk of the hotel. The staff person told me that a protest group was marching against the carpet fibers of the hotel. Supposedly, the carpets were made from the teeth of third-world farm animals. I heard someone kick over the fake plant next to the elevator. Another person got so mad they ate a lampshade and then began yelling because their stomach hurt.

A few hours later Leon was back in the room and I was waking up. I asked him if his brain was still high on cough syrup. Leon opened his mouth and looked at his tongue in the mirror. His tongue looked dry and swollen. He pressed a q-tip to the end of his tongue. The end of the q-tip turned purple. Leon filled a glass with mouthwash and put it in his mouth. He didn't spit it out.

A small glass vase of blonde flowers was placed on each table in the lobby. I poured some maple syrup on a child who was playing with a wheat flake. His father told me not to pour syrup on the child. A poodle licked the child's syrup head.

Leon toasted some bread and told me about a dream he had. The dream involved him wearing a panda costume and eating bamboo twigs that had been sprayed with pesticides in a part of China where poaching was still legal. Leon said, "There were piles of black and white rotting fur throughout the region. After I ate enough bamboo to feel sick I felt a dozen mosquitoes sip on the blood near my ear."

After breakfast, Leon found some cough syrup in his pocket so he ate the pocket. When he finished he said he felt sick and went into the bathroom to lie down next to the toilet. I looked out the hotel window. The dump truck was still burned up behind the taco store.

I turned on the television. A politician was wearing a face wig that made him look like a form of idiocy only found at prestigious and elite universities. He said something violent, and then put his fist in the palm of his other hand.

Someone knocked on the door. I opened it. Maurice smiled and rubbed his forehead. I heard Leon moan in the bathroom. Maurice looked at the bathroom door. I tried to think of an excuse, but my thoughts were slow. Maurice and I looked at each other. I rubbed my forehead. Maurice walked into the hotel room and touched the bed where I had slept. He asked if my bedsheets were comfortable. I nodded. Maurice touched the bed again. I looked at the floor for a few seconds. Maurice said, "Things were going really well yesterday until the dump truck caught on fire and burned up." I nodded. We looked at each other. I asked Maurice if he slept well. He shook his head and said, "Every time I fall asleep I think of my dead wife. I worry that my boys miss her a lot. I am not a very good father because I am busy trying to be a mother. I cannot be a mother. If I become their mother then they won't have a father." We continued to look at each other. Leon moaned in the bathroom again. Maurice said we had to be checked out of our hotel by eleven. He turned and left our hotel room. The door closed behind him.

I heard the water running in the bathtub. I leaned my face against the bathroom door and listened. I could hear Leon talking to the bathwater. I wondered if he was going to kill himself or if he was already dead. Leon said, "I sort of went insane a few years ago, but I think I'm over it." I stopped listening to the bathwater and lay down on a bed. I turned on the television and watched two hours of off-network syndicated programming.

Eventually, Leon came out of the bathroom. The bathtub was still running. He wiped his face with the back of his hand. His eyes looked different. He had a vague shade of cough syrup in his face. We looked at each other for a long time. Leon's altitude seemed to be growing. I could not tell if he was breathing. When he opened his mouth I could not hear his lungs. His mouth began to make noise. I listened. Leon spoke at length about feeling like he was a gift to himself. I continued to watch Leon's altitude grow. Somewhere in Leon's brain, the cough syrup said, "Two years ago I had pneumonia and the doctor said I should go live on a big cattle farm. I thought about building a pueblo where I would be free to raise goats, but then a friend invited me to live in his pagoda so I did that for a few thousand years."

Leon sat in front of the television and pressed his forehead on the screen. He said he wanted to keep his face pressed to the television until the multicolored transmissions began to burn their images into his face.

The cough syrup inside Leon laughed and said, "Men should tie their children to the bottoms of their feet and walk on their children until their children become a worn-out pair of moccasins. When men have finished developing their moccasins they should walk on a narrow trail until they reach a mountain of ornaments."

Leon continued to press his face to the television. He said he could feel the next generation of his existence hatching from the thoughts he had forgotten he had created.

I asked Leon if he enjoyed the cough syrup he was experiencing. He said, "As your legal advisor and travel companion I recommend you tell people your name is Leon Jr. and that you are my son."

After an hour, I grew bored of listening to the cough syrup inside Leon. I didn't want to hang out with his drug speech all afternoon. I was tired of people taking drugs and then acting weird. I wished people would act weird all the time and not wait until they had the excuse of drugs.

Leon took out a voice recorder. He turned it on and spoke into it. He said, "I am mentally capable of making mouth gold right now. It is important that I document my brain. I am having thoughts that no human has ever been capable of creating before. If normal brain function is a daily grinding process of a person's mind taking one long shit over an entire day, then my mental asshole is pooping out rubies."

Leon pressed his face back into the television.

I watched a stranger on the television make faint gestures and vain attempts to forget who they were.

Leon continued to talk. He said, "Maybe my male experiences are in a reality that is impossible for you to identify with right now. I would like to be left alone. Please leave me in the peace of my sprawling island full of mall smog and disco street lamps. I can no longer breathe under the judgment of the most important pieces of my life. I am tired of you eating all the things about me that you will never be able to understand."

I stood up and went into the bathroom to shut off the bath faucet. I looked at myself in the mirror for a little bit. My face could not remember what I had looked like the day before. I felt a small triumph in forgetting the memory of who I had been. The longer I looked at myself and tried to remember the images of what I used to look like the more invisible I felt. When I left the bathroom I found Leon asleep under his bed.

At a quarter to eleven, Leon and I packed our bags and checked out of the hotel. I asked Leon if he was sad we were leaving. He pointed at a man walking a small dog. The dog had just shit. The man was bending down to pick up the dog shit with a plastic bag.

We sat on a picnic table near a tree next to a wooded area behind the hotel. Leon asked the picnic table what it was doing. The picnic table didn't respond. Leon sat on the picnic table for an hour, but our boredom hurt in places we couldn't acknowledge so we left the picnic table and walked over to the gas station next to the taco store.

It was almost noon. There were sandwiches for sale inside the gas station. I decided I was hungry. Leon said, "More and more I find myself listening to the mutterings of a crowd. I am tired of being a part of society's haze-dream, built upon a castle of constructed laziness. I don't want to be forced to live the roars of other people's desires. I feel like sitting here alone and singing a song to no one but myself." Leon began to sing about an aquarium named mommy.

Someone asked me if I wanted tomatoes. I tried to think of something clever to say, but I couldn't so I just said, "Okay." A few minutes later someone handed me a plastic bag filled with bread and meat and said, "When I was eight I tried to make a bologna sandwich. I put mustard and cheese on some bread, but we didn't have any bologna left. For most of my life, I was a moderate example of failure and mediocrity. A few weeks ago, I was unemployed and had no job skills. I was very bad at making sandwiches. Now I have developed skills. I am in love with the opportunity that is the American capitalist system."

142

Leon and I sat at a table inside the gas station. I ate a sandwich. Leon carved something into the table. I leaned over. The table said, "The problem with experience is that it often leaves our carnal thoughts disappointed with the results."

Leon looked up at me and said he was enjoying our present immobility.

A few minutes later, Leon stood up and walked outside. He began talking to a woman who was gassing up her moped. Leon said something and the woman laughed. He pointed at her moped. The woman shrugged and finished with the pump. She climbed onto the moped. Leon climbed on the moped behind her. The two of them left the gas station and went up the road.

I was alone in a gas station in Illinois, eating a sandwich. I felt abstract thoughts form, but I ignored them and watched a man touch his truck with a hose until a machine told the man to stop. The abstract thoughts in the back of my head continued to moan. They tried to tell me to go home and stop pretending I wasn't a tourist. I ignored these thoughts and watched Leon return with the woman on the moped. Leon climbed off the moped and waved goodbye.

A red truck pulled up to one of the gas tanks. Leon walked over to it and began cleaning the windshield. When he was finished I saw him hold out his hand and ask for a dollar. The man who owned the red truck shrugged and gave Leon a quarter. Leon took the quarter and walked across the street to a store that sold cardboard meat. He went inside the store. A few minutes later, Leon left the store. He was holding a small yellow box. The outside of the small yellow box said, "Chicken Sandwich."

A family pulled into the gas station. The mother was reading a magazine. On the cover of the magazine, it said someone was getting married. It also said a person who used to be fat was not as fat as they used to be because they turned their fat into a human baby.

Leon walked into the gas station. He opened the small yellow box that said, "Chicken Sandwich." It was filled with pickles. Leon said, "I love pickles. I bought this whole box of pickles for a quarter."

In high school, after the prom, I saw a classmate throw his hamburger pickles at a guy standing behind the counter at a fast-food restaurant.

Leon took out his phone and poked it. His phone called a guy named Jesse who lived in Vermont inside a log cabin he had built on an island within a small lake. I heard a voice inside Leon's phone. Leon said hello to the small voice in his phone. The small voice said it was eating some high-grade, organic, grass-fed beef. Leon told the small voice he was eating pickles out of a small, yellow, cardboard box.

A cop car pulled up outside of the gas station. Leon hung up the phone and looked at the police officer. A police officer walked into the gas station and asked us what we were doing. Leon looked at the police officer and said, "We're waiting for our mother to pick us up." The cop nodded and said we didn't look like the type of boys who had the same mother. Leon said, "She is on a date with a guy she met last weekend at a church festival. The guy was wearing a dark-floral print suit and a pair of large sunglasses. He was sort of bald. His hair reminded me of someone who glued a piece of lint to their forehead. I think this guy has been sad for a long time because his last girlfriend went to Lebanon and was gunned down. I am pretty sure it won't work out between him and our mom."

The cop said, "We've been getting some complaints about a couple of boys harassing the customers of this gas station." I felt nervous. Leon nodded and said, "I saw some boys earlier playing with the fuel pumps. They really boiled my tongue." The cop began to leave. As he walked away, Leon laughed and said, "I sort of hope we go to jail. I don't think I will miss any of my freedoms. If we go to jail I will just pretend my head is a cloud and then I will let it float away so that the only thing the system will be imprisoning will be my body." The police officer turned around and pointed a finger at us and said, "Our town does not appreciate shitheads and from what I can tell by looking at your faces you've spent the majority of your lives being shitheads."

Leon and I walked back to the picnic table behind the hotel. We found a branch and invented a complex game involving the branch. We played this game for an hour, but then Leon broke the branch. Our game was ruined. I yelled at Leon. He laughed.

A teal van pulled up to the hotel. A man, a wife, and an angry boy got out of the van. The man told the angry boy to stop playing with his video game and help carry some bags. The angry boy threw the video game at the man and ran into the woods behind the hotel. The man told the boy to come back. The boy did not come back. The man looked at us and tried to decide if he needed to give us an explanation. He shrugged and said, "My son has a slight temper." The man and his wife picked up their bags and walked into the hotel. I heard animal noises in the woods and could sense a lot of the trees getting bruised.

Leon said, "An old man once came upon what he thought looked like a holy lake, but when he got naked and tried to step in this body of holiness he realized the lake was a canyon. He fell to the bottom of the canyon. When he landed he did not die. He lay in his broken body for three years. A feathered dog and a white deer ate from the broken parts of his flesh. I am not sure what happened next. I feel hungry. I am too famished to finish the story. I think I want a peanut butter and jelly sandwich." Leon left the picnic table and walked to the fast-food restaurant where he had gotten the box of pickles.

I felt like a young man who had just heard a girl fart for the first time. I wanted to go home and tell my father that I didn't want to be a big man anymore. I was not sure where these feelings were coming from. My emotional baggage seemed to be growing. I tried carefully not to think about anything ever again and felt a twinge of relief. A small goose bump grew near my belly button. I lost sense of what planet I was on. My phone began ringing. I picked it up. Maurice's voice pressed into my idea of civilization. He said, "I could not fix the dump truck." I looked at the area where the dump truck had burned up behind the taco store. There wasn't anything behind the taco store anymore. The dump truck was gone.

Leon returned holding a half-eaten hamburger. He said, "I asked the people inside that store for a peanut butter and jelly sandwich and they gave me a hamburger instead. I was a little upset, but then I realized I could be a personal jesus to these people. It is refreshing to be a god to people who aren't as good as you. I can feel their prayers entering my body. For the rest of existence, it is my goal to be a god option for people who don't have any god options. I look forward to becoming a celestial machine made of white beards connected to extension cords, a machine whose only goal is to suck all the energy from the world's belief in the idea of god. And when god no longer exists I will be an example of something incapable of unconditional love."

At around four o'clock, Maurice's white van pulled into the motel parking lot. I picked up my luggage and walked over to the truck. Leon sat on the picnic table holding his empty hamburger box. Maurice asked if Leon was coming or not. I looked at Leon and asked if he was coming. Leon said, "Just a minute," and held the empty hamburger box to his ear. After a second he got down on his knees and dug a small hole next to the picnic table. Maurice and I watched Leon dig.

A white pickup pulled up behind the white van. Maurice's two sons were in the white pickup. Maurice said, "When I was a child I remember watching a dog sneak into our kitchen to steal a crust of bread."

I looked at the hotel. A maid in her late fifties stood near a back entrance holding a broom and a cigarette.

When Leon finished digging the small hole he put the empty

hamburger box inside the hole and pushed dirt on top of the empty hamburger box. He then walked over to the white van and climbed in.

Our return to the highway was trivial. I looked at the road ahead and felt emotionally tired. We were leaving the dump truck behind. It had failed to get us to St. Louis.

Maurice held the steering wheel. I asked him what was going to happen in St. Louis. He said, "There are a lot of broken driveways in St. Louis. Our goal will be to pave over a majority of St. Louis in black concrete." I looked at Maurice's external appearance. It reminded me of the doubts I had as a child when I realized I was growing older and began to question the existence of giraffes and the ability of frogs to have sex.

The drive to St. Louis took an hour. A blue van passed us when we got near the city. The side of the van said, "People are usually happy with their decision to buy vinyl siding." Leon said, "Everyone in my neighborhood had vinyl siding when I was a child. My parents were the only ones without it. I remember one of my neighbors was always sad because about fifteen years before I was born they had gone to Egypt and they lost some of their luggage and the rest of their luggage got infested with insects."

St. Louis was a pile of everything un-ornamental. Its feeble attempts to be the economic center of the United States had failed. We passed a building owned by a large corporation that built airplanes. Leon said if he owned a jet he would fly it while only wearing a sock on his left foot.

We ended up at a parking lot near some brick buildings. A sign outside one of the brick buildings said, "Temporary housing, rent month to month." Maurice parked and climbed out of the van. He said, "I think I am going to rent a room here."

147

I saw someone drinking a can of soda in the parking lot. He was wearing a gray uniform and nodded at me after I stared at him for a minute.

Leon and I climbed out of the white van. The white truck parked next to us. Maurice's sons climbed out of the white truck. A lot of boys came running out of the brick buildings and began hugging Maurice and his sons. I watched the boys hug Maurice's sons and I thought of a man hugging himself.

•

I thought about whether it was even worth continuing with our adventure. I tried to look at my own brain. I asked it if it was experiencing any sense of pleasure or if it was developing a medium-sized experience that would consume my ability to ever experience anything ever again. Leon asked me what I was thinking, but didn't wait for a response. He pointed at a small water fountain and said, "I think it is a significant Buddhist holiday today."

Maurice was gone for quite a while. There wasn't anything for us to do so Leon picked up a small piece of concrete. We played with the piece of concrete for twenty minutes. As we played we talked about art, business, war, farming, philosophy, politics, money, and natural science. The more we played, the more our game and conversation developed. We began to keep score. Leon was winning eleven to eight when we began to speculate whether or not it was possible that AIDS existed in the 1960s. Then Leon got excited and threw the small piece of concrete on the roof of one of the brick buildings. He laughed. I yelled at him for a little bit and told him to stop ruining all the games we played. He apologized and said, "When my dad was in college he spent a summer in Vietnam. He said he even peed on a section of the Ho Chi Minh Trail."

An hour later, Maurice came out of one of the brick buildings holding a green bottle. He said, "All the brick buildings are rented out already. I will take you to a motel down the street." Maurice drank the rest of his beer and set the empty green bottle in the parking lot next to a gray automobile that didn't have any hubcaps. We climbed into the white van. Maurice dropped us off at a motel and paid for our room. I asked him where he and his sons were staying. He said he was staying with a friend inside one of the brick buildings. Before he left, Maurice said he would pick us up at eight o'clock the next morning.

Our motel room was on the second level. The relationship between geometry and layout in the room told me that we would be spending the next week living in a normal, low-quality location. It was a paradox of old sheets pretending to be clean.

A few minutes after we settled into our new space, Leon walked into the bathroom and said, "The shower curtain is missing, there is no light bulb, and we don't have any bath towels." He told me to go down to the front desk and ask if the missing items could be replaced.

The man in the lobby stood behind a glass window. There was an eight-inch hole in the window. I asked if the glass was bulletproof. The man nodded. I told him I was missing some things. He slid a light bulb, a shower curtain, and two bath towels through the hole. I carried the things back upstairs and put them in the bathroom.

Leon was watching television. I lay down on the bed. Leon said, "The only difference between what we were doing yesterday and what we are doing now depends on the world's inability to understand that everything we have ever done is the same as everything else."

The motel television made small intricate cries all night because no one bothered to turn it off. In the morning, the sun did what it was supposed to do when it was supposed to do it. I was tired of touching my bed so I climbed out of it and looked at all the places in the motel

149

I had touched. Leon was still touching his bed. He was suffering not to wake up. Both his pillows were on the floor. As the morning grew he continued to suffer. I went to the bathroom and looked at the toilet water with a part of my body that often gets dirty.

At eight AM something beeped and told Leon to wake up. He got a little angry at the beep and said, "I wish I was rich and had a personal assistant to do everything for me. If I was rich and had a personal assistant then I would probably become a famous rapper because if I was a famous rapper I would live in a big house. The large house would only have one room. There would be no kitchen. I would eat from a take-out Chinese food restaurant across the street every night. My house would be filled with thousands of televisions and a single recliner. All the televisions would play recordings of women putting my penis in their mouth. I would spend my entire life watching my penis get put in other people's mouths and writing rap songs about my penis. Someone would probably put my penis in their mouth while I watched my penis on all my televisions and someone else would use a video camera to watch my penis get put in someone's mouth so that later I could watch myself on my televisions and then write more rap songs about my penis. I want to reach a point in my life where I only consume my own pleasures. I only want to consume myself. I am not sure why all rich men don't spend the majority of their life putting their penises in other people's mouths while only watching video recordings of themselves getting pleasure."

I thought of Leon sitting naked in a room watching a television that was only broadcasting images of Leon sitting naked in a room full of televisions.

There was a small refrigerator in the corner of the motel room. Leon got out of bed and looked in the refrigerator. It was empty. He asked if there was anything to eat for breakfast. I looked under the bed. There wasn't anything edible under the bed. Leon told me I should go get something to eat. I looked at the clock next to the bed. Someone was supposed to pick us up soon. Leon lay down on his bed and closed his eyes. I thought he was going back to sleep, but he opened his mouth and said, "If I become a famous rapper in the next two and a half years you can be my personal assistant." An image formed in my head of Leon two and a half years into the future. He was not a famous rapper. He was sitting in an apartment somewhere in Brooklyn with a few other guys and a dog as some ambient noises leaked from the background of the apartment.

Leon sat up on the bed and sighed. He looked at a brown stain on the ceiling. I looked at his mouth and waited for it to make enjoyable frequencies. Leon continued to look at the brown stain. He did not sing at enjoyable frequencies. I watched Leon look at the brown stain. The brown stain would eventually infest all the walls in the motel room. This blemish on the ceiling symbolized a person's desire to do something with their life that they would never be able to accomplish. I looked at the brown stain for a few minutes. When all the walls in the motel room turned into a brown stain someone would probably repaint them white. The wall would be painted until it had been reincarnated. As Leon looked at the wall I imagined Leon believing that Leon was infinitely possible. In the back of Leon's head, he believed he would exist for thousands of lifetimes.

I thought of the paperwork that would be required to live more than one lifetime and I became anxious at the expectations people would have of me if they learned I had filed paperwork to live more than once. Reincarnation did not seem worth the effort of not accomplishing what I wanted while I was still alive. The idea of being reincarnated had always felt like an imaginary toy that rich people liked giving poor people to keep them from getting too sad and killing everyone.

Leon asked if I remembered the band we tried to start with the sixty-three-year-old keyboardist. I remembered once holding a guitar, but not being able to make any guitar noises. Leon said, "I wish I could bottle my musical talent and give it to other people to drink. If I don't become a famous rapper by the time I am twenty-five then I will probably impregnate ten different women and then just kill myself. It's reassuring to think that if I had sons with ten different mothers that a few of them would probably turn into musical geniuses."

I thought of Leon spending most of his thirties contemplating suicide, but not doing it. Then one day Leon would be almost forty-seven and he would realize that he was too old to commit suicide. If you kill yourself in your forties it should not be called "suicide" because, at that point in a person's life, suicide is basically the equivalent of dying from natural causes.

At 8:15 AM in the parking lot next to our motel, a barefoot woman in a yellow wedding dress dug a hole and buried her new husband's blue tuxedo. Maurice's white van pulled into the parking lot five minutes later. The woman had finished with her hole. She returned to her motel room to soak her feet.

Maurice was not wearing a shirt. He honked twice and got out of the van to put on a shirt. Leon and I climbed into Maurice's white van while Maurice put on a light blue, button-up t-shirt. There was a name-tag sewn above the right breast pocket. The name-tag did not say, "Maurice." When Leon saw the name-tag he said he went to prep school with a girl named "Jenny," who liked to wear shirts that said, "Ted."

We drove to a suburb and stopped at a gas station. Maurice bought us a bottle of juice and some eggs wrapped in tinfoil. I saw a man with a gray face buying lottery tickets inside the gas station. I asked the man if he liked his beard. He nodded and said, "Yep." I watched him rub his tickets. When he finished he threw all the tickets away. His face mumbled. I asked if he had ever won anything. He said, "I once found some money on a bus, but that was a long time before my face turned gray."

Maurice paused his van near a middle-class neighborhood. In one of the yards, an eleven-year-old girl in a spotted yellow dress poured orange juice on a tulip. When the bottle was empty the eleven-year-old girl went inside a two-car garage. The garage door closed behind her. I watched the tulip drip until a dog walked into the yard and ate the tulip.

There were five thousand households in the neighborhood where Maurice dropped us. We were a little beyond the metro stain of an urban environment. When I took a breath I tasted real air and not the smell of an elderly drip of city sweat. Before the white van drove away Maurice told us to knock on houses in the suburbs and ask these houses for money. Maurice gave us each a few hundred business cards. On the business cards, it said, "I want to repave your lawn."

It was nine AM on a Saturday. I began touching people's houses. None of the houses responded. Everyone in the middle-class suburb seemed afraid of me because I was standing on their porches and I was a large man.
When a large man touches a house the house becomes slightly devalued.

Leon didn't do anything all morning except yawn. He said he didn't want to touch any houses and instead lay down in the middle of a concrete sidewalk. Some lawn sprinklers came on and got Leon wet. He stood up and found a newspaper lying at the end of someone's driveway. The newspaper said, "Local bridge needs repairs so youth baseball team sells cookies to raise money for a statue that will look bored even though it is supposed to symbolize ideas like integrity and courage." Leon threw the newspaper on the roof of an overdeveloped cottage. A bird that had been nesting sighed and flew to a planet called earth and ate a wood leaf out of a piece of oak.

I continued to walk from house to house. At one middle-class household, a woman in her bathrobe answered the door. Part of her bathrobe was open so I could see her navel. I tried not to look at it, but her navel asked why I wanted to fill her lawn with pavement. I shrugged and noticed a child in the living room was trying to eat cereal in front of the television. Every spoonful the child put in their mouth slowly leaked down their face onto the carpet. The woman in her bathrobe closed the door. I walked to the next house.

At ten o'clock, Leon and I stopped at a yard filled with old toys and used household appliances. Everything in the yard was for sale. People who thought used appliances were a good investment were very interested in this yard. Leon put on a pair of ski boots and walked around the lawn. A woman sat in a lime green lawn chair and watched Leon. She said the ski boots cost seventy-five cents. Leon took off the ski boots. The lawn was yellow. Most of the grass was dead. There was an orange bike lying on its side next to a stuffed animal that was missing an ear. Leon asked the woman how much for the orange bike. She looked at the bike and said, "It's not my bike." A couple of wooden bowling pins near the one-eared stuffed animal slowly rotted and decomposed into a dead piece of the lawn. The woman stood up and walked over to the house. She opened the front door and yelled at the house. We watched her walk back to her lawn chair and crawl into it again. She looked at Leon and said, "My son will be out in a second."

A few minutes later a full-grown boy in a blonde wig came out of the house. He looked at Leon and then at the orange bike and then back at Leon. He said he wanted twelve dollars for the bike. Leon looked at the bike and then at the full-grown boy in the blonde wig and said, "Ten dollars." The full-grown boy told Leon that he didn't want to negotiate. Leon only had six dollars in his pocket. He asked me if I had six dollars. I gave Leon six dollars. The full-grown boy in the blonde wig took the twelve dollars and went back into the house. Leon got on the orange bike and rode up the street until I couldn't see him anymore. I didn't see Leon again for an hour. I continued to knock on things and ask people if they would pay me to touch their property with black concrete.

At one house, an elderly woman holding a teacup in each hand answered her door and seemed confused. She asked how I got on her porch. I told her I used the walkway. She said she didn't have a walkway and closed the door. I looked at the parts of the lawn where I had walked. Her lawn was covered with fake grass. I knocked on her house again. A different elderly woman holding a teacup in each hand answered the door. I asked her why the lawn was covered with fake grass. She nodded and said something about the real lawn moving to Thailand to open a recording studio.

I could feel the potential of the day softening. All around me pieces of the suburb seemed to be giving up. Nothing would come from the experience of knocking on houses and asking them for money. It reminded me of a class I took in college. The professor had been replaced with a janitor's mop because the school was trying to cut expenses and it was easier to pay a mop to teach the students than it was for the school to pay a human to be the mop. The class was called, "Can A Mop Teach You Things You Don't Know." I remember looking at the mop's silence for many hours and then coming to the realization that the history of everything would eventually end and that it was okay if the humans gave up on everything they started. Regardless of how hard we tried, the end product of our existence would essentially be the same for us as it was for a janitor's mop. On the second to last day of class, the janitor's mop finally spoke and said, "Time and space were cherished ideas. I gave up on them years ago, but I still exist."

The longer Leon was gone the less I worried about never seeing him again. I continued to think about things my brain remembered. Once an abandoned almond that I found in the bottom of a used backpack at a thrift store said, "It's okay to question your friendship with another person because human nature is incapable of maintaining an idea of friendship for an extended period of time." I took this to mean that it was okay for me to eat the abandoned almond.

Doors continued to open after I knocked on them, but I was tired of speaking to people so I mostly held out one of Maurice's business cards and didn't say anything. A woman inside a red house with a green door seemed to understand this and told me it was okay. I handed her a business card and began to leave, but before I could she touched my shoulder and said, "Look at the detached shape of the sky. It is the color it is because when it was your age it realized what it was, and ever since, it has been slowly drifting away from us. One day we will look at the sky and realize there is nothing in it anymore. At that point, it will be the absence of a vegetable peel that we decided to throw away a long time ago."

I found Leon sitting next to a broken public water fountain. The orange bike was lying on its side next to him. He was holding a piece of paper he found inside a Chinese fortune cookie. The piece of paper said, "A lump of dog eats your peach fuzz off the moon glow resting in the sun's creepy dirt."

Leon said he was hungry. It was almost noon. I called Maurice. He picked us up ten minutes later and brought us to a place that sold chicken. I ate some chicken and watched Maurice eat some cabbage and mayonnaise and drink a diet soda. He asked us how many business cards we handed out. I shrugged. Maurice looked at Leon. I looked at some oak trees growing outside the place that sold chicken. Leon put a little bit of chicken in his mouth and chewed on the meat. Maurice waited for someone to talk. I heard Leon swallow. Maurice smiled and ate some chicken.

After lunch, Maurice gave us more business cards and dropped us off in a different neighborhood. Leon no longer had his bike. He left it in the back of Maurice's van. I began to sweat before I walked up to the first house. My armpits smelled like fried chicken. After I knocked on the door a ninety-five-year-old woman came out on the porch and asked me if I was her husband. I tried to hand her a business card. She wouldn't take the business card and kept saying, "You can't be my husband because the U.S. food and drug administration shot my husband in the head thirty years ago."

I saw a wrinkled man sitting in a bikini that was resting on a lawn chair. He was drinking a beer. A sprinkler made rainbows in the grass around him. I told the man I thought it would be a good investment if he gave me two thousand dollars to spread pavement on his lawn. He laughed and drank four beers. Leon asked if he could have a beer. The wrinkled man told Leon he could have a beer only if he snorted it. Leon said, "Okay." The man gave Leon a beer. He took the beer and ran away. I gave the wrinkled man a dollar. A rainbow from the sprinkler dripped on my forearm.

There were still six hundred business cards to pass out. Leon and I walked to a supermarket and put all six hundred business cards under the windshield wiper of a blue station wagon. Leon said he wanted to buy himself a treat to celebrate. We found gelato. Leon ordered something smeared with pistachio. I asked for a pink cotton candy peanut butter stain. We ate our gelato and played chess inside a café for three hours. The sun began to set. I could taste stale bread. I asked Leon if he could smell the stale bread. He said he didn't smell anything except my body sweat. I looked at my stains. Leon said he was tired and wanted to go home. I called Maurice.

When Maurice dropped us off at our motel he gave us each ten dollars for our day. Leon grabbed his orange bike out of the back of the van. Before Maurice left he said, "On Monday, I will pick you up and we can start paving lawns." I watched Maurice drive away. My eyes got a little sad. Leon asked why I was crying. I watched Maurice's van disappear beyond a place I was incapable of looking.

The hole where the woman had buried her new husband's blue tuxedo had turned into a dead dog. In our motel room, Leon turned on the television. I looked out the window and watched the dead dog turn into a bag of decomposing cheeseburgers from a fast-food restaurant. A fat, barefoot woman picked up the dead dog and put it in the dumpster. She went to her motel room to soak her feet. The parking lot was empty except for a soggy prostitute. She took off her heels and walked up the road barefoot.

Leon asked me to turn off the overhead light. He said there was a movie on television starring Christian Slater. I looked at the television and saw someone I thought was named Keanu Reeves. Leon said, "Oh wait, that's Patrick Swayze." We ate some oreos.

An alarm noise woke me up from a memory of being born, but all the leftover thoughts I had from any of these birth memories was killed by the first morning breath in my lungs.. I touched my arms and realized they were much larger than they had been when I was born.

It was already eighty-five degrees outside. I walked around our motel room without a shirt. I heard Leon breathing within his own dreams. As he slept, I tried to trace his thoughts with a pencil and some white-lined paper. One of my nipples leaked a small tear of sweat onto the paper.

The part of my body that tells me to eat told me to eat. I rode the orange bike to one of the hotels down the street to look at the continental breakfast because our motel didn't have a continental breakfast.

The front desk person at one of the hotels was talking to a phone. I looked at him. He continued to talk to the phone in his hand. He was wearing a blue blazer. I waited to see if he would ask me if I was a guest at the hotel. I was prepared to tell him that I was staying in room "two-oh-six." He looked at me but continued to talk on the phone.

I found a pile of starches in the lobby next to a vase of American-made plastic flowers. The continental breakfast was a normal, unspectacular shape. A man wearing a baseball hat too small for his head complained about the lack of breakfast meats and then picked up the last grape from a bowl of fruit. I felt jealous and asked if I could touch the grape before he ate it. He didn't say anything and only shook his head. Most people in America don't like it when you ask them if you can touch their stuff. I watched the man sit down and eat his grape. He avoided making eye contact with me while he chewed the purple fruit.

158

An opaque man was sitting in front of the television. I could not see what he was watching. I stood up and walked over to him. He looked up at me and said, "No wrinkles." His skin had the soft texture of a young, well-groomed deer. He grabbed my hand and rubbed it against his face. His skin was not the same age as him. He seemed proud. He was eating an egg that he had painted turquoise.

When I got back to the motel Leon was still sleeping. I turned on the television and saw thousands of pigs, bears, and ducks get slaughtered by the horizon of a new species of alien. Leon woke up. I told him about all the animals that had died while he was asleep. He pretended to be upset and then he touched his stomach. I took a raisin bagel out of my pocket and gave it to him. Leon ate his bagel and said he wanted to spend the remaining sunlight hours doing drugs. I told Leon I had never done drugs. Leon told me I should probably smoke cocaine. I could taste some baby formula I had eaten when I was six months old. My ears got nauseous at the idea of doing drugs for an entire day. Leon said we should walk around downtown St. Louis because he heard everyone in downtown St. Louis was either a drug addict or a drug dealer. I looked at a map. Leon turned on the television and tried to snort it. A couple thousand electromagnetic waves entered Leon's bloodstream. His body got dull and he lost interest in the rest of the world. I looked at the map until I figured out where downtown St. Louis was.

•

There was a shuttle van near the hotel down the street. I looked at the person driving the shuttle van for a long time because their face looked like an elk. I asked this elk face if the shuttle van was going downtown. The elk face said, "I am not an elk face." I apologized. The elk face died and was replaced by the skin fat of an overweight human. Leon and I got in the shuttle van.

159

Twenty minutes later we were at the airport. The overweight human driving the shuttle van told us we had to get out of the van. We got out of the van. Leon asked if I wanted to fly to Morocco. I looked at my own face and tried to remain indifferent. Leon asked a person who worked at Delta how much a ticket to Morocco cost. She smelled us and said we didn't have enough money.

Leon and I bought two metro train tickets to downtown St. Louis for seventy-five cents. We waited for a train next to a man wearing a white tuxedo that had evolved into one continuous yellow stain. The man smelled the same way a baby will smell if you leave it in its diaper for a month. I asked the man if he was going to prom. The man opened his mouth and began to moan. He fell over. A metro security guard shot him with an electrical current. The man in the stained tuxedo died. The metro security guard put him in a canoe, set the canoe on fire, and pushed the canoe into a river where it could safely burn.

On the train, Leon met a man named Winston. Leon smiled and took out some money. Winston looked at me and asked me a question. I couldn't hear what he said so I nodded. Leon looked at me and told me to stop pretending I wasn't a real person.

Our train passed a large monument that people believed was significant. When people visit St. Louis they usually take pictures of the large monument and then later tell their friends that they saw a significant object on their vacation.

The train crossed over the Mississippi River. We were no longer in Missouri. I asked Winston where we were going. He said, "Motels are cheaper in Illinois." I whispered in Leon's ear that I was nervous.

We got off the train near a hockey rink and followed Winston to a small park filled with a single, twelve-foot-tall maple tree. Leon told Winston the kind of drugs he wanted and gave him the money. An hour later we were still waiting for Winston to return. Leon kicked a tree. I asked him what he wanted to do. He said he wasn't sure.

Leon and I didn't talk to each other. I was tired from following Leon's drug hunger around all day and Leon was sad because he lost some of his money and was still drug hungry.

Leon walked back to the train and said he didn't like feeling poor. I looked at the empty spot in Leon's pocket where he kept some of the money he didn't have anymore. Leon saw a man and a woman wearing expensive sunglasses waiting for the train. He told them he had been mugged and asked them for fifty-three dollars. I sat on a bench and watched the man and the woman move their heads from side to side.

As the train headed back toward Missouri, Leon's face looked like it was going to cry. I said, "Sunk cost," and tried to explain the logic of not crying about retrospective investments that have already incurred and could not be recovered. He said he had very little interest in economic logic because as a child his parents had a tendency to give him everything he wanted and the small parts of himself had not quite grown up. I nodded and said, "Everything is okay because you're a white, privileged male in an African American, low-income, urban environment. The consumption of drugs is more of a luxury for you and less of a necessity. Your losses are insignificant. The fifty-three dollars you spent in search of drugs have the same effect on your financial stability regardless of whether you actually bought drugs or not. All forms of investment come with inherent risk. If you had bought a fifty-three-dollar ice cream cone and it immediately fell into a river, the outcome would essentially be the same as it would be if the ice cream had never fallen into a river and you had eaten it. Drug use and eating ice cream are luxury investments that have very little practical benefit and provide very limited financial gains. Your life quality index a week after you buy a fifty-three-dollar ice cream is essentially the same regardless of whether you eat the ice cream or you drop it into a river. Once the decision is made to spend your ice cream on drugs it matters very little how much of the fifty-three dollars you smoke." Leon sighed. He shook his head and said he didn't want to take comfort in anything that wasn't drugs.

We rode the train back into St. Louis. It stopped next to the large monument that people thought was significant. Leon and I got off the train. We touched the large monument. Leon said he was feeling nauseous. I watched a mother take eight thousand photos of her son hugging the monument. Leon lay down in the grass near a homeless man who was chewing on an aluminum can. The parts of Leon's body that liked to swallow started to moan.

We walked to a castle that sold miniature hamburgers. I ate thirty hamburgers. Leon ate sixteen. We also ate onion rings. A group of eleven-year-old boys in baseball uniforms showed up and began to yell. One of them rubbed a package of mustard on his baseball glove.

On the train back to the airport, a man told us that he was the most wanted man in America because the government had stolen a billion dollars from him. He said, "I once owned every nuclear reactor in the world and then the government made me sell them all for a penny. Someday they will use all of my nuclear reactors to blow up the moon and when this happens I will be blamed for the destruction of the entire world. I used to be very pained knowing I would be remembered as the person who caused the end of the world, but then one night I was eating a can of beans and when the can of beans was empty its emptiness said it didn't remember who it was. And so, for thirty years, I've been letting the world eat from the can of my body and now I almost don't remember who I am."

At the airport, we found the shuttle with an elk face. It dropped us back near our motel room. Leon had not spoken since we ate the last of the onion rings and left downtown St. Louis. His ear began to complain that his brain was sad.

Our motel room was where we left it. Leon went into the bathroom and lay on the floor. I heard the bathtub running. I asked him if he was okay. He said he was drowning the idea of Winston so that he wouldn't ever have to think about him again. I remembered there was a microwave dinner in our motel refrigerator. I was too tired to warm it up. I turned on the television and ate frozen lasagna. My stomach didn't like me. I ignored everything until I fell asleep.

●

The next morning I yawned and turned on the television. It spoke at a low volume. The sound did not wake up Leon. The television's mouth barely touched me. There was nothing important to watch. Nothing had ever been important. I paused the television on someone's embarrassed diplomatic face. Their face was in the middle of a restrained nod. The television mouth said, "All domestic American politics seem to be incomprehensible and childish. I pity the majority of the country that is caught in whatever fashionable idea has gained political momentum. I'm tired of chewing fresh notions of national flavor. I envy people who do not mind being told what to think and who will never realize they are being told what to think." The television mouth began to drone. I turned it off. I massaged the political opinions in my brain for a little bit. They felt more developed. I got a little sick. I put every political thought I had ever had in a space within my brain where I wouldn't have to think about it anymore.

Leon was still sleeping so I watched him sleep. I touched his cheek gently to see if he wanted to go to one of the hotels down the street for breakfast. He woke briefly and said, "My dunes are un-radiated."

I rode an orange bicycle to one of the hotels down the street.

There was free breakfast food in the lobby. I asked the front desk clerk if there were any walnuts. The front desk clerk blushed and apologized for the lack of walnuts. I ate waffles and fruit. Before I left, I toasted a bagel and rubbed it with cream cheese before wrapping it in a napkin and putting it in my pocket. When I returned to the motel I left the bagel on the nightstand next to Leon's bed and waited for him to wake up.

I still felt quite young and was not sure what to do with my life so I sat on a bed. For the majority of my life, I had been a young person. Another hour of my life was in the process of existing. I was becoming less and less of who I was. The bed was one of billions of ordinary objects that would remain ordinary for its entire existence. I looked at the clock on the bedside table and thought of Maurice.

Leon woke up and clipped his toenails. He left his clippings on the carpet next to his bed and asked me to throw them out. I gathered some of Leon's toe particles in my palm and flushed them down the toilet.

Outside our motel room, I could hear the low whine of a nearby highway. The television was on again. Its mouth told me to hate my father. I looked out the motel window to make sure earth still existed. The only objects in the parking lot were a cooler of beers, a lawn chair, some swim trunks, and a man sitting in two of these objects while he sipped the third. The man looked like a cross between a yellow snowflake and a dead astronaut.

An hour later it was almost ten AM. I looked out the window again. The man was no longer eating beers in the parking lot. He had gone back to his motel room to look at a bowl of ice cream and wait for the sun to set. The empty parking lot became slightly less empty. A teal minivan parked in front of our motel room. A fourteen-year-old boy was driving the minivan. I watched this boy climb out of the van. A few seconds later he was touching our motel door. His shirt was shaped like a middle-aged man's cotton stains. When I opened the motel door the boy said his name was Thomas. He was cloned from a skin fragment of Maurice's immigration experience.

I asked Thomas why Maurice didn't pick us up. He shrugged and then told us a story about the first time he met Maurice. The two of them had been standing in an empty in-ground swimming pool with dozens of other men who were all immigrants. Someone was cooking processed beef on a hibachi near the drain cover of the empty swimming pool.

Leon and I climbed into a teal object that had multiple seats. Before Thomas drove us anywhere he pulled out his wallet and showed us a picture of a woman and said, "This is my mother. She was Maurice's sister. The last time I saw her she was dead." Leon nodded. Thomas looked at Leon and said, "Maurice is having some difficulty gathering business clients. He is lending your services to our pavement operations today." The word "services" lingered in my head.

The teal minivan's thoughts on motion were cluttered, hyper, and slightly out of control. My existence inside the moving automobile with Thomas grew uncomfortable. I felt my chest straining against the seatbelt. I noticed my body tensing as we sped through yellow lights. Thomas pressed the gas. I watched a stoplight turn red. My stomach clenched as we continued to move. I waited for the moment when I would realize I had died inside a teal machine. Motion and existence continued. The teal noise began to grow. Thomas was touching the radio.

The van moved until it stopped in a suburban neighborhood full of stale, oversized houses. I could smell the glue used to hold the large wood synthetics together. A crowd of shirtless men stood next to the bones of a driveway that had recently been scalped.

Four stomach pouches hung over some waistlines. Thomas walked over to this group of four fat, shirtless men. Leon and I climbed out of the van and followed. Thomas nodded at the fat, shirtless men. Leon and I stood a little behind Thomas and waited for something to happen. Lint clung to the sweat stain of one of the fat, shirtless men.

His stain was a few days old. It had begun to mold, and if it were a wound it would have been infected.

Eventually, the four shirtless men looked at Thomas and then at me and Leon. I breathed a smile at them. Thomas told the group he'd found us in the bowels of a motel room. I held out my hand and waited for the fat men to touch it. Their hands were sticky and their names sounded like a wash of slur and drone. One said something that sounded like, "Ribeye." Another said his name was, "Gimmy." A third either grunted or said, "Cork." I looked at the fourth fat, shirtless man. His shorts rode low enough to expose his lack of underwear, but his mouth seemed almost stable. He said his name was "Benjamin." His nipples were larger than the other fat, shirtless men's nipples. He didn't touch my hand when I extended it at him. Instead, he began to yell instructions to all the shirtless workers who were standing near the uprooted driveway.

A lot of the workers began to grab rakes so I grabbed a rake. Everyone rubbed their tool on some dirt. A few men bent down to pick up leaves. Some men found shovels and held shovels. I looked at Benjamin. His nipples seemed to grow larger.

Leon said he was thirsty. We walked around the back of the house and found some guys drinking from a hose. One of the men said, "The last time I was married I got a rash and one of my testicles fell off. This embarrassed me so I called a man who once was a taxidermist. I asked if he could sew something on me that looked like a testicle. He said he couldn't so I tried to do it myself and it turned out pretty good, but sometimes it falls off and I have to sew it on again."

A guy named Bill started to complain that his ear hurt. He asked if I had a q-tip. I did not have a q-tip. He began to pick at his ear with his pinky finger. His black mustache dripped sweat onto his upper lip. I saw the tip of his pinky finger when he pulled it out of his ear. It was orange.

A truck showed up pulling a trailer. A steamroller rested on the trailer bed. I watched Benjamin's fat, shirtless body work as he climbed onto the steamroller. His ass crack grew as he sat down. Everyone had stopped and was looking at the perched, fat, shirtless man straddling the steamroller. We waited for the machine's breath, but when Benjamin fingered the ignition nothing happened. He turned the key again. The machine was dead.

Someone opened the front of the steamroller. There was no battery in the engine's lung. Benjamin asked who stole the battery. No one said anything. Some of his chest sweat leaked into the dead machine. Benjamin stepped down from the trailer and looked around for something else to sweat on. He walked up to Bill's mustache and asked if Bill had stolen the battery so he could buy crack. Bill shook his head from side to side. Benjamin grabbed Bill's face and twisted it until Bill began to cry a small, water-less teardrop. I looked at the pavement as Bill whimpered. When I looked up again, Bill's mustache had stopped moving and was sinking deeper into his face.

Up the street, a woman pulled a newspaper out of her mailbox. She looked at all the men standing around shirtless and may have even heard Bill's whimpers, but she ignored them and looked at her newspaper as she returned to her house.

Benjamin let go of Bill's face. Bill sat on the ground and hugged his knees. Benjamin looked at everyone standing around and waved his arms a little. Everyone began to move and pretended to look busy. Bill rocked back and forth a little on the ground.

A large dump truck full of black pebbles arrived carrying the hot, boiled taste of three thousand years of slow-burning rubber. Someone told Leon and me to grab wheelbarrows. The dump truck backed up to the edge of the driveway, and a hole opened in the rear of the truck. Black pavement fell from the hole. Leon and I filled our wheelbarrows on this hole. I could taste the humidity growing off the hot pavement.

167

Leon's arms grew weak after a few minutes of pushing the wheelbarrow, and he spilled hot pavement in the middle of the lawn. Someone yelled at Leon and took the wheelbarrow away from him. He was given a rake and told to spread the hot smells evenly across the driveway.

I continued my wheelbarrow chores. As the hot pavement came out of the hole in the back of the dump truck, small, black, hot pebbles tumbled into my shoes and burned at my ankles. The skin blistered after it touched these hot pebbles.

Everyone spread pavement for an hour. Leon pushed a few pebbles from one side of the driveway to the other. When the driveway was finished some people got in one van and went somewhere, and the rest of us got in another van and went somewhere else. Leon got in the van that went somewhere. I got in the van that went somewhere else.

I did not leave the suburbs. The van I was in stopped at another old driveway. Someone told us to pick weeds. We picked weeds for an hour. It was almost five. Everyone got back in the van. The van was filled with very loud techno. We stopped next to a driveway where two men were using sledgehammers to beat on the old pavement. The two men stopped working. I realized one of the men was Leon. He got in the van.

Back in the motel room, Leon complained that his hands hurt. He showed me his blisters. I told his blisters to clean themselves with hot water. Leon worried his wounds would get infected and his hands would fall off. He said he didn't want his hands to fall off because then he wouldn't be able to type emails.

We walked to a convenience store so Leon could buy some gardening gloves and vaseline. When we got back to the motel room Leon rubbed vaseline on his blisters and put on the gardening gloves. Leon wore his new gardening gloves to bed.

Before I went to sleep I looked out the window and saw a woman leaning against a door of one of the other motel rooms. She had long, orange fingernails.

At six AM I woke up to the hum of something fat yelling at our motel door. I waited for the yelling to stop, but the hum only grew larger. I touched an alarm clock because I thought maybe it had grown a fat lung and had learned to make loud noises. Leon was in the other bed and told me to stop yelling. I stood up and looked in the mirror to make sure I wasn't yelling. My mouth wasn't open. The yelling continued. I looked out the window of our motel room. Sixteen percent of my face expected to see someone's alarm clock yelling at our motel door, but I only saw a lot of loud skin touching the door. Most of this skin was named Benjamin. His yelling was a symbol of his ability to do whatever he wanted. There were three vans in the parking lot. I opened our motel door. Benjamin told us to get in his vans. Leon and I put on some old dirty cotton and did what we were told to do.

I sat in a van next to a mustache named Bill. He was a low-income crumble. Each day Benjamin paid all the low-income crumbles in the van fifty dollars to touch the hot pavement lawns of suburban neighborhoods. Bill was almost sixty years old, but he told us he was turning eighty-three at the end of the month.

Leon and I both pretended to be crumbles. I looked out the window of the van and saw a man standing in the middle of a fast-food restaurant parking lot crumbling into a bucket of oil filled with used taco meat. The entirety of America was slowly becoming one big low-income crumble.

Our van stopped at a gas station. The food inside the gas station smeared itself on the frail and poor spaces of some Americans who weren't quite human. Bill bought a soda called a "twinkle." His face looked weak as he sipped this soft beverage. A little drink spilled on his chin. His mustache looked guilty and unsure of itself. I felt him whisper in my ear. He told me he had stolen a piece of bread. It was melting in his pocket. Bill removed an orange package of bread from his pants. The outside of the orange package had a picture of a blue circus bear eating peanut butter. Bill's mustache sucked on the melted brown pieces of his stolen bread.

I stood next to a gas tank and felt something spit on me. I looked up and saw a laughter of clouds. Another raindrop dripped. Wet shapes continued to spit. Benjamin's skin got angry. He yelled until he ran out of breath. Some of the low-income crumbles smiled. The rain continued to drip.

Benjamin said the entire day of hot pavement was canceled. Everyone got in the vans. We drove back toward the motel.

An hour later, Leon and I were in our room watching the television mouth. It told us to be satisfied with its limited functions. The motel room grew complacent. Leon held a yawn in his palm and said he wanted to make a photocopy of it. The yawn evaporated. His palm was empty. Something blonde inside the television told everyone in America to buy cheap car insurance. Modern society handed us a frequent rewards card and told us we qualified for a free purple lollipop. A bald man said, "I want to help you be happy for the next ten thousand days you are alive." Something else inside the television said, "Only men who wear paper crowns are allowed to eat." Leon was tired of eating what the television mouth had already eaten. He asked where the nearest mall was. I looked out the window. I could not see any. Leon turned off the television. We left the motel and began walking toward the nearest mall even though we didn't know where it was.

In the dirt, a half-mile from our motel, we found a teal pebble. Leon got scared when he saw the pebble and ran into a nearby parking garage. I found him inside an elevator on the first floor of the garage. He was looking at his hands. One of the fingers on his left hand was blistered. He talked to the blister. I went inside the elevator and waited with Leon. He talked to the blister for twenty minutes. The elevator did not move. I lay on the floor of the elevator and took a short nap.

When Leon stopped talking to the blister on his hand the elevator door opened. We left the elevator. A man in a striped business shirt parked his midsize sedan near the elevator. He was holding a gym bag. Leon and I left the parking garage. We could no longer see the teal pebble. We walked up the road.

The boy behind the counter at the video store had braces and some lip whisker pimples. He told us the nearest mall was ten miles up the road. Leon pointed at a road. The boy behind the counter nodded and picked at one of the pimples near a whisker on his chin.

Leon and I found a bus stop. We waited an hour, but the bus stop didn't seem to be working properly. Leon said he was tired of not moving. We began walking toward the mall. As we walked we held out our thumbs.

A gray Toyota station wagon stopped. It was missing a headlight and its windshield was dirty, with cracks. The inside of the automobile smelled of paint fumes. The driver said, "My name is Walter. I am poor and unskilled. My driving abilities need to improve. A few weeks ago, I crashed my wife's car into a rusted streetlamp. The law mandates that I do three hundred hours of community service before I'm allowed to drive again. I am taking medication. It makes it uncomfortable to wear a seatbelt. The last time I went to the mall I ate a nacho pretzel with barbecue cheese on it. When I think about what the rest of my life will be like I get sad and feel like soaking the left side of my face in alcohol."

Walter dropped us off at the entrance to the mall. Leon said he wanted to buy new socks. We walked around the mall until Leon found twelve pairs of socks for sale. He also bought a t-shirt. On a metal rack, I found a gray sweatshirt. I put on the gray sweatshirt. It fit pretty well. We left the store. Leon pointed at the gray sweatshirt I was wearing and asked if I had stolen it. I looked at the gray sweatshirt. I had forgotten to pay for the gray sweatshirt.

A movie theater employee gave us movie tickets after we gave him money. He told us to enjoy sitting in a dark room filled with people we didn't know. We went to the theater. I sat on a wet cheese doodle. My shorts smelled like food. I asked Leon what I should do. He pointed at a bathroom in the lobby.

At the concession stand in the lobby, I saw a mother with fourteen children. She bought a popcorn kernel for each of her children.

In the bathroom, I took off some of my clothes and rinsed them in the sink until they no longer smelled like food.

When the movie started a lot of things happened. Some people died. A ship floated and then sank. One of the pirates cut off another pirate's head and then wore this pirate's head on his own head as a hat.

After the movie, Leon and I left the mall. There was a bus in the distance, but it didn't hear us when we yelled at it. We walked across the street and waited at a bus stop. Ten minutes passed. We held out our thumbs. A teal van slowed down. Leon and I got excited. We looked in the teal van and saw a mass of skin named Benjamin. He smiled and told us to take off our shirts. We took off our shirts and climbed into the van. Benjamin asked us what we were doing near the mall. I told him my shorts smelled like food. Leon said, "We watched a movie called 'Pirates of the Caribbean 2'."

Leon turned on the television when we got back to our motel room. He watched a rich man complain about money to a picture of a dead parakeet. I looked out the window. An elderly pair of waffles rested next to the dumpster. Leon asked what I was looking at. I shrugged. The image on the television changed. Leon said he wished he could have sex with the image inside the television. I looked at the image. It was wearing short blue legs. The image changed again. The new image reminded me that I had a stomach. I asked Leon if he was hungry. He suggested we microwave a box of lasagna. I found a box of lasagna in the refrigerator and put it in the microwave. The sun went down at some point. Leon and I fed our dinner to the television mouth.

In the morning the wires in the motel stopped working. A pair of denim lay dead on the floor. It was Leon's denim. I put on his denim hoping it would give the machines in our motel room some juice, but the denim did not fit well and gave my legs a fever. I worried the fever would grow into a rash. The television didn't work. Its fabric looked empty and dumb. I took off the denim and rubbed some of it on Leon's shoulder. He was still sleeping. He did not know I was touching him with his own denim. I asked him what he wanted me to do with his denim, but he didn't wake up so I rubbed his denim on a naked light bulb. All the light bulbs in the motel were dead in their plugs. Only the smallest pocket in Leon's travel bag would open. I removed its contents—a pair of fingernail clippers and some toothpaste. I stuffed denim into an undersized location. The smallest pocket on Leon's travel bag wouldn't close after I stuffed it with denim. One of the threads on the denim unraveled and flickered a little in my palm. This loose denim was hungry and told me to plug it into something that wasn't denim. I stuck it in a wall socket. The denim told the wall socket to smell my fingers. I was reminded of the sound dead fish make when you wrap them in stained paper money and burn a pile of old tires on your front lawn. I wasn't sure what to do with the nail clippers and toothpaste so I put them in the sink and turned on the water. Neither of them floated. The toothpaste looked confident in its ability not to drown. I picked up the tube and squeezed it empty onto the fabric of the dumb, empty television. I could almost hear a faint static in the cathode tubes. The television's face softened. I thought of putting a stiff, yellow sponge in my mouth until it was moist and my teeth were no longer wet. When the toothpaste was empty and dumb I tried to stuff it inside a wall socket, but it didn't fit. The sink drained. I played with the nail clippers until I accidentally clipped off all the small areas near my cuticles. The tips of my fingers were empty. It was too dark to see anything so I had to get down on my knees and rub the carpet with my fingers to find all the clippings. Most of the clippings seemed lonely so I tied them all together with a few hairs I plucked from the scalp of my face. Leon was still sleeping. A dribble of spit leaked out of his mouth onto the pillow while he slept. I leaned over him with the system of hair and fingernails. I dipped the end of it into the wet area of his pillow and then I wrapped them in a tissue and flushed them down the toilet. When the toilet stopped running I could hear the television talking in the non-toilet location of our motel room. The motel wires were no longer empty. Their juice gave our machines the ability to give us faith in the objects we weren't aware we were praying to.

I found a few pitchers of coconut milk next to a toaster. There was breakfast music playing in the lobby. An old man was using the waffle machine. I drank three flutes of coconut milk while I waited for the old man to finish making his waffle. After the third option of coconut milk, I felt a little sick so I leaned over a large glass bowl of sliced watermelon until the sick parts of my body were digested. I heard the waffle machine beep. The old man peeled his waffle out of the machine and rubbed it with syrup.

Leon was already up when I got back to our motel room. He could smell the coconut milk on my teeth and asked why I didn't bring him back a jar. I took a raisin bagel out of my pocket and set it on the nightstand next to the clock. Leon said he wasn't hungry. He seemed disappointed. The television mouth was talking again. Leon walked over to the bureau where we kept some of our food. He looked inside one of the drawers until he found an oreo. He sat on his bed for a long time looking at this oreo. I waited for him to eat it, but he didn't. Instead, he sighed and put the oreo back in the bureau where he found it.

Next to a dried tobacco stain on the nightstand, I found three granules of sugar. I wasn't sure where they had come from so I didn't eat them. I put them in an envelope and decided I would mail the three granules to my father. He would put them in a coffee cup and then wait for the inside of his cup to turn black.

At nine AM Leon shut off the television and put on his gardening

174

gloves. He was wearing a new pair of socks. We climbed into a teal van filled with low wage labor. I noticed some dirt on the floor of the van that had not been there the day before. I picked up a piece of the dirt. In my palm, the dirt was the shape of wet coffee grounds. Benjamin sat at the front seat of the van. He was not wearing a shirt. I asked his large, fat, shirtless body why he was always fat and shirtless. Benjamin laughed and reached under his seat. I waited for him to answer. When he pulled his hand out from under the seat it was holding a cashew.

The van moved and then stopped near the smell of plastic sweat and old children. Everyone climbed out of the van. I looked across the street and saw two boys chewing cigarettes next to a public swing set.

Someone picked up a shovel and scratched a few words into the dirt. I bent down and picked up the dirt. It said, "calm plot."

A woman came out of the house and stood on the porch. Benjamin put on a shirt and talked with her. She pointed at the area in her yard that was black and crumbling. Benjamin nodded and said, "You will be pleased with everything that happens to your yard." The woman got in a mid sized automobile and drove to a place where she was paid to sit between the hours of nine AM and five PM.

Benjamin took off his shirt and hung it from a branch in the front lawn. He walked over to the garden. I watched a large, fat, shirtless man unzip his shorts and pee on a daffodil. When he finished he grabbed his shirt from the tree and told everyone to get to work. I picked up a shovel and watched Benjamin walk back over to the van. There were three other men in the van, all the same size and shape. One of them looked like he was eating a handful of amphetamines.

The guy working next to me said, "I'm a Midwestern transplant." I asked him what that meant. He said, "I remember my grandmother sitting on a porch somewhere in Ohio, wrapped in shawls. Then a few years later she was dead and I was too sad to look at her dead body so

I moved to New York City. I lived near a lake in New York City until the lake turned black and all the fish died."

After using a shovel for a little bit Leon complained that his hands hurt. He took off his gardening gloves and walked over to the house. There was a spigot connected to a hose. Leon touched the hose and drank from it. His mouth got tired. He removed his mouth from the spigot and looked inside the house. He didn't move for a long time. When he walked back to where everyone was working he said, "There is a sofa and a television in the living room." I developed a little bit of amnesia and forgot how to think so I didn't say anything. Leon said something else, but I wasn't paying attention to him because I was looking at my brain.

A helicopter flew overhead. One of the guys stopped working on the pavement and yelled something at the helicopter. The helicopter worked for the government. A lot of the guys working on the driveway didn't like the government. One of the guys holding a rake said, "I hate when the government snoops around looking for my drug plants. I can't wait until the republicans cut the government down to the size of a peapod and there are no regulations on drugs anymore."

An hour passed. I removed a small corner of the driveway. The rest of the driveway dug itself up. Leon took a lot of breaks and moved only a few pebbles. Someone asked him why he was wearing gardening gloves. He shrugged and said he was allergic to shovels.

A few of the workers went behind the house and smoked crack. They said they were glad they were poor because if they were rich they would just spend all their money on crack and then end up being poor anyway.

At eleven AM Benjamin told four of us to get into the teal van. Leon, three other guys and I climbed into the teal van. The van began moving very fast. I looked at the speedometer. We were driving fifty-five miles-per-hour through a residential neighborhood. I saw a sign that said we were only allowed to drive twenty-five miles per hour.

It did not take us long to get to the next job site. The three other men and I got out of the van. Leon stayed in the van with Benjamin and the others. I waved goodbye to Leon. The teal van drove away.

Four of us looked at the crumbling piece of pavement we had to dig up. Our tools were limited. We only had three shovels and an axe. I picked up the axe while the others used shovels to chip at the corners of the deteriorating pebble. When I swung the axe against the remains of the driveway I could feel my insides strain. For the rest of the afternoon, my fingers and hands were filled with an old pain that was starting to crumble. Every few minutes I paused and looked at my hands to make sure they hadn't fallen off. When I began to move the axe again, a cloud of sweat grew off me.

One man was wearing a red, collared shirt with only one button. I could feel the atoms of the red shirt slowly wearing down. Soon there would be no buttons left on the shirt.

A guy was moving a shovel near me. I asked him if he graduated high school. He said, "I dropped out of school when I was four." I asked him if he ever thought about college. He nodded and said, "Sometimes I want to get educated so I can own a big house." I told him I was sort of educated and I didn't own a big house. He shrugged and lifted his shovel. I could feel my thighs sweating.

Hours later the teal van returned. It was almost four o'clock. Most of the driveway had been removed. Leon climbed out of the teal van. He sipped on a cup from a fast-food restaurant. There were four men in the teal van. They were all holding bags of cardboard meat. I watched them hold these bags and worried they would eat all the food themselves, but they got out of the van and set the bags of cardboard meat down in the street and told us it was lunchtime. Everyone dropped their tools and grabbed a handful from the brown paper bags.

I sat on the curb and ate a hamburger.

Leon sat down next to me. He smiled and said he had been riding around all afternoon with the large, fat shirtless men. Leon said, "At one point, the teal van paused at a stoplight and Benjamin yelled at a man in a red pickup. The man ignored him. Benjamin kept asking if he could buy the man's truck for five thousand dollars. He didn't stop yelling at this man until the light changed and the red pickup drove away."

I filled my face with the meat from my hand. I felt a little sick. I tried not to think of the pile of chemicals that had been used on the hamburger. Instead, I thought of a piece of cardboard slowly turning into something edible. I took another bite. It tasted good. My brain was confused. It knew the thing I was eating was not a good thing, but the noise it made in my mouth sounded good and I could not help wanting to swallow more. When I finished eating the hamburger I wanted to eat more hamburgers, but there were none left. I was disappointed. I drank soda from a plastic cup.

An empty dump truck arrived. Benjamin told everyone to start throwing the old pieces of the driveway into the back of the truck. I began to pick up the old driveway. Leon put on his gardening gloves. Benjamin and the other men watched us work. When all the pieces of the old driveway had been put in the back of the dump truck I sat down on the curb and watched it drive away. A raindrop landed on my bottom lip. The aftertaste of something unhealthy rested in my stomach. It was almost five PM Everyone climbed into the teal van.

On the ride home I sat next to one of the guys who had smoked crack earlier. I asked him if he owned a rifle. He said he once owned a rifle, but then the rifle got bored of domestic life and moved to a motel in Angola where she looked out her bedroom window and watched millions of civilians die each year. I asked him if he missed his rifle. He said, "Sometimes at night when I don't have any money or crack I wish I still owned a rifle because I often have an urge to shoot every raindrop that has ever fallen."

At the motel, Benjamin gave Leon and me each fifty dollars. Leon said we were the perfect example of a capitalist society and that our positive contributions to the idea of democracy were the reason that America existed. He paused and then said, "I think the most important part of our journey is how we are distorting the relationship dynamic that exists between a father and his son." I looked at Leon and tried to remember if he was either my father or my child.

Nothing much else happened that night. Leon removed his gardening gloves. I turned on a shower. We cooked a box of lasagna in the microwave. I felt the remains of the fast-food hamburger get excited when my stomach introduced the microwave lasagna to it. Leon said he regretted not going to a college like Yale. I ate twelve oreos. Leon told me not to eat anymore. I found some milk. I drank the milk. Leon looked at me for a long time and then said, "I wish you were an upscale, female prostitute." I went to the bathroom and looked at the toilet seat. I heard Leon laugh because something on the television made him laugh. I looked in the mirror and pinched some color into my cheeks. When I came out Leon told me he didn't like me leaving my wet, dirty socks on the chair near his bed. I picked up the socks and threw them out. My hair felt longer than it had been the day before. I could feel my hair continuing to grow. As I climbed into bed I felt my stomach look at the television and sigh.

It took me a long time to fall asleep. At one point I had to take my biological clock out and gently rub it until it stopped being so anxious. As I fell asleep I could hear a woman and a man making sex noises somewhere in the motel. Or maybe it was the sound of a human giving birth to a stillborn child.

In the morning I rode the orange bicycle to the edge of the Mississippi River and washed my face. When I got back to the motel I found Leon microwaving a wet sock. He pressed his face very close to the microwave window. I asked him why his sock was wet. He took a deep breath and didn't say anything. I sat down on the bed and waited for Leon to give me advice about something. Leon's chest moved. He took another deep breath. I thought of blowing on Leon's lungs with my lungs until he floated away. The microwave stopped making heat. Leon took out his sock and put it on his left foot.

Leon said, "I think this motel used to be a man about our age who wanted to travel, but he gave up and accepted the boring existence of being a motel. If we continue living in the motel we will also turn into cheap motels."

I imagined poor people living inside of me. I could almost feel my heart turn into an old paint can. My body was growing bored with itself and my brain felt ready to give up and be poorly reconstructed into something that it didn't want to be.

Leon's ears breathed as he waited for me to say something. I shrugged. Leon told me I should talk more. I nodded and said, "Okay."

A few hours later, Leon and I were still in our motel room. It was almost ten AM. The motel was getting its late morning smell. The fat men who usually picked us up had not picked us up. I looked at a blank spot on the wall. Neither of us said anything. The television mumbled and touched a part of our brain that would not remember being touched. Leon said he was tired of waking up in St. Louis. He began putting his dirty clothes in a bag. I found a pile of dirty clothes and put them in the same bag. When everything dirty was in the bag Leon handed it to me and told me to go to the laundromat. He got on the orange bicycle and rode it to a pawn shop. I was alone in the motel room. I picked up the bag of all our dirty clothes and walked to the laundromat.

At the laundromat, I put everything in one of the machines. The shirt and shorts I was wearing were dirty. I took them off and put them in the washer. My underwear was dirty. I looked at the woman standing behind the counter. She was watching me. I turned on the machine and sat down in a yellow chair. My phone beeped. Someone had sent me a text message. I looked at my phone. The text message was from Leon. It said, "I sold the orange bicycle to someone for a nickel. I now have a nickel in my pocket."

Twenty minutes passed. The machine finished its cycle. Leon walked into the laundromat and asked why I was wearing dirty underwear. I looked at myself and shrugged. Leon picked up a magazine and began reading it. I put our clothes in the dryer. Leon asked me if I knew the three ways to infallibly pleasure an older woman. I shrugged. Leon began to read the magazine out loud. I took deep breaths and tried not to pay attention. When the clothes were done I put on a clean shirt and shorts.

Leon asked a man leaning against a Chrysler minivan outside the laundromat for a ride back to our motel. The man didn't reply. Leon told me to get down on my knees and kiss the minivan's front left tire. It was almost noon. We walked back to the motel with our clean bag of laundry.

A pair of twenty-year-old college students in yellow shorts and sports bras ran past us. Leon pointed at them. We looked at their butts. I was not sure which area of the butt was the best part to look at so I looked at the right butt cheek. One of the girls was wearing headphones. The song she was listening to had been reduced to a wizard's mumble. I could feel the small throb of a synthesized drum in her earlobe. At some point in her life, she would be sitting in an office, drinking coffee, trying not to yawn. The last whisper of her music earphones beeped into the space expanding between us.

Whenever I see girls running I always think about buying a pair of expensive jeans, but then thousands of mechanical Chinese factories grind out a piece of fabric that costs a dollar and I forget about the time I had a thought about an expensive pair of pants.

A mile up the road one of the girls got thirsty, kneeled next to a puddle, and sipped.

Leon and I packed our luggage. I got sentimental when I noticed a stain in the carpet near the small refrigerator. It looked like a dead piece of milk. I asked Leon what he thought of the carpet stain. We both put our faces near whatever old liquid we were looking at. It smelled of bleached mustard and reminded me of a boy from high school named "the perm chronicles." The longer I looked at the stain the more it felt like my brain was going to weep. Leon stood up and touched a trashcan. The stain began to sweat. Leon turned the trash can upside down and covered the stain.

In an hour, we'd leave the motel and a linen dentist would clean our room. Everything about the motel would forget we ever existed.

I found three oreos under my pillow so I put them in my mouth. There were four cans of tuna in one of the drawers of the motel bureau. They were next to a can of kidney beans. I looked at the can of kidney beans for a long time. Everything in the world was touching my emotions and asking for sympathy. My face began to sweat a little. I put the kidney beans and tuna cans in my luggage.

Before we left, Leon wrote a note to the immigrant who had driven us to St. Louis. The note said, "Dear Maurice, you were a kind and gentle man who helped me develop my human experience into a more fully realized object. I'm sorry we broke our promise and are now leaving St. Louis. Thank you for being a good person. It's a shame our relationship could not be infinite and handsome. Maybe someday we will use the same public restroom again. I will always remember you as the only leaf of grass I ever met who did not grow from one of the domestic lawns of America." When Leon finished the letter he walked over to the upside-down trashcan and slid the letter under it.

There was still some uneaten food in the refrigerator. Leon took out the last microwave lasagna and opened the package. He took a bite and handed it to me. It was frozen. I took a bite and let the cold lasagna sit in my mouth until it got warm. Then I swallowed. Leon and I sat on a bed and passed the frozen lasagna back and forth until it was gone.

We walked to the highway. I was worried a large, fat, shirtless man would see us and make us get into his van. As I walked I felt like a pile of disassembled furniture. Leon and I no longer seemed to know what we were doing. The reason for the journey had been lost. I asked Leon if he was tired. He said he was tired of nothing happening.

Before we had set out, America had been a blank slate. It was a void I thought I needed to fill. America was the father responsible for every idea I had ever believed, but whose presence was nonexistent, leaving me in this void, alone, with only my own brain to explain the deep emotional complexities of what it felt like to be an object that grows and develops. Being an American isn't quite the same as being a human. There is a divide between the two that doesn't quite overlap. For a long time, I was invested in this idea that I was an American. It gave me a false sense that I was capable of god behaviors, but when I realized I wasn't a god I also understood that my belief in being an American was flawed. No one in America is truly capable of living up to the ideal of being an American. For many years the white citizens of this land have believed that being American is equivalent to being a white god. The majority of white Americans believe in their individual ability to be their own white god even though no one in America has actually ever been a white god. The fact that these people living in America put their faith in the idea of being American even though they are incapable of ever truly being the thing they believe they have been their whole lives is, in short, a dehumanizing consequence of their existence. Because being American and being human is no longer the same thing, everyone in America who believes they are an American is by default not human. On our last day in St. Louis I realized I didn't quite feel human. Before leaving on the journey, it had felt rational to be a young man and travel, but as our days of travel progressed I was growing less and less interested in rational thought. My desire to wander had shifted. I no longer wanted to fill the blank slate of America with my presence. I had seen an America that was a product of miles and miles of highway nothingness. The American landscape had lost its allure. All I wanted to do was find a small, empty room where I could sit and let my lack of possessions fill the room. I wanted to sit in this empty room, alone, with myself, to relearn what it meant to be a real person.

•

I asked Leon what we should do next. He wasn't sure but thought maybe we could go to Guatemala and find an indigenous tribe that had never seen white people and ask them to feed us. I nodded.

We continued walking to the highway.

The highway did not look special. Leon took out his camera and took a picture of the side of the road. I looked at the spot he photographed. He said, "This picture will document the emotions we were feeling when we continued our journey from St. Louis and stepped deeper into the American soil of the road." I looked at where we were standing and then at the passing cars. I thought of the photograph Leon had taken and imagined looking at it in twenty years. I doubted the photograph had captured any single emotion I had ever felt. It seemed impossible to photograph what we were experiencing. To properly capture even one single human emotion of an individual thought, someone would need hundreds of hours of film. To understand the moment when Leon and I returned to the road you would have to stare at the same yellow line painted on a black piece of asphalt for hours, only listening to the silent roar of large metal objects as they ignored the ability of humans to be human.

An automobile drove by. A woman in the automobile looked at us. I made eye contact with her and understood the history of her entire life. She had once been inside her mother. When she left her mother she had to wear a dress. A boy removed this dress. The woman bought something because it was on sale. She ate a bean. She used the internet. She bought a car, but the car needed to be fixed. She dumped gasoline on her life until it was fixed. Everything tasted like plastic because the only thing she could afford to eat was plastic. And then the sun went down so she went to sleep.

Leon and I stood next to the highway for an hour. It was ninety-six degrees. There wasn't anything for us to do but sweat, count the automobiles, and look at the nearest pebble of asphalt. We were in the road's lung. I felt some cars breathe on us. Leon said, "It's too hot. I feel like grease." I watched more cars make unhealthy sounds. Leon suggested we give up on the road for a little bit and go sit in a fast-food restaurant. I shrugged. Leon and I left the highway.

I did not feel like giving up our lives to go live inside a fast-food restaurant, but I followed Leon.

A television inside the restaurant said things that were sort of true. A man named "CNN" talked about how a fire was burning in California and probably wouldn't stop burning until someone put it out. Leon and I got fountain drinks with unlimited refills. I drank a cup of a clear soda and then I drank something blue. My stomach began to hurt so I bought an apple pie and an ice cream cone. Leon bought a piece of meat. He didn't agree with my decision to buy an apple pie because his prep school girlfriend once told him that the apple pies at fast-food restaurants were the most unhealthy food substance that you could purchase in America. I felt like a bad man as I ate the most unhealthy substance I had ever eaten. Leon watched me eat and said, "It is highly probable that you will feel slightly ill for the next hour and then fifty years from now you will develop cancer and die."

When I finished eating the apple pie I felt okay.

Leon and I walked back to the highway and stood on the side of the road for seven minutes.

A gray Honda pulled over. The man inside was wearing a blue collared shirt and a tie. He said his name was Shawn. Leon and I climbed into the gray Honda. Shawn said he worked for a company that made airplanes. Leon asked Shawn if he had ever flown an airplane. Shawn said, "Once, me and my girlfriend stole a car from a dealership the day before Thanksgiving and then spent the holiday weekend driving to Chicago." The gray Honda began to move.

Other cars moved near us. Shawn leaned over while he drove and opened the glove box. He pulled out a thin piece of cardboard and said, "Albert Pujols." He held up the cardboard. On it there was a picture of a goatee wearing a man's face. Under the goatee the words, "Albert Pujols" were printed in yellow. Shawn put the baseball card in his breast pocket. He said, "I sucked a man's penis for that baseball card. It's probably worth eleven thousand dollars." Leon told a story about when he was in second grade and he traded three tootsie rolls for a Lenny Dykstra baseball card.

Shawn stopped listening. He took out a crack pipe and began smoking some crack. After he smoked a little he asked us if we wanted to smoke crack. I didn't say anything. Shawn looked at Leon. I thought Leon might tell another story about being in second grade, but instead Leon said, "Sure." Shawn smoked a little more and then handed Leon the pipe. While Leon smoked some crack, Shawn said, "A lot of people don't like crack because most bad people smoke crack. If better people smoked crack it would have a better reputation. If I was Albert Pujols I would smoke a lot of crack and then more people would respect crackheads. I think the average American is afraid of drugs. I've been smoking crack recreationally for almost my entire life. I have a good job and a nice car. I am a positive example of what crack can accomplish." Leon handed Shawn the crack pipe. Shawn put the pipe in his mouth and smoked some more. A few minutes later the gray Honda pulled off the highway and stopped at a gas station.

Leon and I were alone again along the side of the highway. I asked Leon why he smoked crack. He looked at me for a long time and then said, "The only thing humans were made to do was moderate the rate at which they destroy themselves. I felt like destroying a piece of myself today."

It was no longer ninety-six degrees. I felt a raindrop. Leon and I took out our ponchos. I asked Leon if he liked smoking crack. He shrugged and said, "I have a small urge to birth a premature, three-ounce baby." I thought of my parents and wondered if they had ever smoked crack in any of my precious development stages. Another raindrop fell. I touched the large parts of myself to make sure I weighed more than three ounces. I was still a big man. I took a deep breath. My lungs were not the shape of a half-deflated plastic goldfish. I was not raised inside a dumpster that had been converted into a mobile home behind k-mart. I took another deep breath. I swallowed a raindrop. I asked Leon if he was worried about getting pregnant from smoking crack. Leon picked up a piece of grass and put it in his mouth. I watched him chew the grass. The silence of his mouth gazed out at the landscape around us. There was nothing for him to reflect upon. The dirt, the fields, the billboards, and the passing automobiles were a horizontal wash whose place in the world would barely echo beyond its present murmur.

I looked at the sky. It was dark, moody, and indifferent. We were going to get wet. Leon said, "I've never met a crack baby. All my friends are made from the advanced stages of a mediocre, suburban form of tooth decay. Everyone I knew as a child was a mutation of this dental plaque."

The emptiness of our surroundings held a fascination in there being nothing fascinating about it. A growing nostalgia within me yearned to look upon a simple mass of trees. I had not seen a healthy patch of forest in almost a week. I only felt the abstract blah of the highway. Its sprawl through the open spaces of America made my life seem like an imitation. I was a two-dimensional image glued onto a sense of insignificant grandeur that hadn't yet figured out that everything was meaningless.

More raindrops fell. I heard Leon yell something. I looked up and saw him running toward a car that had pulled over next to the highway. Our lives would continue to have motion and we would accept this as a feeling of importance.

A man named Don laughed and said, "It's raining." We climbed into his Buick. He took a sip from a coffee cup. Large rain sprinkles touched the Buick's windshield. Leon said something about his father owning a Buick in college before he met Leon's mother. Don said his mother had bought the car for him. The Buick began to move. Don asked us where we were going. I pointed west. The windshield got wet. I looked out the window and half-expected to see a naked man running through the field bordering the highway. The Buick accelerated.

Don talked about a hurricane in Mississippi. He said, "I planted three spruce trees after my friend's yellow barn fell over in the storm."

We passed a puddle filled with pigeon feathers. The clouds continued to be emotional. The seat cushions in the Buick were maroon. A white dove sat on the side of the road and spat at our vehicle. Don asked us if we had ever heard of someone named "Brett Favre." We nodded. Don said, "Once, Brett Favre and I touched the same golf club."

A light blue pickup passed Don's Buick. There were a half-dozen gimpy dogs crouched in the back of the light blue pickup. These gimpy dogs barked at the raindrops. The drips leaked into our miles.

Don continued to drink at his coffee cup. He had a difficult time maintaining a constant rate of speed. The Buick slowed down to forty-five miles per hour. A parade of lamp posts spread themselves out along the highway. Some of them were bruised with rust. We exited the highway to get gas. Don put six dollars worth of gas in his engine.

While Don was inside paying, Leon said he thought Don was drunk. I looked at Don's coffee cup until he climbed back into the Buick and took a sip. We returned to the highway. Don said, "I once was homeless in Minnesota and spent a winter eating hamburgers from the dumpster behind a fast-food restaurant."

A few miles passed. The Buick slowed down again. I asked Don if he wanted me to drive. He took a sip off his coffee cup and began driving faster. Leon asked Don about the ring he was wearing. Don looked at his ring and said, "In college we won a National Championship. I was a pretty good hockey player. I was on that Olympic team that beat the Soviets. After the game, I wrapped myself in an American flag and cried and then I just lay on the ice and didn't ever want to move again. For the next couple years I mostly partied. Everyone loved me because I was a symbol of pure American triumph. I guess I represented everything that people wished they were. America is full of a lot of people who want to do heroic things, but most people fail to ever accomplish anything. A few weeks after we won the gold medal I was at a party with Axl Rose and Bono. The three of us did a bunch of cocaine. Axl gave me the red leather coat he was wearing. I was probably going to be a millionaire because a lot of teams in the NHL wanted to pay me a lot of money to play for them. The Winnipeg Jets talked to my agent so I bought a yellow Porsche because I like the color yellow. Then someone made me pee in a cup and I failed the cocaine test. The NHL said I was doing too many drugs to play hockey. My mother got really upset. It was all over the newspapers. She said I was an embarrassment. All my mother's friends made fun of her. She took my yellow Porsche and kicked me out of my own house. I had to move to Florida because no one liked me anywhere else. Everyone had heard about my cocaine use and if they hadn't then my mother would call and tell them. Florida was okay. No one in Florida had heard of hockey. My mother tried calling people in Florida, but I think all the numbers she tried calling were disconnected. My life got better. Every morning I would feed the manatees on the coast and this big guy would watch me. Eventually, he asked if I wanted to smoke weed with him. It turned out he was a professional football player for the Miami Dolphins. His name was Ricky."

An hour later, Don stopped at a rest area to use the bathroom. Leon and I stood outside the bathroom. I told Leon that no one named Don was on the Olympic team that beat the Soviets. Leon nodded and said he didn't think Don was very good at telling the truth. Don came out of the bathroom. We climbed back into the Buick.

Don talked about the length of his urine. Then he talked about a woman he was going to meet in Kansas City. Leon asked if the woman was pretty. Don said, "A peach is a fruit."

In a ditch, I saw a dead tire on fire.

Don said the woman in Kansas City was blonde. I imagined a blonde woman in a red sweater. Don said, "She used to have drug problems." I imagined a blonde sweater trying to chew on a long red piece of frayed yarn. Don asked us if we wanted to spend the night with him and a former drug addict in Kansas City. Leon nodded.

Don stopped for gas again. As he was pumping gas an old man said hello to him. Don and the old man had a brief conversation. When Don got back in the Buick he said he was worried. The Buick moved toward the highway. Don said, "That old man is going to call everyone in Kansas City and tell them to hurt me. I don't want anyone to hurt me. I wish people didn't hurt other people." The Buick got back on the highway.

A few minutes later I saw some buildings grow from a place that was Kansas City. Don pulled off the highway a few exits before we entered the growth of the city limits. There were suburban neighborhoods sprouting on the edge of the urban rubble. The Buick slowly rolled through these neighborhoods. Don mumbled toward the steering wheel. One of the mailboxes in the suburban neighborhood was painted to look like an ear of corn. Don took a sip from his coffee cup and said, "I really wish I had never seen that old man." The Buick swerved a little. We almost ran over a gas station. Don gripped the steering wheel. He rocked back and forth and said, "All that old man does is hurt me."

Don stopped the car next to an oak tree and took a sip of the coffee cup. He was looking straight ahead. He began shaking his head and said everything in Kansas City was hopeless. The oak tree began to rain small leaves on the Buick. Don said, "There's a good chance that old man has already called everyone in Kansas City, and now they're all waiting to hurt me."

Leon suggested that maybe we should get out of the car. Don nodded. Leon and I climbed out of the Buick. Don moved the Buick in a direction we were not going. Leon and I watched the car disappear. Leon shrugged.

We were near a store that sold fried chicken and seafood. Leon and I went inside and ate some grease and soda. When we left the restaurant, clouds began to sweat on us. We did not have a place to sleep. It seemed like our first night alone. Every other night on our trip someone had either given us a motel room or a blanket. Leon and I didn't know anyone in Kansas City.

I saw an RV parked next to an auto garage. I tried to climb into the RV, but all the doors were locked. Leon and I walked behind the auto garage. There was a black truck parked behind the auto garage. The truck was unlocked. Leon and I climbed into the truck. We reclined our seats. It began to rain harder. Some lightning blinked and was followed by mumbles of thunder. I listened to the mumbles until they stopped mumbling.

The sun flicked our cheeks at six AM. We felt our eyelids yawn. Kansas City was breathing on us. The floor of the GMC Jimmy where we had slept was filled with cigarette pebbles and some old fast food skin. Leon and I didn't want to move from the abandoned truck we had found, but the truck began to cave in so we climbed out of it and walked until we felt the highway breathe on us again.

Yesterday's sweat talked to my struggling morning thoughts. My feet were slow. I wanted to yawn until the day was over, but my mouth was not capable of eating an entire day. Leon rubbed his ears and said he no longer felt like a good person. I saw a piece of long grass and asked Leon what he thought of it. Leon shrugged. He seemed bored. I picked up the piece of grass and realized it wasn't as long as I thought it was.

A white pickup truck stopped. Leon and I climbed inside and found a pink man named Clancy. He had long blond hair and thick forearms. His pink mouth told us he was unemployed. A week earlier he had been a house painter, but he lost his job when his penis crawled inside someone's wife. Leon asked Clancy if he put his penis in a lot of females. Clancy said, "I probably put my penis in something yesterday." Leon asked Clancy if he used any special penis techniques. Clancy said, "One of my favorite techniques is to sit next to a lake and rub oil on my chest." I asked Clancy how many penises he had. Clancy gave me a strange look and held up one finger.

The white pickup slowed down. We had only gone a few miles. Clancy apologized and said he had to go to the unemployment office downtown. Leon asked how much money they were giving him. Clancy laughed and said, "Fifteen billion dollars." The white truck opened. Clancy held up two of his fingers and said goodbye. We watched the pink man float away somewhere.

Leon and I weren't sure what to do with our lives. We decided we were hungry. I looked on the ground for something nutritious to put in my mouth, but I only found a crumb of asphalt. Leon said his face hurt because he was tired. The highway didn't offer us any food so we left its motion to look for something that we would enjoy swallowing. Our legs carried us deeper into Kansas City.

Next to a thirty-foot tall building, a fire hydrant was leaking into the street. A man wearing only a trash bag pointed at the water and told us that the city was bleeding. Another man wearing a light blue tuxedo dropped a bowl of cereal into the wound of running water. My face began to sweat. I opened it and watched the fire hydrant bleed a little bit more. It drowned most of the trash bags waiting on the sidewalk.

Leon said he wanted a piece of blackberry pie. We looked for pie. None of the buildings looked edible. I found a package of candy on the ground. I put something orange in my mouth. Leon asked what I put in my mouth. I offered him a piece of candy. He shook his head. I noticed someone holding a cell phone delicately near their face. I asked the delicate person if she wanted a yellow candy. Her face nodded. I tried to put something sweet in her mouth, but she took the candy and held it in front of her left eyeball. I could not see her pupil anymore. The yellow candy had replaced her pupil.

Most of the people in Kansas City looked homeless, but a small percentage of the people I saw were dressed like they wanted everyone to think they went to business school. There was a large banner hanging outside a hotel welcoming all the regional glue salesmen to an annual business conference.

A low moan began to creep out of Leon. I asked him if he had a rare, inoperable form of cancer that would kill him in the next ten to fourteen hours. Leon stopped walking and continued to moan. He touched his empty pockets. I told Leon I would kiss his inoperable forms of cancer until they felt better. Leon ignored me and began looking through his bag. A few homeless people sucked on their own lips as they watched Leon touch his luggage. When he finished going through his stuff he said, "I think I might start crying." I tried not to blink in case Leon started to cry and his image became wet and blurry. Leon began to cry. I tried to protect his face from his tears by stepping on them when they fell on the ground. Each teardrop I stepped on was not capable of climbing back on Leon's face and eating him. He looked through his bag again. There were more tears. I watched Leon and tried to figure out why he was crying. I thought maybe he had lost a small bird the size of a golf ball. I began to cry a little but pretended it was sweat and instead asked Leon why he was crying. He said he wasn't crying. I asked him if he had lost a small bird the size of a golf ball. Leon said he didn't have a small bird the size of a golf ball. I felt all the tender innocence within me die. Leon looked through his bag again. He took everything out of his pockets. Everything Leon owned at that point in his life was on the sidewalk.

I watched some traffic lights change. I pretended the green light and the red light were two puppies fighting over the love of a medium-sized lemon cookie.

Some of Leon's tears dried up. He said he couldn't find his digital camera. I watched Leon slowly pick everything up. The digital camera had belonged to his prep school girlfriend. Leon had stolen it from her after they broke up. With the camera gone, Leon was crying at the realization that he would never get back together with this prep school girlfriend.

His face looked like a worn travel bag that had not been fed or held in a long time. I asked Leon's face if he wanted a hug. He sighed and pointed at a bus station. Leon said he was tired and wanted to go home. I nodded.

We walked to the greyhound bus station. In the bus terminal, Leon said, "I think I want to go back to the truck where we slept and look for my digital camera." He started to walk toward the highway. I

194

followed. After a few steps he turned around and said, "It'll be easier for me to go alone." Leon started walking again.

I sat down in a bus station. Some boys were playing a video game. Some other boys were peeing in a drinking fountain.

When Leon returned he said, "I caught a ride with a small astronaut inside a Toyota Corolla. He brought me back to where the truck had been abandoned behind the auto garage, but when I went behind the auto garage the truck was gone. I asked one of the mechanics if he knew where the truck was. The mechanic laughed for a long time. Eventually, I realized the mechanic was wearing a dress and was actually an ugly old woman." I started to tell Leon about the small boys peeing in the water fountain, but Leon ignored me and said he wanted to walk downtown to the unemployment office. He thought he might have accidentally left his camera in Clancy's white truck.

I stayed at the greyhound bus station and watched people guard their luggage. Some people looked at me while they protected their luggage. A large man wearing two hours of weight slowly shed this weight as he talked on his cell phone to something that sounded like a shopping cart slowly filling itself with highly processed high fructose corn syrup. I watched this man's conversation grow stale. A pile of the large man lay on the floor around him.

When Leon returned he was not holding his digital camera. He curled up on one of the bus station benches and tried to fall asleep. We did not move for two days. All we ate were small stale pretzels from a vending machine.

At one point, I asked an employee at the bus station how much it cost for a bus ticket home. The employee said, "Three hundred dollars." I asked if we could get a discount. The employee said, "There's a shelter down the street. Sometimes they will buy bus tickets for people who can't buy their own bus tickets."

I walked to the shelter down the street. A man at the shelter said he didn't have the resources to buy me a bus ticket, but said I could sleep on a cot at the shelter, and then in the morning I could leave the shelter and walk around Kansas City for the rest of my life pretending that I was homeless. He handed me a yellow slip and said that I could exchange the yellow slip for a cot when the shelter opened its night services. I walked back to the bus station. Leon was no longer curled up on a bench in the bus station. He decided we should steal a car.

We left the bus station. Near a broken street lamp we found an empty automobile. Leon pulled on the handle of the car. The door of the green automobile opened. Neither of us knew how to make this automobile move. Leon said he wished he knew how to hotwire an engine. He reached under the steering wheel until he found a wire. He pulled on the wire. Nothing happened. He pulled on the wire again. The car did not move. Leon stopped pulling on the wire.

After an hour of stumbling around Kansas City, looking for cars to steal, we found our way back to the highway. A deer carcass lay in the grass next to us. The sun was setting. I could see the airport. A brown van pulled over. Leon and I climbed in. As the brown van left Kansas City I turned around and watched the city's image shrink. We crossed a river. We were no longer in Missouri. I thought, "If anyone ever asks me what I think about Missouri I will tell them it is the bad place that made my friend's eyeballs wet."

The object that owned the brown van was named Lloyd. He was driving his brown van to Wichita because he was tired of living in a van parked in his sister's driveway. He had been living in his sister's driveway for two years. He still liked living in his brown van because he could stay up late and watch television. His television plugged into the ashtray. I asked Lloyd if his battery ever ran out of juice. He nodded. We didn't talk much after that. The sun went down. Leon sat in the back of the van. He could not hear anything Lloyd and I said. A mix of guitars and mustached voices filled the brown van. I heard

Leon nodding his head to the music. I asked Lloyd why he was going to Wichita. Lloyd nodded and said, "A girl I used to have a crush on in third grade is living in Wichita and she recently separated from her husband."

A blue reflection of the dashboard blurred out Lloyd's eyes. He wore an old pair of bifocals. I asked him if he liked wearing glasses. He shrugged. I told him I had lost my glasses. Lloyd said, "I once was stung by a bee and my glasses fell off, but then I picked them up before I started to swell." I told Lloyd I had a friend who was allergic to bees. Lloyd said, "I used to have a child who was in love with a girl whose father owned a funeral parlor, but then one day my son got stung by a bee and died." I looked at Lloyd. I thought of the time my mother rented a movie and the two of us watched it and I cried at the end of the movie because a little boy died.

Lloyd dropped us off at a gas station somewhere in the middle of Kansas. It was eleven PM. We shook his hand and wished him luck in Wichita. For a few minutes, I watched the brown van get plump with gas and then Leon and I walked across the street to a fast-food restaurant.

Leon said, "Good morning" to one of the people standing behind the counter and then ordered a beef patty and a soda cup. I took a can of tuna from my luggage and ate the tuna. Some of the other customers looked at me while I ate from the can of tuna.

There wasn't anything for us to do except sit in the fluorescent glow of the gas station parking lot and ask people for rides. Leon made a sign that said, "West." Large mosquitoes floated toward us but lost interest when they realized we weren't damp spots of the gasoline that had soaked into the concrete.

An hour passed. Leon bought some red candies from the gas station and gave me two pieces. I asked him if he had ever soaked a piece of candy in a cup of soda for a week before eating it. Leon said, "When I was eight, my friend had a birthday party and I ate a lot of cake. I remember I gave my friend a plastic brontosaurus. He licked the dinosaur's head and then stuck the head in a bowl of rainbow sprinkles. When he removed the dinosaur's head from the bowl of sprinkles it was wearing a rainbow haircut."

A little after midnight a boy named Andrew asked us if we wanted a ride. Leon and I got into his car. He said he had a hotel reservation in a town an hour west of where we were. A few miles of silence piled into the car.

Andrew said he was probably going to spend most of his night sitting alone in his hotel room drinking alcohol. Leon asked Andrew why he wanted to sit alone in a hotel and get drunk. Andrew said, "I work forty hours a week at a fast-food restaurant. The work is okay, but sometimes it makes me want to be alone and drink a lot of alcohol." Our conversations barely mumbled above the noise of the highway. Leon sometimes looked at Andrew while Andrew held the steering wheel with two hands.

Andrew said, "If I ever traveled cross-country I would bring a Swiss Army knife, four popsicles, and a wireless router." He said he had never left the state of Kansas because he didn't know anyone else in the world.

We drove the next twenty minutes in silence.

When Andrew dropped us off, Leon asked if we could drink alcohol with him in his hotel room. Andrew nodded, but then said, "I'd prefer to be alone."

I saw a large store. It was almost two AM. The large store was open twenty-four hours. Leon said we should go in and play the video game where you have to shoot deer with a rifle. Leon and I went inside. The deer hunting game was broken.

Leon said he was tired and wanted to go to sleep. We found some lawn furniture and lay down. Ten minutes later, an employee of the large store told us we could not sleep on the lawn furniture.

I was hungry so I bought some carrot cake. Leon asked me where we should sleep. Next to the large store there was a large field. I looked at the field to see if there were any long pieces of grass in the field. I did not see any long pieces of grass. The field was entirely empty except for the pieces of dirt.

I told Leon that we could sleep in the large field. Leon thought of what dirt felt like and said, "I don't think I want to sleep in a field." I tried to remember if I liked dirt or not. Leon said, "Do you remember the time when we slept in a field and a snake curled up next to you and then I saved your life by grabbing the snake and cutting off its head?" Near the flat, empty pile of dirt, there was an auto dealership. Leon and I walked over to the auto dealership and climbed into the back of separate pickups. Leon lay in the back of a silver pickup. I lay in the back of a red pickup. For a few minutes we talked to each other from our separate trucks, but our conversations struggled to stay awake. Soon we fell asleep.

I climbed out of the back of the red pickup at six AM. Leon was still asleep. I heard some voices. I crouched down. On the other side of the dealership, I saw a man talking to another man. I could not hear what they were saying because they were too far away. I reached into the truck where Leon was sleeping and poked him. He told me it was too early to get touched.

We walked to a gas station and washed our hands in a sink. I ate some leftover carrot cake. Leon looked at the moon and said, "I can still see the moon even though I am awake and most of the time when I am awake I cannot see the moon."

The highway was where it had been the day before. It had not gone to sleep. The nearest on-ramp had waited for us. We stood in a place made of dirt, insects, and asphalt. Leon looked at his phone. He said, "I got a text message from my prep school girlfriend last night." I waited for him to say something else. He picked up a small pebble and threw it at me.

A woman in a blue Honda looked at us. Her machine was filled with piles of old sweaters. Her hair smelled like it had been shaved off and replaced with toasted wigs. She said, "I only have room for one of you." I looked at Leon. He stared at the woman's automobile nest. I was nervous Leon would climb into the blue Honda and leave me. He sighed and opened his mouth, but didn't say anything. The woman leaned her face from the blue Honda. Leon opened his mouth wider. The woman leaned further from her car. I thought maybe she would continue to extend her head from her automobile until it was resting on the teeth hole of Leon's face, but then Leon finished his yawn and the woman slowly began to creep away.

Ten minutes later a black SUV told us to crawl inside of it. The woman driving said her name was Susan. She worked at the post office. Sometimes her boss ate muffin crowns. She said, "He is a big and toothy man." Leon asked Susan if her boss ever tried to put his mouth on her. She said his mouth only worked on food.

The black SUV merged onto the highway. We passed a foreign, mid-sized decision of luxury. A gray child chewed on a fried clam potato chip and watched us from the backseat of the foreign, mid-sized decision of luxury. As the black SUV droned into the hum of the road, Susan told us a story about the time one of her coworkers got sexually harassed by a manila envelope and the government mailed this coworker six ice cubes to rub on their manila wounds.

I looked out the window and saw two moons, but one of the moons was just my eyeball's reflection in the passenger-side window. The other moon was normal. I could feel the moon in my face get sad for no apparent reason and leak a teardrop.

Susan changed lanes. Leon asked her if she liked to drink raindrops from antique chimney boots. Susan said she liked drinking coconut milk from the fresh udder of a tropical vacation. A cow walked up to the side of the highway and licked a chunk of black rubber lying in the breakdown lane.

Leon asked Susan if he could tell her a secret. She said she was technically trained to gather confidential information from people she didn't know. Leon admitted that when he was in first grade he once put a stamp on a dime and then swallowed it. Susan laughed and said, "It sounds like your mother was a bad parent." Leon nodded and said, "I have been a federal criminal from a very young age."

A piece of grass on the side of the highway watched the black SUV and had a desire to be a black SUV.

I thought about the dead mouse I once put in a blue postal mailbox when I was sixteen.

Susan said she had never left the state of Kansas. Her mouth was glad we were in her black SUV. A pause filled the automobile. The three of us didn't do anything except breathe for a little bit. Susan broke the silence by asking me if I had eaten a carrot cake recently. I nodded. She said, "Your fingernails and breath smell like carrot cake."

Susan began to talk about her husband. She said he raised goats and sometimes felt helpless because her abilities as a woman were superior to his male instincts. I looked at Susan and thought about what it would feel like to be an unborn child living in her womb.

The black SUV pulled off the highway. We had only traveled a few miles. Susan apologized and said she had to go to work. We climbed out of her machine. She handed us each twenty dollars and a bag of cookies. As the black SUV drove away I put some things in my mouth and looked up at the moon, but the sun had eaten the moon and its heat was plump and bored and didn't have anything to do the rest of the day except stare down at Leon and me.

●

We stood on another on-ramp next to the highway. The on-ramp was dirt. Leon and I were stranded on a dirt on-ramp. An hour passed. The dirt on-ramp remained empty. We left and walked to the highway. None of the passing cars on the highway noticed our thumbs. I said something about being enthusiastic about the rural financial systems of America. Leon pointed at a gas station next to an empty field. Across from the gas station there was a diner. A mosquito once landed on the roof of this diner and drank the breakfast oils until its wings got fat. Leon said he wished there were more beach resorts in Kansas. Most of the state seemed to be an empty fracture on a limb that had detached from any idea of financial growth. In its emptiness, I thought about a multinational corporation's ability to build multiple skyscrapers in Kansas. If my human body ever liquidated its assets into the form of a multinational corporation I would make a lot of poor investments in Kansas.

A truck drove by. The mouths inside the truck were talking too loud about things that weren't important. Leon noticed something that would give us trouble and pointed at it. I thought he was pointing at a dandelion, but then I realized there were no dandelions and he was pointing at something else.

A highway patrol officer stopped and asked us what we were doing. I thought about pointing at the ground and saying, "Earth," but instead I answered his question. We were told we weren't allowed to be where we were. Leon wondered where our bodies were allowed to be human. The highway patrol officer said, "You can stand and wait on the pieces of earth that aren't shaped like highways." He wrote up his observations of us on highway patrol stationary and asked if we understood the information he was presenting. We nodded. Before leaving, the highway patrol officer said, "If I find you on the highway again I will make you both literally swallow a bullet."

Leon was hungry so he walked to the diner and ate some eggs and home fries. I followed. The waitress had boobs and a perm. She refilled our water glasses twice. Leon drank some orange juice with a straw. When our plates were empty we walked back to the dirt on-ramp.

Leon picked up a pebble and threw it at me. The pebble hit me in the lip. I picked up a pebble and threw it at Leon's mouth. The pebble hit Leon in the shoulder. We continued to throw pebbles at each other's faces for the next hour. A truck drove by carrying hazardous wastes.

Leon got tired of throwing pebbles at my face. He said he wanted to drink some gasoline. I watched him walk to the gas station. I waited on the on-ramp and looked at all the pebbles Leon had thrown at my face. I could no longer see Leon. I thought of him getting raped in the bathroom of the gas station. I began to cry. I picked up the largest pebble I could find and threw it at a nearby sign. I missed. I picked up the second largest pebble. I missed again. My right arm yawned. My left kneecap twitched. I watched a truck filled with ten thousand grass-fed tomatoes move toward the highway.

Twenty minutes passed. I figured Leon was either dead or he had met a girl. A car stopped next to me. I looked at the gas station where Leon had gone to talk to the gas pumps. I did not see him. I looked at the car that had stopped next to me. I looked back at the gas station. A tear grew a mouth at the corner of my left eyeball and said goodbye to Leon. I picked up my luggage. Pieces of my body felt sick at the thought of never seeing Leon again. In a few days, I would have to send Leon's mother a postcard and tell her that Leon had died a few hours west of Kansas City.

The car that stopped was red. When I opened the passenger's side door I found Leon sitting in the passenger's seat. He laughed when he noticed the teardrop near my left eyeball. I climbed into the back of the car. The man driving the car had a small haircut. His name was James. He said he would drive us to Denver. I looked at one of James's eyeballs in the rearview mirror. The whiteness of his eyeball was a fog trying to consume a brown stump.

I knew someone in Denver named Jake. We had played on the same youth hockey team. When he was younger he was a little fat, but then he lost some weight and got handsome. I thought Jake might give us a few pillows and some cornbread. I looked at my phone. It was dumb. It did not know Jake's phone number. I called a guy named Jason, but when he answered I realized he didn't know Jake so I pretended I was calling to ask how his life was. Jason said, "My life is pretty good, I sweated yesterday, but I have not had sex with my girlfriend in two months. Once, I made her dinner and she said the next time she wasn't tired we would have sex."

James continued to drive. Most of Kansas was a green corn sprout. A song about turnips and religion came on the radio. We passed a field of sunflowers. I opened my mouth because the field of sunflowers excited me. Leon asked James if he liked Jesus. James said, "My father was Amish. He taught me how to eat wool. When I was five he let me cut my own hair. A few years later he got a job driving a large truck. He bought a CB radio. The other Amish dads told my Amish dad that he was no longer allowed to be an Amish dad."

I fell asleep for an hour. James and Leon talked about politics and the small pink American elephants that look like pigs. When I woke up James said he needed gas. We stopped at a gas station. I bought some trail mix. James paid for his gas with a thin piece of plastic. We got back in the car. James continued driving west.

I tried to think if I knew anyone else in Denver, but I had trouble thinking so I decided that I had never known anyone. Leon said, "What about that girl we used to know who moved to Denver after college?" I looked at my phone to see if I had the phone number of any girls who moved to Denver after college, but after a few minutes of looking at my phone, I decided to give up and never think about the girls again.

A calm breeze drifted down from the sun. James said, "I have a house a little north of Denver. I live with two roommates, but one of them is out of town. We have a cat. It likes to poop in the corner of any room with carpet." Leon laughed and said he used to hide in the corner of the bathroom and watch his prep school girlfriend poop.

We passed through Denver. James didn't stop. He said we could spend the night in his condo. I looked out the window at Denver and saw a pile of construction equipment. Next to this machinery, a man with a goatee shaved his head and chewed on a mechanical shovel.

James lived in Longmont, Colorado. Longmont was twenty miles north of Denver. It was founded in 1871 by a man named Heatpipe. Originally, Longmont was called, "The membership colony for men who live in this town." In the 1960s IBM killed a bunch of cattle and built a large factory in their place. Longmont is near a river that takes up only five percent of the city. The river is five thousand metric units above a place where there are no metric units.

The neighborhood where James lived was dry and brown. There were some blades of grass, but they were shaped like small, bleached stones. James lived in a two-story house with three bedrooms and two bathrooms. He said we could sleep on the floor in the computer room. Leon and I put our luggage on the floor in the computer room. I saw some cat poop in the corner.

One of James' roommates was wearing a white shirt. He said he was a food chef. I noticed an old stain near the left nipple of his white shirt. James' roommate left to go cater a high school graduation party.

After his roommate left, James said, "I like that guy, but sometimes he leaves his dirty socks in my room." I thought of Leon microwaving a wet sock in St. Louis.

James asked if we wanted to eat some nachos. We ate some nachos. He pointed at a bathroom and told us to shower. We showered. It was three PM. James said he was tired and went upstairs to lie down.

We left James' house and walked down the street toward a grocery store. A man watered a large rock in his front lawn. I asked Leon if he wanted to buy some bread. He said he wanted some drugs and ice cream. Outside the grocery store there was a man sleeping in his truck. Leon asked the man if he knew where to buy drugs. The man yawned and said he wasn't a drug dealer. Two girls in a red Saab drove by. Leon said, "We should try to have sex with those girls." They parked near the grocery store. We walked over to the red Saab and Leon said hello. The girls smiled and said we both looked creepy. I saw an ice cream cone across the street from the grocery store. The two girls went inside the grocery store and bought goat cheese. Leon said, "If I lived in the Middle East I would own an antelope." We walked across the street and bought some ice cream.

On the way back to James' house we got lost. Leon found a playground and kicked a swing set. He then looked at himself and said, "Not as much has happened in my life as I thought would happen." I nodded. He told me to lick the swing set. I looked at it and wondered if anyone had ever licked it before. Leon said I should write a book about him and then told me I could be his personal biographer until someone more famous offered to be his biographer. I thought about writing a book about Leon but figured the book wouldn't be any good because my interest in Leon wasn't as strong as it once was and my interest would probably continue to slowly decrease the longer I knew Leon.

The playground was silent for a few minutes and then Leon asked if I ever caught my father touching my bedroom stuff. I couldn't ever remember my father touching my bedroom stuff. Leon said, "When I turned sixteen my father started going in my room when I wasn't home and touching things I didn't want him to touch. After a year of this, I decided he wasn't allowed to be my father anymore so my parents sent me to prep school."

I thought of the day I decided my father wasn't quite my father anymore. He was in the bathroom cleaning his teeth with a q-tip. When he finished I told him I was leaving soon and would not return until I had become my own father.

It took us an hour to find our way back to James' house. James was still asleep. It was six PM. We spent the next five hours watching television in the living room. Someone we both knew from high school called because he heard we were hitchhiking across America. Leon talked to them for a little while and then hung up. Our mouths got hungry so we looked in the refrigerator. We found some fried chicken and put it in our mouths. The television continued to watch us looking at it. Around midnight we went to the computer room. The cat poop was still in the corner. We lay down on the carpet and fell asleep.

I woke up to a cat pooping in the corner of the room where I was sleeping. I turned on the computer and went on the internet. Leon was still asleep. I looked at a map of Longmont. We were no longer on a major highway heading west. We had two options. We could either go south to Denver and move west toward Los Angeles or we could go north to Cheyenne and end up in San Francisco.

I gently rubbed Leon's shoulder and asked him where he wanted to go. He lifted his face off the floor and said it was too early to have thoughts. I looked at his left ear. Leon turned his head and pressed his left ear into the carpet. I asked Leon's right ear a question. It said,

"Once, I read an interview in a magazine with a famous author who said humans are no longer capable of relying on their own individual modes of reason to explain earth's reality and instead humans must rely solely on sources of non-human thought to make sense of our existential beings." Leon turned his head and rested it face down on the floor. I stopped touching his shoulder. Leon went back to sleep.

The computer looked at me until I went online. Not many people were online. I messaged a girl who made parts of my chest feel weak. I told her I had given up on reason. She said, "oh" and then "cool." I looked at the space where our conversation was taking place. Nothing else happened. The conversation box became empty. I clicked on a website that listed the local weather, but as I thought of the idea of daily forecasts and knowing the future I felt a little sick so I closed the window before the page loaded.

The computer continued to look at me. I asked it what its plans were for life after college. My chest felt a little weak. A conversation box in the computer said, "I think I want to find a middle-aged man and give him a child. I will probably be more attractive than him. After we are married we will settle into a nice lifestyle. If our marriage stops doing well then we will go to a luxury spa and fix our marriage." I did not have any marriage plans so I was unsure what to say. I typed, "cool" but then erased it and didn't type anything else.

A girl from Utah was online. I remembered once going to a party at her dorm suite. The party had been boring so I stole a light bulb from a lamp in the hallway. A few minutes passed. I sent her a message. The computer looked at me. Nothing happened.

The lack of interest in my sense of being at that particular moment made me wish I wasn't where I was. I regretted hitchhiking across America. I wished I had sent out more press releases to major news organizations telling them that I was hitchhiking across America. I had vague thoughts of turning thirty and sending out press releases about a cross-country bike trip but instead of riding my bike anywhere I would hide in my parents' shed for a month and post doctored photos of myself on the internet.

The girl from Utah said, "Hi." I asked her if she still lived in Utah. She said, "I live in Ogden with my parents and my brother. Our neighbors have a pony." I told the girl from Utah that I might be in Utah soon. She told me to call her when I got to Utah. I asked her if she liked Denver. She said, "I have been to Denver many times. It is a very beautiful place, but I am tired of it. The beauty is starting to feel like tiny plastic flamingos and palm trees even though it has nothing to do with those things. Maybe I will go to Denver again after I find a suitable marriage and I am beyond the pregnant years. I think Denver is a good place to take a family if you want to do outdoor leisure activities that don't quite feel like outdoor leisure activities."

I looked at a map of Denver. It did not look like a tiny plastic lawn flamingo. I looked at a map of Cheyenne. I thought of a child drawing horses that were shooting pistols at dead goats. Cheyenne felt like the only place in America that no one had any interest in ever going to, which made it more appealing. I said goodbye to the computer and turned it off. When Leon woke up I told him we were going north to Cheyenne.

James drove us twenty miles north to a rest stop. We thanked him for being a special kind of person who had fed us nachos and leftover fried chicken. Before he drove away he gave us a wrinkled drawing of Jesus he had made with a brown crayon. His small haircut had grown a little since the day before, but the growth was negated by the indentations the bed had made on his face while he slept. A plane passed overhead. It was on its way to a city. Some of the people in the plane would take a picture of a skyscraper when they got to the city.

There were four hundred boy scouts at the rest stop. A dozen of them were in the tall grass looking for dead turtles. One of them found a white plastic spoon and put it in his mouth. He said he felt sick. One of the other boy scouts gave him a pigeon feather and told him to eat it, but the sick boy scout began to cry until one of the scoutmasters sewed a leaf-shaped patch onto his shirt. The sick boy scout smiled and puked a little on his own shorts.

As the boy scouts were climbing back into their bus I asked one of the scoutmasters if Leon and I could get in the bus too. The scoutmaster looked at us and said, "I am afraid of men." A gentle tone trickled off my bottom lip. I told the scoutmaster that my favorite shirt in third grade was a faded turquoise floral pattern and that this shirt was one of many positive examples in the history of my calm nature. The scoutmaster began to slowly creep backwards to the bus. The gentle tone in my mouth turned into a pleading mumble and I began to talk about my experience as a large athletic being that was capable of providing a positive male influence to boys who were undecided about their adolescent options. The scoutmaster ignored these large mumbles and climbed into a mobile object that would soon turn into a river filled with hundreds of inflatable canoes.

As I watched the bus drive away I realized all the boy scouts would remain children for the next few days, but eventually they would sprout little twigs from their faces and these twigs would grow into children of their own who would also end up becoming slightly overweight boy scouts.

I enjoyed the thought of a slightly overweight adolescent slimming down in its late teenage years only to regain the weight in middle-age.

Leon lay down in the grass. He said he was tired and told me to find us a ride. I stood outside the rest area bathroom and poked people who were full of road juice. Some of the people I poked looked scared and didn't respond. Some of them didn't like the added pressure my presence made in their urgency to use the bathroom. A few people asked me why I poked them and I told them I was looking for a ride to Cheyenne. Everyone I poked responded with excuses wrapped in a blanket of fear.

One honest woman said, "I don't quite trust you because hitchhiking has gotten a bad reputation and you are a large man who might do bad things to me if I let you in my car."

I went into the men's room to look at the stains. At the foundation of the inside of the brick structure where everyone left their road juice there was a crinkle of liquid. It reminded me of what it would look like if I decided to boil cornmeal in olive oil for an entire year. I left the men's room. I became less interested in the people using the rest area bathroom and more interested in the insects living near the toilet house. One of the insects chewing on the concrete of the rest area bathroom was green and had once been a tall piece of grass in Nebraska. It was talking to a half-eaten chicken nugget the shape of a cricket.

A priest stopped at the rest area to use the bathroom. I asked him if he trusted the idea of two boys he didn't know filling the empty space inside his automobile. His white collar looked at me and said, "I'll think about it." He went into the bathroom. As I waited for the priest to finish in the bathroom I watched the cricket eat itself until it took the shape of a chicken nugget that had been entirely eaten. The charm of its disappearance was kept alive in the ambiguous memory of its existence. When the priest came out of the bathroom he said, "Alright. I'll drive you to Cheyenne."

His name was Anthony. He was on his way to Wyoming to start a college for people who were interested in learning basic survival skills. He believed in the infinite nature of human life but worried that the existence of humans would be forgotten when young people lost their ability to do anything except click buttons on their computer.

Anthony said, "Our college will teach young people how to exist in a world without technology." I asked Anthony if he had ever been alone in the woods for an extended period of time. He said, "I once spent fourteen years of my life sitting naked in a pine tree."

Anthony dropped us off near something that extended west. He continued north, deeper into Wyoming to start his college.

Leon and I stood next to another on-ramp and waited. Nothing happened. A thread of substance we could feel both emotionally and physically did not present itself.

Leon said, "I am the interstate. I am a long ribbon of hot pavement. I am almost unwound."

A large truck passed us. A guy in the passenger's seat opened the window of the truck and threw a bag full of nickels at us. Leon picked up the bag and counted the nickels. He said there were eight dollars worth of nickels in the bag.

A geometric pattern radiated in the shape of mild pressures on our ability to move. Leon said he was hungry and asked me for a piece of carrot cake. I gave him the last of my carrot cake.

Leon ate the carrot cake, wiped his face with a napkin, and threw the napkin on the ground. I told him not to do what he had just done. He shrugged. The napkin began to blow away. I picked it up and tried to put it in Leon's mouth.

We began to wrestle.

As we wrested, I told Leon he was a creamy bikini that made everyone around him feel dirty. He called me a dented ping-pong ball.

We stopped wrestling when our muscles were tired of wrestling. Neither of us could remember why we started wrestling.

Leon began walking west. At an exit two miles up the road, we found a telephone pole and not much else.

We left the highway and walked down a long on-ramp to the outskirts of Cheyenne. At the bottom of the on-ramp we found a gas station with a soft ice cream machine and a rack of feathered headdresses.

A middle-aged woman with a short haircut stood behind the counter. She looked like she was trying to slowly creep into another body without anyone noticing.

I bought two ice cream cones, a burrito, and a feathered headdress. Leon bought an ice cream, a bag of skittles, a burrito, and a toy hatchet. We ate our ice creams while we walked back up the on-ramp to the interstate.

I put on my feathered headdress, but it immediately turned into a small flock of dust pigeons and flew away. Leon and I ate our burritos. We had a race to see who could finish first. I lost. Leon told me that because I lost I had to run out into the prairie and touch one of the cows. I looked out at the prairie bordering the highway and saw a herd of black cows. Leon gave me his toy hatchet. I ran across the prairie. The black cows ran away from me. I tried to catch them, but I couldn't. I threw the toy hatchet at them.

I returned to the highway. Leon questioned my ability to properly exist in America. He said I lacked the proper consciousness to be an open-minded person.

We were paused in a rural conglomeration of the northern outskirts of the Midwest. I looked for a grain silo, but I didn't see one. The lack of grain silos disappointed me. I felt like I wasn't experiencing a real place. Leon pointed at a hawk. We watched it fly until we could no longer see it.

A highway patrol car stopped to look at us. The man in the car got out and told us we couldn't do what we were doing. I looked at the highway patrolman and waited for him to turn into a grain silo. He did not turn into a grain silo. The patrolman told us we weren't allowed to hitchhike on the interstate in Wyoming, but we could sit on the dirt and wait for someone to pick us up as long as we didn't hold out our thumbs.

The highway patrol car drove away. Leon and I sat in the dirt on the side of the road. A piece of wind touched my ear and I could feel a piece of winter in its breath even though it was the middle of summer.

No one stopped. Leon and I drew pictures of each other in the dirt. We made miniature sculptures out of pebbles. Leon said his stomach hurt. I looked at my stomach, but it didn't hurt. He said, "I think the burrito I ate was made from the meat of a bad stomach." I thought of an insect growing inside Leon. I squinted and looked up the road to see if there was a hospital nearby. I only saw a road and some prairies. Leon opened his luggage. I waited for him to puke in his suitcase, but he took out a pair of socks and closed his suitcase. He walked into the prairie. I watched him pull down his pants and sit down on a malformed tuft of grass. For twenty minutes, Leon crouched in the prairie as he waited for something to happen. When he was done he dug a hole in the prairie and buried the dirty socks.

We sat on the dirt next to the interstate for another two hours. No one stopped. Our stomachs had grown empty so we walked back to the gas station to get something to eat and ask people for a ride. The woman with short hair working behind the counter told us we could eat as much ice cream as we wanted. We filled our pockets and then went outside to sit on the curb and wait for someone to give us a ride. Train tracks ran parallel to the highway. We could see the trains heading west as we sat and waited for a ride.

Leon asked a carload of elderly teenagers if they had any drugs. A boy in the front seat took out a small plastic bag of drugs. Leon asked if he could have some. The boy gave Leon a small pinch of what was in the bag. He thanked the boy. The carload of elderly teenagers drove away.

Leon went behind a pine tree and did drugs. The sun went down. Leon said the drugs were stale and not very helpful. A man stopped and gave us a peanut covered in chocolate. A dozen trains passed. No one gave us a ride west.

At ten PM Leon stood up and said he wanted to climb on a train. We began walking toward the trains. As we walked Leon touched his stomach and said, "If I fall asleep tonight I bet I will dream about a lima bean that likes to eat ice cream."

Under a bridge we found some hobo scribbles. On a piece of concrete, a hobo named Red River Slim had scribbled, "I am an acoustic jungle." Leon and I both added our names to the hobo scribbles.

We walked past a gas station. People were doing gasoline things. Two guys and a girl sat in their car and listened to trashy music. I told Leon that I liked to listen to trashy music sometimes. He asked me to define trashy music. I said, "Trashy music is the repetitive dribble throb that a car makes when I turn on the radio and drive too fast."

Leon pointed at an abandoned mobile home near the train tracks. He said we should sit behind it and wait for a train. We walked behind the old mobile home. Leon and I sat on something that looked like a concrete drainage pipe.

Trains moved past us very slowly, but none of them stopped. Leon asked if I wanted to jump on a moving train. I told him I didn't think I had the brain functions to make that decision. He nodded and said he preferred stationary objects as well. We left the concrete drainage pipe and kept walking toward downtown Cheyenne.

The city of Cheyenne was a boot that wanted to be a river, but then someone in elementary school called it a fat buffalo and the city spent the rest of its adolescence concerned that it would develop weight issues. In fourth grade, it had to write a report on an Indian tribe and it picked itself, but the night before the report was due it watched a movie about some crows that existed in the shadow of an apocalypse. All the crows were named "Patrick Swayze."

Leon and I sat on a metal platform and waited for the next train heading west to stop in the rail yard. Leon asked if I remembered the movie about the guy that liked to dance and every middle school girl who watched it developed an erection.

I told Leon I had never gotten an erection.

Leon said, "It's sort of sad that Patrick Swayze was once Charlie Sheen's brother, but then Charlie Sheen did so much cocaine that Patrick Swayze developed cancer and died."

I saw a train move east. It was traveling at thirty-five miles per hour. It moved toward a blinking light. The train looked like it was going to hit the light. The train began moving faster. I watched the train pass within two inches of the light. I remembered once I had seen a subway move through a tunnel and this subway train was less than an inch from the sides of the tunnel. This memory reminded me of the time when my father took me to the aquarium and I pressed my face on the same piece of glass that an octopus was sucking on. Our human existence had developed close proximities with objects that we weren't quite mathematically able to explain.

Leon peed on some dirt next to some train tracks. He told me to pee too. Leon watched me pee near the spot where he had peed.

A train stopped. I could hear my heart rate begin to talk very fast inside my chest. Leon said his heart rate had the aesthetic of a twitching, high-pitched whistle. We both existed as young American men in the dried substance of something that bore no resemblance to the thing it was trying to maintain. We ran over to the train and climbed on the platform at the front of a freight container. There was a metal bench. We wedged ourselves under the bench and lay there waiting for the train to move.

Neither of us spoke or moved for twenty minutes. We were stationary on a stationary metal object. I remembered stories of people who got severely beaten when they tried to ride trains. I waited for something affiliated with the railroad to yell at us and beat us with a piece of metal. Somewhere up the tracks I began to hear the slow thump of a piece of metal against something else that was metal. I imagined a railway employee walking up the tracks tapping a metal pipe on the side of the freight boxes. The sound of the metal thumping on metal grew closer. I felt a small movement underneath me. I continued to hear the sound of metal on metal. We began to move. I realized the metal sounds were from the freight cars stretching and pulling against one another as the train began to move. The train continued to move. I looked at Leon in the dark lying next to me. He was looking at me. We were on a moving train.

•

As we left Cheyenne, Leon and I sat up on our freight platform. We passed the gas station where we had sat most of the day. Leon and I were both laughing. We were both glad no one had hit us in the face with a metal wrench.

Leon and I both looked at each other. He asked me what we should do now. I shrugged. It was almost midnight. Cheyenne was behind us. We were moving into complete darkness. The air was cold as the train cut through it. We put on sweatshirts and took out our sleeping bags. There was nothing else for us to do, but lie down and go to sleep.

In the night we passed over the Rocky Mountains. Leon and I were both wedged onto a metal platform at the front of a freight car. The cold invisible presence of the night troubled our sleep. I woke up multiple times and found myself lying on a bitter piece of metal with no visual sense of where we were. As the train pushed through the night I was not entirely sure if Leon was still there. Sometimes when I woke I would reach out and touch him to make sure he had not fallen off the train.

At six AM we pulled into a rail yard and didn't move for a half hour.

The metal platform had pressed indentations into my face where it had rested while I slept. Leon and I lay wrapped in our sleeping bags, but the morning light exposed us to whoever bothered to look at the waiting train.

I worried about railway employees doing bad things to our faces. I stared at a blinking light. When the train began shifting under us I heard the slow thump of the freight cars fighting this attempt at momentum. Eventually, our freight lurched and we were moving again.

Another hour passed. The sun ate up the rest of the night's breath. I put away my sleeping bag. We were passing through a desert somewhere in Wyoming or Utah. I saw cattle roaming from one small tuft of grass to the next. A few deer were talking to an antelope that was eating a large-eared rabbit.

The dirt was a color I hadn't ever seen before. It reminded me of the unfriendly look a stranger might give to a person they don't know and will never see again. Small wounds of trickling water occasionally broke up this unfamiliar color. I asked these streams if they were friends with any turtles or goldfish, but the drips of water did not respond.

As the tracks curved I could see the front of the train we were on. It was close to a half-mile in length. I looked at the pieces of the train that trailed us. The train seemed over a mile long.

A train passed us heading in the other direction. When the train was gone, Leon stood up and peed off the side of the train. A wind sprayed his juice in multiple directions. It almost looked like a pleasant twinkle. When this faucet yawned and stopped dripping Leon put himself away and sat down on the platform.

We had not spoken to each other all morning. We both sat in a disheveled image of ourselves. Our clothes and fingers wore a filth we weren't used to. The platform where we slept was frosted with years of train sweat. The metal had blackened under the stress of hundreds of thousands of miles of rail. I asked Leon how he slept. He looked at his hands and said, "I don't think I almost fell asleep once last night."

The beauty around us soon grew stale. The dirt was no longer a color I had never seen before. It had become a relentless pattern that was not gentle on our eyes. As we tried to adjust to the growing shine around us we sat and realized there wasn't much else for us to do but sit. Leon acted self-consciously aware that we were on a train. He asked me to take a picture of him. His smile reminded me of a boy I once saw at Disneyland.

The train continued pushing forward. I wondered why no one ever built an amusement ride that lasted twenty-four hours and passed through a desert and gave its passengers the experience of what it would feel like to be a hobo riding a train.

I took out a book. The sun rose above us. I could feel it eating away at my skin. We passed through a tunnel. Leon and I ate clouds and clouds of the train's black lung. I felt lightheaded. Leon liked feeling lightheaded. He laughed and said, "If we pass through a tunnel that is two miles long we will probably die of smoke inhalation."

Neither of us knew where the train was headed. It flowed west, but there was little else for us to know.

As the day rose over our heads I continued to look at the book I was reading. I tried not to move. I didn't want my body to remember it was a body and that my body was hungry. I had not eaten breakfast. My body was confused and didn't know where it was. All we had left to eat was a can of tuna and a can of kidney beans. Leon's water bottle was empty. My drip jar was half-filled.

Around noon the train stopped. I saw a highway running parallel to us. Leon asked what highway it was. I shrugged and said it was maybe interstate 80. The train did not move for two hours. I imagined the train conductor had gotten tired and stopped to eat a sandwich. The longer we didn't move the more it felt like the sun had decided to only stare at us. Leon jumped onto the freight car in front of our freight car. I continued to read a book and sweat. The heat ate at me until I got a little delirious.

A mountain to our right seemed to be pointing at me. Its mountain drone preached. I pointed at the mountain and told Leon that its sermon was trying to get our attention. Leon didn't know what I was saying. I opened my luggage and found our only bottle of water. I took a sip. I gave some to Leon. He asked if I was hungry. I looked at our can of tuna and the can of kidney beans. I asked Leon how far he thought we were from California. He guessed we still had a day of travel left.

We didn't have a can opener. I cut open the can of tuna with a swiss army knife. I thought about draining the tuna water off the side of the train but instead drank the tuna juice. The first bite from the can felt dry in my mouth. I had trouble swallowing, but my hunger forced down the meat and I quickly emptied half the can. I handed the rest to Leon. Some of the tuna had red spots. Leon ate the rest of the tuna. There was no more tuna. There was only a can of kidney beans left.

Next to the train, a warm meadow sprouted. I saw a fence between us and the highway. I put the book down and stood up. This was the third time I had stood up all day. Leon pointed at the sky and asked if I saw the yolk. I didn't understand. He laughed and said, "I meant to say 'hawk'."

I noticed a dirt road on the other side of the train running parallel to the railway. It looked like a service road. A yellowish cloud of dust grew up from this dirt road. I squinted. A truck appeared from the dirt cloud. The side of the truck said, "Union Pacific Railroad." Leon asked what I was squinting at. I told him a truck from Union Pacific had probably seen us.

We climbed down from the train and hid behind a bush in the warm meadow. We waited for someone from the rail company to show up. I again imagined the rail employee would be holding a large metal pipe.

A small stream with not much faith in its ability to be a stream drifted through the warm meadow. I wondered if we should drink from the stream or fill up one of our empty bottles. I pointed at the stream. Leon looked at the stream and then talked about a wooden ox he had once seen. He said it had been made from a cedar tree.

No train employees holding metal pipes showed up.

The train began moving before we had a chance to get back on. Leon and I had been looking at a cricket in the warm meadow and didn't notice when the train began moving. We ran along the side of the train, but the train quickly began moving too fast and we were afraid to climb on. It was no longer an object we wanted to ascend into.

When the train finally drifted away Leon's face had trouble not looking concerned. He said something about forgetting a small pouch of dried spicy mangoes on the train. I thought of Leon nibbling from a pouch of dried spicy mangoes. I was disappointed he hadn't shared this pouch with me.

We waited in the warm meadow between the highway and the train tracks for a few minutes. Leon said that maybe another train would come through. It seemed doubtful. Our train days were over. We would return to the road.

I looked at the flow of passing automobiles. The road would be jealous of our train sweat, but it would treat us fairly. There was nothing else to do. We climbed a small fence and walked toward the highway. I looked back at the rail tracks. I was disappointed and glad we weren't still on the train, moving toward Nevada with nothing to eat and drink except a can of beans and a half a drip jar of water.

When we felt the highway's automobile heat we stuck out our thumbs and waited for our next ride.

The noise of the highway replaced the sounds our ears had been making earlier. Leon found an empty wine bottle in a ditch and held it up. I imagined him someday drinking ditch wine in Europe. I waited for Leon to throw the empty bottle at a passing car, but he didn't throw it at anything. He set the wine bottle back down in the ditch.

The highway ignored us. We began walking west. Our thumbs tried talking to the passing automobiles, but they wouldn't listen.

These brief attempts to hitchhike in Utah were becoming modest, individual moments of failure.

My face diminished to the shape of a weak smile similar to the one I wore after my six-year-old birthday party when all I got was some wool bricks and a single gray clothespin.

Our legs found a sign that told us we were fifteen miles from a town called "Ogden."

•

I knew a girl in Ogden named "Frou Frou." She had been an art history major in college. Her ex-boyfriend once offered to sell me a piece of tofu that had soaked overnight in parmesan cheese. He said he would give me the tofu if I gave him sixteen thousand dollars. At the time I only had a couple pennies and an illuminating christmas reindeer. He said he would frame the tofu and mount it in my dining room. I slowly avoided talking to him ever again. He ended up selling the tofu to a museum whose curator used it as bait to catch a trout the size of a peacock.

Leon said he was thirsty. I handed him what was left in our water drip jar. He drank it. I looked at the highway. Our movement was paused. We seemed to be the only things left in the world not capable of moving.

I touched one of my foreheads. The one above my left eyebrow. It was already toasted. Soon it would fall off and I would have to wait for a new forehead to develop.

When I called Frou Frou she sounded like she had just finished looking at a magazine filled with recipes that were supposed to make women not feel fat. The body on the cover of this magazine probably had developed a system of attraction that made other people feel bad about themselves. In America, there seemed to be a tendency for people who feel bad about themselves to look at magazines until they feel so depressed that all they want to do is go shopping.

Frou Frou said she had spent the summer making snow globes and drinking juice pouches on speedboats. I asked her if her ex-boyfriend was still selling dirty tofu. She said he got a job as a molecular finance analyst because his dad knew someone who invented the first business molecule. I felt guilty because my father had sort of stopped knowing people after he'd dropped out of college to be a bible minister. The last businessman my father knew was a bible salesman who overdosed on cocaine.

After I hung up, I said, "Once when I was in college I helped a girl named Frou Frou do her math homework. When the math was finished we lay on her bed and looked at the ceiling for an hour. When I leaned over to kiss her she told me I had to leave because her roommate would be back soon and she didn't like the smell of the kind of boys that Frou Frou let into their room."

We continued to walk and hold our thumbs out. My thoughts began to feel light. I asked Leon what he would do if I passed out. He said he would leave me in a ditch and then call the authorities to let them know there was a person in a ditch somewhere. I decided not to pass out because I would probably die in a ditch and never see Leon again.

I looked at our empty water drip jar. I was very thirsty. Leon began walking faster than me. I had trouble keeping up. He told me that sometimes when he felt lightheaded he looked directly at the sun. I looked directly at the sun until my face hurt. I felt nauseous. Leon laughed and continued to walk faster than me. A mile up the highway

Leon and I found an exit. We left the highway and walked up the off-ramp. At the end of it, neither of us knew which way to go so we stood at the end of the off-ramp and waited. A guy on a three-wheeler approached. He noticed that we did not know where we were and paused next to us. There was an ink spot on the breast pocket of the shirt he was wearing. He pointed up the road and said, "Sip sip."

We found a small market a mile from the highway. A pile of day-old sandwiches wrapped in styrofoam and plastic told us to eat them. I drank four cups of white bread cola.

For an hour, Leon and I ate sandwiches under an umbrella outside the place where we bought old sandwiches. I watched my sweat pool in the dirt under my chair.

Leon finished his sandwich and went to the bathroom. When he got back he said, "I flushed it a little."

Frou Frou called while I was sipping my fourth cup of white bread cola. She asked where I was. I told her I was at a small market near the highway.

Twenty minutes passed. A blue SUV parked next to our table.

Frou Frou was wearing large sunglasses that covered most of her face. Leon and I climbed into her car. Normal conversation filled the automobile. At one point Frou Frou said, "I was reading the internet earlier today and some guy compared the potential financial landscape to a very handsome little beetle that is a quarter of an inch long with dark green spots and cinnamon brown legs, but which no longer lives on land and is instead kept on a boat inside two clamshells that have been tied together."

When we got to Ogden, Frou Frou said, "I live with my parents. My dad is a thread of mist who struggles to convince people to buy real estate from him. My mother married my father because she knew he would age well and also because she is a doctor and doesn't have to worry that much about her financial well-being."

As we drove through Ogden, the town reminded me of an antique buffalo skin that someone had traded for a six billion dollar gift card to a grocery store that sold organic berries. Frou Frou said that once a homeless person tried begging for change outside of a convenience store in Ogden and then the sheriff hung him from a lamp post near the tall white religious steeple that was built in honor of someone who may not exist.

I looked at Ogden until I got bored of looking at Ogden and then I looked at Frou Frou's teeth until she noticed me looking at her teeth.

Frou Frou lived in a well-positioned neighborhood. Her parents' house was an excel spreadsheet with figures that added up to a sum of three million dollars. I was sort of jealous of the ease in which their refrigerator door provided crushed ice, but Leon didn't think this was a big deal and said his parents' refrigerator door had a similar function.

My armpits were pretty dirty when I got to Frou Frou's house so I took a two-hour-long shower.

Everyone was in the living room looking for Frou Frou's younger brother. He was three. No one could find him, but we could all hear him whimpering.

At dinner, Frou Frou's parents asked Leon and me if we had studied hitchhiking in college. We opened our mouths and pretended we knew what our mouths were saying. At various points in the night I found myself putting a steamed vegetable in my mouth.

Frou Frou's mother drank some wine and said, "Someone who went to high school with my brother hitchhiked home from Vietnam and a few weeks after he got home his younger sister tried to hitchhike to the mall and ended up getting run over by a bus. This traumatized the boy for a few years and then when he stopped being traumatized he went to work in a tomato canning factory for the rest of his life."

Frou Frou's mother seemed emotional when she finished telling this story. I looked at Frou Frou's father. He was grinning. His face had been grinning the entire meal. He kept asking us if we wanted more steak. He was very generous with his family's meat. He put a lot of meat near his face. Sometimes while he was chewing he talked about things he used to do when he was younger.

After dinner, Frou Frou asked if we wanted to drive around Ogden in her father's SUV and listen to trashy pop music on the radio. I looked out a window. The neighborhood where Frou Frou lived was quiet. A pink bicycle lay in someone's front yard. The rest of the neighborhood was empty. I did not feel like being anything. I just wanted to relax in a large suburban attitude and do nothing for the rest of my life. I touched my forehead. It was toasted and would peel off soon. Large portions of me didn't want to keep hitchhiking.

I thought about marrying Frou Frou and spending the next forty years eating meat with her parents. I looked out the window again. The pink bicycle had turned into a FOR SALE sign.

I asked Frou Frou if she still talked to anyone we had gone to college with. She shrugged and then said she recently got an email from her ex-boyfriend that said he had mounted a peacock on his living room wall. He had caught the peacock somewhere in Northern Canada and it was the shape of a trout. I noticed Leon yawn. Frou Frou said there was ice cream in the refrigerator. We all sat down on a couch and put spoons in our mouths. There was a movie on television about the guy who invented the hula-hoop. I fell asleep at the part when a guy in an elevator started talking to another guy in the elevator.

227

Leon and I slept next to a treadmill in a room with blue carpeting somewhere in the luxury of a suburban home filled with air conditioning. I woke up at six AM and went upstairs. Frou Frou was asleep on a king-sized mattress. Some bedsheets covered most of the naked pieces of her body so I looked at her bare chin until I got bored with her face.

I sat on a porch for a few minutes and watched automobiles leave their driveways. Everyone seemed in a hurry because they were late for appointments that probably weren't very important. The American journey through life no longer seemed tedious or dangerous.

An empty house that was for sale smiled at me. It said, "American comfort offers no further wisdom into the strange, unknown object that is life. Human minds tend to grow dull when lost in years of calm routine. The brain will never be satisfied with being a concept of the American suburban lifestyle because the mind always needs some new, odd experience to push against and there is nothing strange or odd left in the majority of the lives we lead."

I saw a piece of grass next to an aluminum can. Both objects were talking politics. One of them tried to sing the Chinese national anthem. A dog walked up, sniffed, and then drizzled on the piece of grass next to the aluminum can. I left the porch and walked to a creek. I thought about drinking from the creek, but a log was already taking a sip and I didn't want to wait around for it to finish. As I made my way back to the suburban home where Frou Frou and Leon were sleeping I noticed multiple houses in the neighborhood were for sale. Each of these houses had a sign on its front lawn that said, "Call Shirley."

A shirtless man stood in his kitchen. Frou Frou's dad was not wearing a shirt. He poured milk on a cracker. I watched him talk to his spoon. He took some bacon out of the refrigerator and asked the bacon if it wanted to get sexy. The stove began making heat. Some oils inside a flat piece of metal got angry with the stove heat. Frou Frou's dad sipped on a bowl of coffee. One of his eyebrows looked very excited.

He began talking about the internet. He said, "I found this website where everything is cheap. Yesterday, I bought eight lampshades."

Leon woke up at nine AM. There was no bacon left except for the greased lips of my face. Frou Frou's dad also had greased lips. We tried to hide our mouths from Leon so he wouldn't get jealous. I giggled a little. Leon didn't notice there was no bacon left. He still had dream twinkles in the corner of his right eye.

Frou Frou's dad put a rotten mango into the garbage disposal.

Leon sighed and said he didn't want to do anything the rest of his life except eat margaritas and rub his face in drunk beans. Frou Frou came into the kitchen wearing a t-shirt and some socks. She asked Leon and me if we wanted to go to a lake and eat some fried chicken. One of her socks fell off. I picked it up and told her a story about how one of Leon's socks once got wet and he put it in the microwave. Frou Frou's dad said he had three brand new microwaves in his bedroom closet. No one said anything. He left the kitchen. Frou Frou opened the refrigerator and took out a single grape and peeled off the skin. She nibbled on what was left of the grape for a few minutes and then put the grape skin back in the refrigerator. Frou Frou's dad came back into the kitchen holding three brand new toasters still in their boxes. Frou Frou asked her father if she could borrow his SUV. He nodded and put the toasters in the freezer.

We found a little boy at the lake. His name was Smokey. He went in the water and pointed at some goose feathers. He played with these bird flakes until they dissolved. The skin on Smokey's chest got pink and irritated. He tried to make himself feel better by rolling in the sand. Frou Frou gave him an apple. He took a bite and then dug a hole. He dropped the apple in the hole. When the hole was filled in he began to cry. Frou Frou asked the little boy where his mother was. He said he didn't have a mother and ran away from Frou Frou.

Frou Frou's dad showed up and swam in the lake for a little bit. He did the backstroke. Frou Frou said her father once got a swimming scholarship from a school in California. When Frou Frou's dad came out of the lake he asked if anyone wanted to build a sandcastle.

An hour later Frou Frou's dad went home. Leon and I ate some fried chicken. Frou Frou was still wearing one of her socks. She took it off and filled it with sand. When Leon and I finished nibbling on the fried chicken we buried the chicken bones. Frou Frou called someone she knew who owned a speedboat. Leon said he liked speedboats because he felt like they were symbols of his ability to be more famous than all his classmates from high school. Frou Frou said she had once ridden on a speedboat made from the oil of the last turquoise whale left in the world.

When the speedboat pulled up to the dock we climbed on it. The guy who owned the speedboat asked us if we wanted anything to drink. He opened a cooler. It was filled with pouches of pink Hawaiian milk and citrus farm blood. Leon and Frou Frou drank some pink milks. I found a straw in the cooler. I leaned over the side of the speedboat and sipped on the lake water.

We drove around the lake in a speedboat for three hours. The guy who owned the speedboat talked about a girl named Linda he met at a dance club. He said, "She has a really nice body and her hair hides the fact that she has a masculine face." I asked the guy who owned the speedboat how fast the speedboat could go. He said, "I once was hauling this speedboat across Nevada with my uncle's pickup and I was driving at least one-hundred-and-fifteen miles per hour."

On the way home from the lake Frou Frou stopped at the grocery store to buy tomatoes. Leon found a bowl of garlic potato chips near the entrance of the grocery store and began to eat them. I stood a comfortable distance away from Frou Frou and watched her pick out four tomatoes. I asked her if the tomatoes were made out of beef. She ignored my question and picked up a bag of lettuce. She looked inside the bag of lettuce for a long time. I asked her what she was looking at. She said she wanted to make sure there were no toads in the bag of lettuce.

When we got back to Frou Frou's house everyone got naked and stood in the shower until everything was clean. There wasn't much to watch on television but the three of us looked at it for an hour. During a commercial for marshmallow light bulbs, Frou Frou asked if we wanted to drive to Salt Lake City and eat a burrito. I shrugged and looked at Leon. He smiled. We climbed into Frou Frou's father's SUV and drove to Salt Lake City. There was a Mexican restaurant inside an abandoned fast-food restaurant. I ate nine tacos.

Salt Lake City was a clean syndrome of heartache. Everyone seemed to be suffering from the same pain, but no one could figure out what that pain was so everyone just pretended everything was okay and drifted through their lives with a moral smile resting on their lips. Most of the people in Salt Lake City were short white males with toned legs who wore very short shorts.

Frou Frou asked if we wanted to go to a mall. Leon said he liked malls. We went to a mall in Salt Lake City. There was ice cream for sale in the mall. Leon bought a shirt and a pair of white sunglasses. When he put the sunglasses on his face they made his face smile. He looked like he was trying to be the golden boy of his generation. A girl standing in front of a store that sold large soft pretzels said she liked Leon's new sunglasses. He blushed and then told Frou Frou he was very experienced at receiving compliments.

In the window of a store called "Karl Malone," there was a picture of the crucified body of Michael Jordan.

Around nine PM, we left the mall and went to a bar to watch people hold a microphone. The first guy who held the microphone said, "When I am an old man I hope I am a giraffe." Someone asked him why. He shrugged and stopped touching the microphone. Another guy picked up the microphone and said, "Yesterday I coughed on an elephant and it threw a banana peel at my four-year-old daughter." Everyone in the bar looked at this man until he felt uncomfortable and let go of the microphone. The next guy who held the microphone said he was afraid of microphones and didn't say anything else. He began making emotional face noise. The shape of his eyebrows reminded me of a guy I once saw shoot a basketball and completely miss the backboard. Someone in the audience thought the emotional face noise of the man holding the microphone was funny so this guy laughed until he farted loud enough for everyone in the bar to hear. The last guy to hold the microphone said he was in the process of driving a van to Oregon and had only eaten cheese doodles for the last three weeks. He said he was tired of making jokes and wished he was of an age where a crayon was still an acceptable writing utensil.

After everyone finished touching the microphone I walked up to the last guy who held the microphone and asked him if I could have a ride to Oregon. He looked at me for a long time. Then his mouth apologized and he held out a picture of a sad giraffe drawn with an orange crayon on a yellow napkin.

Before we left Salt Lake City, Frou Frou stopped to buy gas for her father's SUV. She put the premium brand of gas into the SUV. I went into the gas station and bought some lip moisturizer. Leon bought a can of cheese queso and a bag of corn chips. We climbed back into the SUV and returned to the luxury of a suburban home with air conditioning.

The next morning I found a pocket I hadn't looked at in a few weeks. Inside the pocket was a seedling of a variety of tree that I had eaten many times. I put this seedling in the corner of the room where I had slept. The blue carpet of the guest bedroom was frayed in the corners and I was able to pull up a piece of the flooring and plant the seed. Leon did not notice the disruption of the carpet and continued to sleep. When the seedling was as deep as it would get into the guest bedroom floor I replaced the carpet.

A bird outside the guest bedroom window beeped. I poked Leon in the part of his face that ate beeps. Then I poked him in the left ear and asked if I had given him ear damage. He said he was not sure if human existence was capable of experiencing more damage.

I heard someone in the kitchen. I left the guest bedroom. Frou Frou's father was making breakfast. He said he had a business meeting in Salt Lake City and would drop us off next to the highway. I went back into the guest bedroom. Leon was packing his luggage.

Frou Frou came down to the kitchen before we left. She was wearing a pair of pink shorts and a baggy t-shirt. I was holding a piece of bacon. Leon was eating the local news from a ten-inch television next to the microwave. A weatherman inside the television said, "There is a three percent chance of precipitation. Temperatures will rest in the mid to upper nineties." Frou Frou's father was concerned that our bodies would shrivel somewhere in the deserts of Nevada. I ate the piece of bacon I was holding.

Frou Frou's father was late to his business meeting. He dropped us off on the west side of Salt Lake City. A few minutes after Frou Frou's father dropped us off Leon went behind a pile of small shrubs and did some drugs. When he crawled out from behind the pile he said the drugs he had smoked were stale and not very good.

I saw a helicopter. Leon waved at the helicopter. An automobile approached. I picked up my luggage figuring it would stop. The automobile stopped.

Leon and I climbed into a black truck. A man with some missing teeth and long, twisted knots of hair shook our hand and said his name was Raul. The first enchilada I had ever eaten was also named Raul. The black automobile began to move. Raul said he was on his way to a salt factory to pick up his last paycheck. He had recently been laid off. Leon asked what he was now going to do for work. Raul said he would probably collect unemployment for three months until the salt factory began hiring again. He drove us only a few miles. Near the edge of Utah, he said, "My truck is low on gas. I have to fuel up." Leon and I got out of his black automobile and were alone with each other under the sun again.

●

Five seagulls were floating in a pond next to the on-ramp. Leon walked over to the pond and took a sip. A seagull flew away. I watched Leon walk back to the on-ramp and hold out a finger. A lot of vehicles were moving at high speeds. Leon said, "When I was three I found a seagull asleep in the garage." More automobiles moved at high speeds. I could feel their movements under my feet. The day continued to burn.

A large tractor-trailer stopped. The driver stuck his arm out the window and waved. We waved back. The driver continued to wave. Leon and I walked up to the tractor-trailer. The driver asked if we wanted a ride. We climbed into the large truck. I sat on the mattress behind the driver's seat. Leon sat in the passenger's seat. The driver held out his hand and said, "My name is Cory." We shook his hand. He said he was going all the way across Nevada to Reno. The large truck began to move.

Cory didn't say anything for the next fifty miles. We were no longer in Utah. Every once in a while Cory took a can of Mountain Dew out of the cooler next to his seat and pressed it on his lips. There were three empty cans on the floor when we got into his truck.

Somewhere in Nevada we passed a fuel pit. Cory pointed at the fuel pit and said, "There's nothing in that gasoline town except whores and prostitutes." Leon asked Cory if he had ever slept with a prostitute. Cory laughed and said he only liked to pay for Twinkies. I asked him what a Twinkie was. He looked at me in the rearview mirror and raised an eyebrow.

Leon asked what Cory was hauling. He sighed and said he wasn't hauling anything. I got nervous. Cory grinned and said that when he got to Reno he would pick up sixty pallets of lettuce and drive them back to Salt Lake City. Leon asked if he ever did any under the table jobs. Cory nodded and said, "Once someone paid me twenty thousand dollars to drive a truck down to Arizona. No one ever told me what was in the truck. I got half the money when I picked up the truck and the rest of the money when I dropped it off."

Cory put the truck on cruise control and rested his feet on the dashboard. He was straddling the steering wheel as he drove. Leon said he saw a movie where a girl put her legs on the dashboard of a car, but then the car got in an accident and her legs fell off. Cory asked if the girl had pretty legs. Leon said, "I don't remember what her legs looked like, but I saw this other movie where a guy ate some nachos." Cory turned on the radio. A song by a popular band was playing. Cory said he saw the popular band play live when he was thirteen.

I fell asleep on the mattress I was sitting on. Twenty minutes later, I woke up to Cory telling Leon about the last girl he dated. He said he found her in bed with another man. Leon said, "The girl I dated in prep school once kissed my friend's parakeet."

I looked at Cory's teeth in the rearview mirror. There were yellow stains on Cory's teeth. Leon continued to talk about his prep school girlfriend until the radio began to fade. Cory turned some dials and found another station. He yawned and took his feet down from the dashboard. He said, "At some point in Nevada the radio stops working." Leon asked Cory what he did when the radio stopped working. Cory shrugged and said, "Nothing."

Cory pulled off the highway and parked next to a gas tank. Leon and I went into the gas station and each bought a rib sandwich. Cory bought another six-pack of Mountain Dew.

I saw an old lady putting her old teeth into a slot machine. I asked her if she ever won any money. She grinned. I saw an empty hole in her face. The empty hole said, "Once, twelve years ago, my husband found a dead pig in the middle of the road and we ate pork chops for a year." The old lady continued to put her old teeth into the slot machine. I asked her where she got her teeth. The old lady smiled at me again and said, "Once a month, my daughter brings me a box of six-hundred new sets of teeth."

Cory was standing next to a fish tank that was next to a row of slot machines. Leon asked Cory if he liked fish. Cory looked at the fish tank and said, "No."

An hour later, Cory pulled off the highway again. There was a fast-food restaurant near the off-ramp. Cory said, "I want to eat some chicken nuggets." He parked next to the dumpster. As he climbed out of the truck he said, "I hate this hamburger shit, but whatever." We went inside the fast-food restaurant and stood in line. There was a cardboard cutout of someone famous holding a meat twig. When it was Cory's turn to order he asked for a box of twenty-five chicken nuggets. A few minutes passed. Someone gave Cory twenty-five chicken nuggets. We got back to the truck. Cory ate five of the chicken nuggets very quickly and then said, "I hate these crusty fuckers," and threw the rest of the chicken nuggets out the window.

I looked out the window for a shape that reminded me of a green lawn. There was nothing green anywhere in Nevada. The radio was no longer working. I tried to think of something to say to Cory, but I couldn't think of anything. Some sand drifted over the road. We drove over a large hill that was the shape of a mountain. Cory asked us what we were going to do when we got to California. I told him I would probably just turn around and go home.

236

The sun was starting to set. Cory told us that Reno would sprout soon. Leon asked Cory if he had a girlfriend in Reno. Cory said, "I once slept with a girl from Reno who was average, but she was disappointed because I didn't make her orgasm." Leon told Cory that I had never had an orgasm. Cory looked at me in his rearview mirror. I nodded.

An hour later, Cory pulled off the highway and dropped us off at a gas station in Reno. Leon asked me where we should sleep. I suggested we walk until we find a pine tree. He shrugged and went inside the gas station and bought a hot dog.

It was almost eleven PM We couldn't find any pine trees to sleep under. Leon said he wanted to sleep in a car. He began pulling on door handles. I imagined us going to jail. Leon pulled on the handle of a white Corvette. It was locked.

We passed the Nevada State Historical Society. I noticed the building wasn't very tall. I walked over to it and stood on the railing next to the front door. My fingers grabbed the edge of the roof. I pulled myself onto the roof. Leon handed me our luggage and then climbed up on the roof with me. The entire roof was empty. We put down our sleeping bags. Leon lay on his sleeping bag and said, "This might be our last night of sleeping on the road." I kissed his forehead and lay down on my sleeping bag.

The tar on the roof of a Nevada Historical Society building in Reno rubbed against our sleeping bags most of the night.
I woke up to the black roof surface resting against my face. I could feel the skin on my forehead trying to sweat itself clean of the tar smudged onto my head. It was a little after six AM. The heat of the day was already loud. We quickly rolled up our sleeping bags and climbed down from the roof.

There was very little traffic. We walked up the road. I looked at a mountain because there was not much else to look at. Leon said, "Last night, I dreamt I lived in a fourteen-bedroom mansion and one of the maid's names was Cecilia." We walked past a university. One of my heels began to bleed. I took off my right sock and put on a band-aid. I threw away the bloody sock. Leon asked if I needed to go to the hospital. I told him I was okay. He asked if I was feeling nauseous or if my stomach was ill. He placed a hand on my forehead and asked me if his hand felt cold. I told him his hand felt like a normal hand. We kept walking. We did not find any hospitals. My heel stopped bleeding.

A mile up the road we found a highway. We were fifteen miles from California. The drone of people inside automobiles filled our morning. We waited next to the on-ramp for half an hour. No one stopped. Leon said he was thirsty.

Leon and I walked over to the gas station across the street. I put a dollar in a machine and pressed a button. The machine said I lost. A man behind the counter laughed and said, "No one ever wins on that machine." His face was full of young wrinkles. I could not tell if he was a teenager or an old man. He smiled. His face seemed to take both a step forward and a step backward in its daily growth. He did not seem to be a product of linear time.

Leon and I sat outside the gas station sipping on fountain drinks. We watched a man park his brown van and go into the gas station to buy mayonnaise. A few minutes later he left the gas station. He got in his van and set the mayonnaise on the seat next to him.

People used nozzles at the gas station. A girl wearing a blue diaper sat in a car seat and ate ravioli out of a glass jar with her fingers. The size of her mouth seemed to grow as a ravioli stain spread across her face.

The city where we waited looked like it wanted to shrivel up into itself. My lungs swallowed layers of dust every time I opened my mouth. The filthiness of Reno lacked the damp humid taste of east coast cities.

I asked Leon what he thought of Reno. He said, "One thousand years ago someone cracked open a coconut and left it out to dry. It was forgotten. The meat of the coconut crusted and flaked. A buzzard nibbled on the fruit for one hundred years, but then the buzzard got tired of being a buzzard and lay down next to the coconut. A couple hundred years later someone decided to pave over the coconut and buzzard. It wasn't long before another person came along and built some condos on the empty pavement."

Leon and I did not wilt.

Leon was looking at a piece of trash on the side of the road that looked like a dead beer can. He pointed at it and said it was a boutique of plastic flowers. Our yawns extended into the late morning.

America continued to shift its economy to help only a few people get richer.

Somewhere a peasant dined on one of the twelve pennies in his pocket. Our progress seemed to be changing.

A black SUV pulled over.

We climbed into our last ride. A medium-sized man with a goatee sat behind the steering wheel. We asked if he could drive us to California. He said he would. We tried to be happy, but the glory we thought we would feel didn't exist. We sat in the black SUV and realized we would soon be in California.

In a few minutes, we would be able to tell people we had hitchhiked across America, but it didn't really matter because all we had done was move from one place to another place.

The trip was over. We still did not know what to do with our lives. The road had not provided us with an answer. The modern freedoms of American society would continue to plague us.

A long time before I was born there was a hierarchical order to human society. People were locked into the same roles, places, and occupations as their parents. In America, this structure has long been abandoned and replaced with the whine of youthful ignorance complaining about how their lives have no meaning and are impossible to figure out.

Looking back, it was maddening for us to think that we would somehow find order in our lives by throwing ourselves at the mercy of the American highways. We thought by giving up control of our future that our future would find us. After thousands of miles nothing had changed. We were still a couple of small boys trying to not be small boys. The only thing that had changed was that I was not quite as clean as I once was. And I was older. I would probably continue to grow older and fatter.

Our lives would continue to not quite accomplish what we wanted. The days would continue to grow to a point where all we could do was look back at them with regret.

Since we left these roads I've often found myself wishing we had done more with our roads, but our roads were done and there was nothing more we could do.

NAME: Mark Baumer

ASTROLOGICAL SIGN: Sagittarius

BIRTHPLACE: Indiana

CURRENT CITY: Providence RI

HEIGHT: 6'3"

NUMBER OF TATTOOS/PIERCINGS: 0

WHO WAS YOUR FIRST CELEBRITY CRUSH: Mandy Moore

WHAT IS YOUR BIGGEST FEAR: I have a recurring dream where I'm late for a hockey game and I can't tie my skates.

WHAT IS YOUR BIGGEST PET PEEVE: People not doing life right.

WHAT IS THE MOST EXPENSIVE THING YOU'VE BOUGHT RECENTLY: A house

WHO DID YOU GO TO PROM WITH: I went to prom with the softball hero of the entire state of maine. She threw like 6 consecutive no-hitters and was in sports illustrated.

WHAT ARE YOU WEARING RIGHT NOW: My one pair of pants, a striped shirt, and a blazer.

HAVE YOU EVER STOLEN SOMETHING: In high school I got suspended for being a bad man.

WHAT IS YOUR FAVORITE DRINK: kombucha, iced coffee, or water

HOW DO YOU LIKE YOUR EGGS: I eat them raw sometimes, but only if the chickens are pastured.

WHO WAS YOUR FIRST LOVE: Dale Murphy

WHAT WAS YOUR AIM SCREENNAME: wyldstyleee & dragonxcrew

HAVE YOU EVER BEEN IN A FISTFIGHT: I got suspended in third grade for punching someone but it was only one punch to the face.

WHAT IS THE MOST EMBARRASSING ALBUM YOU'VE OWNED: teenage mutant ninga turtles 3 soundtrack

WHO IS YOUR FAVORITE PROFESSIONAL WRESTLER: junkyard dog

WHICH ONE WORD WOULD DESCRIBE YOUR LAST RELATIONSHIP: special

WHAT IS YOUR FAVORITE FAST FOOD
FRANCHISE: whole foods

DO YOU THINK YOUR CHILDHOOD DREAMS WILL
COME TRUE: sure

DO YOU FLOSS DAILY: yep

WHAT'S YOUR FAVORITE SCARY MOVIE: jeepers
creepers

WHAT SHAMPOO DO YOU USE: dr. bronners

WHAT IS THE BEST PARTY YOU'VE EVER BEEN TO:
the one on earth

DO YOU EVER WRITE: yep

ACKNOWLEDGMENTS

"Eleven Holes from Hole Patterns of Behavior" originally appeared in *Fog Machine*

"Yachts" originally appeared in *BOMB*

"Cow" originally appeared in *The Fanzine*

"killing/deathing/bombing" originally appeared in *Dark Fucking Wizard*

"Invisible Mosquitos" originally appeared in *Hobart*

"b careful" originally appeared in *Black Warrior Review*

"Not Ted Cruz" originally appeared as Mark's Tinder profile

"An Age of Doubt Adrift in Half-Knowledge" originally appeared in *Dirty Chai Magazine*

Holiday Meat was originally published by *Quarterly West*

Meow was originally published by Burnside Review Press

Cover Letters (original files here- http://thebaumer.com/tagged/coverletters)

The Mark Baumer Sustainability Fund exists
to fund important community projects that raise awareness
about the environment and promote social justice, as well as
involving under-served populations directly in renewing their
communities. Your gift to the Mark Baumer Sustainability Fund
helps build a world for everyone, not just those in power.

http://markbaumersustainabilityfund.org/

The FANG Collective leads direct action campaigns
to create a more just world, working intersectionally to bring
communities together to enact powerful change.

https://thefangcollective.org